TH

MICHAEL MCDOWELL was born in 1950 in Enterprise, Alabama and attended public schools in southern Alabama until 1968. He graduated with a bachelor's degree and a master's degree in English from Harvard, and in 1978 he was awarded his Ph.D. in English and American Literature from Brandeis.

His seventh novel written and first to be sold, *The Amulet*, was published in 1979 and would be followed by over thirty additional volumes of fiction written under his own name or the pseudonyms Nathan Aldyne, Axel Young, Mike McCray, and Preston MacAdam. His notable works include the Southern Gothic horror novel *The Elementals* (1981), the serial novel *Blackwater* (1983), which was first published in a series of six paperback volumes, and the trilogy of "Jack & Susan" books.

By 1985 McDowell was writing screenplays for television, including episodes for a number of anthology series such as *Tales from the Darkside*, *Amazing Stories*, *Tales from the Crypt*, and *Alfred Hitchcock Presents*. He went on to write the screenplays for Tim Burton's *Beetlejuice* (1988) and *The Nightmare Before Christmas* (1993), as well as the script for *Thinner* (1996). McDowell died in 1999 from AIDS-related illness. Tabitha King, wife of author Stephen King, completed an unfinished McDowell novel, *Candles Burning*, which was published in 2006.

MICHAEL ROWE's first novel *Enter, Night* was a finalist for both the Prix Aurora and the Sunburst Award. His second novel *Wild Fell*, a classic ghost story set in northern Ontario, has drawn comparisons to the work of Ann Radcliffe and Edgar Allan Poe and is a finalist for the 2013 Shirley Jackson Award. He lives in Toronto and is at work on his third novel. Visit him at www.michaelrowe.com.

By Michael McDowell

NOVELS

The Amulet (1979)*
Cold Moon Over Babylon (1980)
Gilded Needles (1980)
The Elementals (1981)*
Katie (1982)
Blackwater (1983; 6 vols.)
Jack & Susan in 1953 (1985)
Toplin (1985)
Jack & Susan in 1913 (1986)
Clue (1986)
Jack & Susan in 1933 (1987)
Candles Burning (2006) (completed by Tabitha King)

PSEUDONYMOUS NOVELS

Vermilion (1980) (as Nathan Aldyne)
Blood Rubies (1982) (as Axel Young)
Cobalt (1982) (as Nathan Aldyne)
Wicked Stepmother (1983) (as Axel Young)
Slate (1984) (as Nathan Aldyne)
Canary (1986) (as Nathan Aldyne)

SCREENPLAYS

Beetlejuice (1988)
Tales from the Darkside: The Movie (1990)
The Nightmare Before Christmas (1993)
Thinner (1996)

* Available from Valancourt Books

THE ELEMENTALS

MICHAEL McDOWELL

With a new introduction by
MICHAEL ROWE

VALANCOURT BOOKS

The Elementals by Michael McDowell
First published as a paperback original by Avon Books in 1981
First Valancourt Books edition 2014

Published by Valancourt Books, Richmond, Virginia
Publisher & Editor: James D. Jenkins
20th Century Series Editor: Simon Stern, University of Toronto
http://www.valancourtbooks.com

All Valancourt Books publications are printed on acid free paper
that meets all ANSI standards for archival quality paper.

ISBN 978-1-941147-17-7
Also available as an electronic book.

Cover art by M.S. Corley
Set in Dante MT 11/13.2

NOONDAY DEVILS

An Introduction to Michael McDowell's THE ELEMENTALS

Re-reading Michael McDowell's *The Elementals* again after my first reading of it, more than thirty years ago, what immediately returned to me was the vivid, annihilating heat of the Alabama summer at Beldame, the compound of three Victorian mansions perched on an ocean of glittering white sand on the Alabama shore —mansions that never existed in real life, but which were conjured to life by the writer whose novel you are now holding in your hands.

As someone not unfamiliar with gothic horror fiction, especially ghost stories, I am struck, today as in 1981, by that sunstruck Gulf shore brightness. Gothic horror fiction traditionally has depended on darkness and cold. *The Elementals*, among other things, a terrifying ghost story in which the ghosts are not exactly 'ghosts' in the accepted sense of the word, is notably unbound by that cliché, and its horrors are as likely to reveal themselves under the blazing noonday sun as they are to do so once the sun has gone down. The heat and the light in *The Elementals* is as much of a character in the novel as any member of the Savage or McCray families, as much of a character, indeed, as any of those three terribly-occupied houses at Beldame.

Michael McDowell, once hailed by Stephen King as "the finest writer of paperback originals in America today," was a master of *place*. Other writers will have their own take on his aesthetic when it comes to *place*, but my (very joyous) task here is to introduce *The Elementals*, not any of his other novels that comprise one of the finest oeuvres in 20th century speculative fiction, and one of the books most formative to my aesthetic as a horror writer.

I read *The Elementals* in the late autumn of 1981. I had just graduated from boarding school and was trying to make a life for myself in Paris. As a Canadian living in Europe, I was already two geographic and cultural steps removed from the languid deep-south world of McDowell's novel. Though a lifelong fan of horror fiction, in those pre-Internet days I knew nothing about the novel's author, and had not read any of his other books yet.

What I *did* know was that, reading *The Elementals* in my apartment with the red-and-gold flocked wallpaper, while the cold Paris rain beat against the mottled glass of the apartment's windows, I felt literally transported to high-ceilinged rooms where the heat baked in from outside, stopping breath, cutting off any hope of relief, while the shifting, living sands filled the rooms, assuming the shapes of the dead with a malign intelligence beyond the ken of the living—the world of Beldame.

And it stayed with me for more than thirty years, retreating into my subconscious, occasionally suggesting itself in dreams, and always feeling like a place I *visited*, not a place I'd merely *read about*. The people I met there—the McCrays and the Savages—became people as real to me as those in my own life. Re-reading the novel in 2014 was more like a reunion of old friends than merely a revisiting of a book I'd read as a very young person on the brink of my own adult life.

Which is, after all, one of the hallmarks of a masterpiece.

What I know now, but didn't know then, was that I was living through a certain later golden age of paperback horror fiction. There had been other such ages, but the flourishing of horror novels between the late '70s and the late '80s was a time of immeasurable richness. It was a time when it was not only possible, but likely, to pick up a book like *The Elementals* in all its southern gothic glory at the now-inconceivable price of $2.95. Perhaps the reason I never understood the disdain for horror fiction—literally never even *connected* to it as an abstract concept—is that my sensibility was nourished on work like this. The fact that they were in mass-market paperback didn't matter, because with work like McDowell's, which could just as easily have been published in hardcover by Knopf as southern gothic, the reader was in the hands of a gifted novelist. Of course there were hacks working in horror in the early '80s, as in any era, but for anyone with a whit of discernment, there were the Michael McDowells and the Charles L. Grants. The sheer volume of the work being produced at that time, in that format, meant that it was also a moment when a horror reader (or aspiring horror writer) with taste had a treasure-trove through which to sift.

In an interview with critic Douglas E. Winter for his superb interview collection, *Faces of Fear*, McDowell famously quipped, "I would be perfectly willing if a publisher came up to me and said, 'I need a novel about underwater Nazi cheerleaders and it has to be 309 pages long and I need fourteen chapters and a prologue.'"

It's a terrific line, and certainly apropos for a writer of McDowell's prodigious output, but the reason the line actually works it that McDowell's writing never reads like the work of the author of underwater Nazi cheerleader novels.

Among other things, McDowell was a master of *place*, and *The Elementals* is an unequivocally southern novel. While it's very true that Michael McDowell (who wrote about many different locales over the course of his career) was never bound by region, and that the success of *The Elementals* derives from his extraordinary gifts as a storyteller, not his extraordinary gifts as a southerner, it might also be true that the confluence of those two identities combined to create something extraordinary in this case.

It opens exquisitely with the funeral of the matriarch of an old Alabama family with its own particular tradition of bizarre burial rites. The matter-of-factness with which these rites are taken for granted by the clan is itself a preemptive cultural assertion. The entire opening sequence—the funeral, the dialogue between the various family members in the wake of the passing, the rite itself, a parrot that screams a jolting, terrifying refrain, *"Savage mothers eat their children up!"*—is in direct line of literary descent of the best of the southern gothic tradition, let alone the tradition of the very best horror fiction.

In the hands of a lesser writer, that aspect could be culturally distancing to non-southerners, or at least remarkable in a slightly jarring sense, but McDowell's canvas, with its glorious descriptions and its artless, pitch-perfect dialogue, makes the experience of reading *The Elementals* an embracing one. The reader relaxes back into the prose, and travels.

The Alabama panhandle, he writes, *which consists only of Mobile and Baldwin counties, is shaped rather like a heavily abscessed tooth.*

Mobile Bay represents the large element of decay that separates the halves, and at their northern extremities the counties are further divided by a complex system of meandering rivers and marsh.

Terrifying elemental spirits that can take on the shape and aspect of either the living or the dead, at any hour of the day or night, haunt Beldame itself, revealing themselves at first to India McCray, the visiting daughter of Luker McCray, one of the heirs. An assiduous follower of McDowell's later work might think they had seen the bones of India McCray lying beneath the portrait of Lydia Deetz in *Beetlejuice*, a slightly jaded Upper West Side sophisticate wielding a Nikon as a shield between her own vulnerability and the often frightening and confusing world of adults around her.

But the world of Beldame and its three identical houses perched on an island of brilliant white sand on the edge of the Gulf hides horrors beyond anything that even India McCray can conceive.

In the words of Odessa Red, the family retainer housekeeper who serves as the novel's "Van Helsing" figure, *"What's in that house, child, knows more than you know. What's in that house don't come out of your mind. It don't have to worry 'bout rules, and behaving like a spirit ought to behave. It does what it does to fool you, it wants to trick you into believing what's not right. It's got no truth to it. What it did last week it's not gone be doing today. You see something in there, it wasn't there yesterday, it's not gone be there tomorrow. You stand at one of them doors thinking something's behind it—nothing's behind it. It's waiting for you upstairs, it's waiting for you downstairs. It's standing behind you."*

And all of this under a blazing Alabama summer sun where shade and shadow are hard to come by.

Earlier I mentioned that the sheer bounty of paperback horror fiction in the '80s was a treasure. In many ways it was, but my own, very personal view is that, when the treasure became a glut, it killed it.

Eventually it became impossible for readers to immediately distinguish, on the surface, between work like the novels of Michael McDowell and his genuine peers, and the offal of increasingly bad fiction by talentless writers, published by publishers without discernment or taste, trying to stuff the maws of the book-buying public with what had basically become product. In spite of the same sorts of titles, the same sorts of covers, and even, in some cases, the same sorts of plots, the reading public eventually clued in to the fact that they were being sold a bridge. It wasn't to say there weren't still wonderful, literary horror novels being sold as paperback originals, just that it had become impossible to distinguish between them, and the sterling variety, until it was too late.

The republication of the best of these novels by Valancourt Books is an occasion for joy for any of us who truly loved that era, and miss it every time we visit what remains of the bookstores, let alone the remains of the bookstores that sell horror fiction.

In my opinion, this very noble and worthwhile undertaking is perfectly exemplified by this edition of Michael McDowell's brilliant The *Elementals*. This is a horror novel for the ages, a 20th century haunted house that belongs in the company of Hill House, Hell House, or the Marsten House. Classic literary horror fiction simply doesn't get better than *The Elementals*.

It has its peers, but Beldame and its inhabitants—both living and dead—cast their very own, very long, shadow.

MICHAEL ROWE
Toronto, Ontario

April 29, 2014

To lead us farther into darkness, and quite to lose
us in this maze of Error . . . the Devil maketh men
believe that apparitions, and such as confirm
his existence are either deceptions of sight,
or melancholy depravements of phansie.

— Sir Thomas Browne
Pseudodoxia Epidemica

In memory of
James and Mildred Mulkey

PROLOGUE

In the middle of a desolate Wednesday afternoon in the last swel-tering days of May, a handful of mourners were gathered in the church dedicated to St. Jude Thaddeus in Mobile, Alabama. The air conditioning in the small sanctuary sometimes covered the noise of traffic at the intersection outside, but occasionally it did not, and the strident honking of an automobile horn would sound above the organ music like a mutilated stop. The space was dim, damply cool, and stank of refrigerated flowers. Two dozen enor-mous and very expensive arrangements had been set in converging lines behind the altar. A massive blanket of silver roses lay draped across the light-blue casket, and there were petals scattered over the white satin interior. In the coffin was the body of a woman no more than fifty-five. Her features were squarish and set; the lines that ran from the corners of her mouth to her jaw were deep-plowed. Marian Savage had not been overtaken happily.

In a pew to the left of the coffin sat Dauphin Savage, the corpse's surviving son. He wore a dark blue suit that fit tightly over last season's frame, and a black silk band was fastened to his arm rather in imitation of a tourniquet. On his right, in a black dress and a black veil, was his wife Leigh. Leigh lifted her chin to catch sight of her dead mother-in-law's profile in the blue coffin. Dauphin and Leigh would inherit almost everything.

Big Barbara McCray—Leigh's mother and the corpse's best friend—sat in the pew directly behind and wept audibly. Her black silk dress whined against the polished oaken pew as she twisted in her grief. Beside her, rolling his eyes in exasperation at his mother's carrying-on, was Luker McCray. Luker's opinion of the dead woman was that he had never seen her to better advantage than in her coffin. Next to Luker was his daughter India, a girl of thir-teen who had not known the dead woman in life. India interested herself in the church's ornamental hangings, with an eye toward reproducing them in a needlepoint border.

On the other side of the central aisle sat the corpse's only daughter, a nun. Sister Mary-Scot did not weep, but now and then the others heard the faint clack of her rosary beads against the wooden pew. Several pews behind the nun sat Odessa Red, a thin, grim black woman who had been three decades in the dead woman's employ. Odessa wore a tiny blue velvet hat with a single feather dyed in India ink.

Before the funeral began, Big Barbara McCray had poked her daughter, and demanded of her why there was no printed order of service. Leigh shrugged. "Dauphin said do it that way. Less trouble for everybody so I didn't say anything."

"And nobody invited!" exclaimed Big Barbara.

"Dauphin is even making the pallbearers wait outside," Leigh commented.

"But do you know *why?*" demanded her mother.

"No, ma'am," replied Leigh, ignorant but uncurious. "Why don't you ask Dauphin, Mama? He's sitting right here, hearing every word that you speak to me."

"I thought you might know, darling. I didn't want to disturb Dauphin in his sorrow."

"Barbara, shut up," said her son Luker. "You know very well why it's a private funeral."

"Why?"

"Because we are the only people in Mobile who would have come. There's no point in advertising a circus when everybody hates the clown."

"Marian Savage was my best friend," protested Big Barbara.

Luker McCray laughed shortly and punched his daughter in the ribs. She looked up and smiled at him.

Dauphin Savage, who had attended not very closely to this exchange, turned without rancor and said, "Y'all please be quiet, here's the priest."

They knelt to receive the priest's summary blessing, then rose to sing the hymn "Abide With Me." Between the second and third stanzas, Big Barbara McCray said loudly, "It was her favorite!" She turned to Odessa across the aisle and a curt bobbing of the dyed feather confirmed this opinion.

As the others sang the Amen, Big Barbara McCray said, "I miss her already!"

The priest read the service of the dead quickly, but with appealing expression. Dauphin Savage rose, moved to the end of the pew—as if he were unworthy a place nearer the coffin—and spoke briefly of his mother.

"Everybody who was lucky enough to know Mama real well loved her very much. I wish I could say she had been a happy woman, but that wouldn't be the truth. She was never happy after Daddy died. She raised Mary-Scot and Darnley and me with all the love in the world, even though she always said she should have died on the day that Daddy was buried. And then Darnley died too. Everybody knows she had a hard time of it in the last few years—chemotherapy really does something bad to you, everybody knows that, and even then you're not sure it's working right. Of course we're all sorry she's dead, but we cain't be sorry that she's not in pain any more."

He took a breath and glanced at Marian Savage in her coffin. He turned back, and in a sadder softer voice, went on: "The dress she has on is the one that she wore when I got married to Leigh. It was the prettiest dress she ever had, she said. When she took it off after the reception, she hung it up and said *this* was what she was saving it for. She would be real happy to see all the flowers here today, to see how much people cared for her. Ever since she died people have been calling up at the house and asking whether they ought to send flowers or make a donation to cancer research, and Leigh and me—whoever answered the phone—would say, 'Oh, send flowers, Mama didn't care anything about charity, but she always said that when she died, she hoped there would be a churchful of flowers. She wanted the smell to reach right up to heaven!'"

Big Barbara McCray nodded vigorously, and loudly whispered: "Just like Marian—just like her!"

Dauphin went on: "Before I went to the funeral home I was all upset thinking about Mama dead. But I went in there yesterday and I saw her and now I'm fine. She looks so happy! She looks so natural! I look at her and I think she's gone sit up in that casket and fuss at me!" Dauphin turned toward the coffin and smiled tenderly at his dead mother.

Big Barbara grabbed her daughter by the shoulder. "Did you have a hand in the eulogy, Leigh?"

"Shut up, Barbara," said Luker.

"Mary-Scot," said Dauphin, looking toward the nun, "there anything you want to say about Mama?"

Sister Mary-Scot shook her head.

"Poor thing!" whispered Big Barbara. "I bet she's just bowed down with grief."

There was a troubled pause in the proceeding of the funeral. The priest glanced at Dauphin, who still stood at the end of the pew. Dauphin looked toward his sister, who only fumbled with her rosary. The organist peered over his railing above them, as if waiting for a cue to play.

"*This* is why you need a printed program," whispered Big Barbara to her son, and looked at him accusingly. "When there's not a printed program, nobody's got the least idea in the world what to do next. I could have used a printed program for my scrapbook."

Sister Mary-Scot stood suddenly in her pew.

"Is she gone speak after all?" asked Big Barbara in a hopeful voice that everyone heard.

Sister Mary-Scot did not speak, but her rising was evidently a signal. The organist, with a clumsy foot sounding discordantly on a couple of bass pedals, clambered down out of his loft, and disappeared through a small side door.

After nodding to Dauphin and to Sister Mary-Scot in somber conspiracy, the priest abruptly turned on his heel. His footsteps echoed the organist's out of the sanctuary.

It was as if these two functionaries had suddenly determined, for a specific and overpowering reason, to abandon the ceremony before it was finished. And the funeral was certainly not over: there had been no second hymn, no benediction, no postlude. The pallbearers still waited outside the sanctuary. The mourners were left alone with the corpse.

In her vast astonishment at this unaccountable procedure, Big Barbara turned and said loudly to Odessa, who was a dozen yards distant, "Odessa, *what* do they think they are doing? *Where* did Father Nalty go? *Why* has that boy stopped playing the organ—when he gets paid *special* for funerals, I know he does!"

"Miz Barbara . . ." said Odessa with pleading politeness.

"Barbara," said Luker in a low voice, "turn around and just shut up."

She started to protest, but Dauphin said to her in a pained unhappy way, "Big Barbara, please . . ."

Big Barbara, who loved her son-in-law, sat still in her pew, though the effort cost her.

"Please, y'all, pray for Mama for a few minutes," said Dauphin. Obediently the others bowed their heads.

From the corner of her eye, India McCray saw Sister Mary-Scot pull from beneath her scapular a long narrow black box. She held it tightly in her hands before her.

India flicked a long painted fingernail against the back of her father's hand. "What has she got?" she whispered to him.

Luker looked over at the nun, shook his head in ignorance, and whispered back: "I don't know."

For many seconds then there was no movement in the sanctuary. The air conditioner started up suddenly, drowning the traffic outside. No one prayed. Dauphin and Mary-Scot, embarrassed and evidently most uncomfortable, stood staring at each other across the central aisle. Leigh had shifted a couple of feet down and turned sideways. With her elbow resting on the back of the pew, she held her veil raised so that she might exchange perplexed glances with her mother. Luker and his daughter grasped one another's hands to communicate their wonder. Odessa stared fixedly ahead of her, as if she could not be expected to evince surprise at *anything* that was done at the funeral of a woman mean as Marian Savage.

Dauphin sighed loudly and nodded to his sister. Slowly they moved toward the altar, and took stations behind the coffin. They did not look down at their dead mother, but stared grimly ahead of them. Dauphin took the slender black box from the nun, unlatched it and lifted the top. All the McCrays craned but could see nothing of its contents. In the faces of the brother and sister was something at once so terrified and so solemn that even Big Barbara refrained from speech.

From the box, Sister Mary-Scot withdrew a shining knife with a narrow pointed blade about eight inches long. Together, Dauphin and Sister Mary-Scot held the dagger by its polished handle. Twice they passed it over the open space of the coffin, and then turned the point of it down over their mother's unbeating heart.

Big Barbara's astonishment was so great that she must stand; Leigh clutched her mother's arm and rose as well. Luker and India followed suit, as did Odessa across the aisle. Standing, the mourners were able to see into the coffin. They half expected Marian Savage to sit up in protest at this extraordinary proceeding.

Sister Mary-Scot let go the handle of the knife. Her hands trembled in the space above the coffin, her lips moved in prayer. Her eyes opened wide as she reached down into the coffin and pulled apart the linen grave-clothes. Marian Savage's unpainted flesh was distinctly yellow; Sister Mary-Scot pushed aside a prosthesis and uncovered the mastectomy scars. Drawing in his breath sharply, Dauphin raised the knife high.

"Lord, Dauphin!" cried Sister Mary-Scot, "get on with it!"

Dauphin pressed the blade an inch deep into the corpse's sunken breast. He held it there the length of his shuddering.

He withdrew the knife slowly, as if fearful of causing Marian Savage pain. The blade emerged coated with the mixed coagulated liquids of the unembalmed body. Shuddering anew at the sensation of actually touching the corpse, he placed the knife in his mother's cold stiff hands.

Sister Mary-Scot flung away the empty black box and it clattered on the polished wooden floor. Quickly she pulled together the graveclothes and without ceremony dropped the top of the coffin over the mutilated body of their mother. She rapped loudly three times on the lid. The sound was distressingly hollow.

The priest and the organist reappeared through the small side door. Dauphin and Mary-Scot dashed to the back of the church together and dragged open the great wooden doors to admit the pallbearers. The six men hurried down the aisle, lifted the coffin on their shoulders and, to the accompaniment of a thunderous postlude, carried it out into the fiery sunlight and blasting heat of that Wednesday afternoon in May.

PART I

SAVAGE MOTHERS

CHAPTER 1

The house in which Dauphin and Leigh Savage lived had been built in 1906; it was a large, comfortable place with generous rooms and careful and pleasing detail in such things as hearths, moldings, frames, and glazing. From the windows on the second floor you could see the back of the great Savage mansion on Government Boulevard. Dauphin's house was the secondary Savage residence, reserved for younger sons and their wives. Patriarchs, older sons, and dowagers got the Great House, as it was called. Marian Savage had wanted newly-wed Dauphin and Leigh to stay with her in the Great House as long as they remained childless—she possessing no affection for infants or small children—but Leigh refused this invitation politely. Marian Savage's daughter-in-law said that she would just as soon settle into a place of her own, and pointed out how much more efficient the air conditioning was in the Small House.

And, despite the heat of that Wednesday afternoon, when the temperature at the cemetery had been over 100 degrees, the glassed-in porch at the back of Dauphin and Leigh's house was almost uncomfortably chilly. The harsh sunlight that prevailed at the front was here filtered through the two great live oaks that separated the backyard of the Small House from the extensive grounds of the mansion. In this generous chamber, filled with heavily upholstered furniture covered in large-patterned chintzes, Big Barbara had removed her shoes and stockings. The quarry tile was cold beneath her feet, and she had plenty of ice in her scotch.

Right now it was only Luker, Big Barbara, and India in the house. Leigh's two maids had been given the day off in deference to the dead. Big Barbara sat at one end of the great soft sofa, going through a Hammacher-Schlemmer catalog, turning down pages for Leigh to examine particularly. Luker, who had removed his shoes, lay stretched out upon the couch with his feet in his mother's lap. India sat at the long trestle table behind the couch, reworking on to graph paper the patterns she had memorized in the church.

"House seems empty," remarked Luker.

"That's 'cause nobody's here," said his mother. "Houses always seem empty after a funeral."

"Where's Dauphin?"

"Dauphin went to take Mary-Scot back to Pensacola. We're hoping he's gone be back by suppertime. Leigh and Odessa are taking care of things at the church. Luker, listen . . ."

"What?"

"I don't want *any* of you to go dying on me, because I just can't *begin* to tell you how much trouble it is to arrange a funeral!"

Luker didn't reply.

"Big Barbara?" said India, when her grandmother was knocking the last ice cube into her mouth.

"What, child?"

"Do they always do that at funerals around here?"

"Do what?" asked Big Barbara uneasily, not turning around.

"Stick knives in dead people."

"I was *hoping* you hadn't been paying attention at that time," said Big Barbara. "But I assure you, child, it is *not* a common occurrence. In fact, I have *never* seen it done before. And I am as sorry as I can be that you had to see it."

"Didn't bother me," shrugged India. "She was dead, wasn't she?"

"Yes," said Big Barbara, glancing at her son, hoping that he would interrupt this unhappy exchange. Luker's eyes were closed, and Big Barbara knew that he meant to give the impression that he was asleep. "But you are still too young to have to know about that sort of thing at all. I went to my first wedding when I was nine, but they wouldn't let me into a funeral until I was fifteen—and that was after Hurricane Delia, when half the people I knew in the world got blown twenty-five miles up in the air and toothpicks got driven all the way straight through telephone poles. Lots of funerals that month, I can tell you!"

"I've seen dead people before," said India. "One day I was walking to school, and there was a dead man in a doorway. My friend and I touched him with a stick. We wiggled his foot, and then we ran away. And then one afternoon, Luker and I were having dim sum in Chinatown—"

"You were having *what*? Is that innards?"

"We were in Chinatown having lunch," India said more simply, "and when we came out of the restaurant we saw two little Chinese girls get run down in the road by a water truck. It was disgusting —we saw their brains and everything. After that I told Luker I would never eat a brain again—and I haven't, either."

"That's terrible!" cried Big Barbara. "Those poor little girls— were they *twins*, India?"

India didn't know.

"What a terrible story!" cried Big Barbara, pushing Luker's feet out of her lap. "That's just the sort of thing that happens in New York. Now that you're divorced I don't see why you still live there."

"I love New York," said Luker without opening his eyes.

"So do I," said India.

"When you got your divorce from . . . *that woman*, you should have come back home to live."

"I hate Alabama," said Luker.

India didn't say anything.

"Luker," said Big Barbara, on to her favorite subject, "the happiest day of my life was the day you called up and said you were getting a divorce. I said to Lawton, 'Lawton,' I said, 'I—'"

"Don't get started," warned Luker, "we all know what you think about . . . *that woman*."

"Then get up and get me some more scotch. Grief has *always*— ever since I was a little girl—grief has always made my throat dry."

Luker got up slowly. "Barbara, it's not four o'clock yet. You guzzled that first drink—"

"I was just trying to get at the ice, I was so thirsty. That cemetery ought to have a water fountain. I don't know why it doesn't. People get thirsty at funerals just like they get thirsty everywhere else."

From the kitchen Luker called, "You're a drunk, Barbara, and it's time you did something about it!"

"You've been talking to your father!" cried Big Barbara. She turned to India. "Do you treat him as badly as he treats me?"

India lifted her red pencil from the graph paper. "Yes."

"Then you're a rotten child!" exclaimed Big Barbara. "I don't know why I waste my love on either one of you!"

Luker brought his mother her drink. "I made it weak. It's all ice cubes and water. You don't have any call to be drunk before the sun goes down."

"My best friend in the world is dead," replied Big Barbara. "I am toasting her memory."

"She'll be toasted all right," said Luker in a low voice. He threw himself back on to the couch, and again dropped his feet into his mother's lap.

"Lay 'em flat!" commanded Big Barbara, "so I can put the catalog down."

There was quiet for some minutes. India continued her painstaking work with a handful of colored pencils; Luker apparently slept; Big Barbara sipped at her drink and turned the pages of the catalog that was propped against Luker's feet.

"Good God!" said Big Barbara to Luker, and pummeled his knees with her fist. "Did you see this, Luker?"

"See what?" he murmured without curiosity.

"There is an ice cream machine in here that costs seven hundred dollars. It doesn't even use rock salt. It probably doesn't even use milk and cream. For that kind of money you just plug it in, and four minutes later you got a half gallon of cherry-peach-vanilla."

"I'm surprised that Leigh hasn't got one then."

"She does!" said Big Barbara, "but I just had no *idea* that it cost seven hundred dollars! For seven hundred dollars you could make a down payment on a recreational vehicle!"

"Recreational vehicles are in bad taste, Barbara. At least you can hide an ice cream machine in the closet. Besides, Dauphin's got all the money in the world. And now that Marian Savage has finally had the good taste to kick off, he's going to have even more. Are they going to move into the Great House?"

"I don't know, they haven't decided yet. They're not gone decide till we get back from Beldame."

"Barbara," said Luker, "whose idea was it for us all to go down to Beldame? I mean, Marian Savage died at Beldame. You think it's going to do Dauphin a whole lot of good to be down there where his mother died about three days ago?"

Big Barbara shrugged. "You don't think *I'd* suggest something like that, do you? It wasn't Leigh either. It was Dauphin's idea—Dauphin's and Odessa's. Odessa had been down there with Marian, of course—these days when she was so sick, Marian wouldn't walk across the hall unless Odessa went with her. And anyway, Dauphin and Odessa seemed to think it'd do us all good to go on down there and get it out of our system. You 'member when Bothwell died down there, nobody went back for six months—and that year had a *beautiful* summer!"

"Bothwell was Dauphin's father?" asked India.

Big Barbara nodded. "How old was Dauphin when Bothwell died, Luker?"

"Five. Six. Seven," replied Luker. "I don't remember. I had forgot that he died at Beldame too."

"I know," said Big Barbara. "Who thinks of poor old Bothwell any more? Anyway, it wasn't as if Marian had been down there all that long either, it's not as if all her suffering took place down at Beldame. She and Odessa hadn't been down there more than a day and a half when Marian died. It was real strange. She stayed in the Great House for almost two years, hardly stirring from that room, sleeping all day and awake all night complaining. Then all of a sudden she up and decides that she wants to go to Beldame. Dauphin tried to talk her out of it. *I* tried to talk her out of it, but Marian gets something in her head, it doesn't get out again. So she just ups and goes down to Beldame. Dauphin wanted to go with her, but Marian wouldn't let him. Wouldn't even let him drive her. Johnny Red drove her and Odessa down. And they weren't gone hardly twenty-four hours before there was a state trooper beating on the door to tell Dauphin that Marian was dead. It was just horrible."

"What'd she died of?" asked India.

"Cancer," said Big Barbara. "She was eaten up. It was just strange that she should have lasted two years up here, and then die all of a sudden-like soon as she got to Beldame."

"Was Odessa with her when she died?" asked Luker.

Big Barbara shook her head. "Odessa was cleaning upstairs or something, and Marian had a stroke out on the verandah. When Odessa came downstairs the swing was still rocking, but Marian was dead on the floorboards. Odessa dragged her inside and put her in the hammock and then walked to Gasque and called the highway patrol. She tried to call Dauphin but wasn't anybody at home. Listen, Luker," said Big Barbara in a lower voice, "India has got me to thinking—have you figured out yet what that knife business was all about?"

Luker had turned so that his face was buried between the cushion and the back of the couch. Big Barbara rolled him over.

"Yes I have," he replied.

"Well?"

"Dauphin and Mary-Scot were just sorry they hadn't stuck a knife in her when she was still alive, and it was their last chance."

In the corner of the room, in a cage suspended six feet from the floor, was a large red parrot. It screamed.

Big Barbara pointed. "See. Nails understands every word you say. Marian loved that bird, don't you dare say anything mean about Marian in front of Nails! He doesn't like it."

"What is that thing doing here anyway?"

"Well, they couldn't just leave it at the Great House, it would have pined away in three hours without Marian around."

"They should have buried it with her."

"I thought parrots could talk," said India.

Nails poked his beak through the wires of the cage and screamed again.

"This one's doing a perfect imitation of Marian Savage, right now," said Luker.

"Luker," exclaimed Big Barbara, grabbing a handful of his toes and twisting them, "I do not understand why you talk so mean about the woman who was my best friend in the world."

"Because she was the meanest bitch that ever trod the streets of Mobile."

"I *wish* you wouldn't use language like that in front of a thirteen-year-old girl."

"She can't see me," said Luker, who was invisible from where India sat, "and she doesn't know who said it."

"Yes I do," said India, but then added to her grandmother: "He's said worse. And so have I."

"I'll just bet," sighed Big Barbara.

"Barbara, you know how mean that woman was," said Luker. "Poor old Dauphin, she treated him like dirt as long as Mary-Scot was around. And then when Mary-Scot joined the convent, she treated him like shit."

"Shhh!"

"Well you know she did." Luker shrugged. "And that's the way it's been for two hundred years in that family. All the men are very sweet and good-hearted, and the women walk around with armor plating."

"But they make good wives," protested Big Barbara. "Marian was a good wife to Bothwell for as long as he lived. She made him happy."

"And he probably liked getting nailed to the wall and beat with a bicycle chain, too."

"*You* do," said India to her father. Big Barbara jerked her head around, dismayed.

"India's lying through her teeth," said Luker evenly. "She doesn't know anything about my sex life. She's only thirteen," he said, lifting himself so that he could grin at his daughter. "She doesn't even know what fucking is yet."

"*Luker!*"

"Oh, Barbara, listen, as long as I've got my feet in your lap, why don't you rub 'em for a while? Those shoes pinched today."

Big Barbara peeled off her son's socks and began to massage his feet.

"Well," said Luker, "granted that the Savage women make okay wives, the fact is that as mothers, they're the pits."

"No they're not!"

"Barbara, you don't know what you're talking about. Why are you trying to defend a dead woman?"

"Marian Savage—"

"*Savage mothers eat their children up!*" cried Luker, and the parrot screamed again.

CHAPTER 2

Big Barbara, Luker, and India remained on the glassed-in porch for another hour, waiting for Leigh to return. Luker slept, still with his feet in his mother's lap, and turned disturbed only when the parrot Nails screamed. India brought her grandmother a stack of catalogs to be looked through while she herself worked free embroidery in green and purple threads on a blue work shirt. The sun continued bright and green through the live oak foliage at the back of the house. A square of leaded stained glass dangled before one of the windows, and now and then the sun, breaking momentarily through stirred foliage, pierced that square of glass and painted India's face gold and blue and red.

At last Leigh arrived: they heard the car in the gravel driveway, they heard the doors of the car slam, they heard the opening of the door to the laundry room downstairs.

"Was there that much to do?" asked Big Barbara of her daughter, who came through the kitchen. "You were gone such a long time."

"Get up, Luker!" said Leigh. "I've been on my feet the whole day." Luker rose wearily and unsteadily from the sofa. Leigh kicked off her shoes and took his place. She unpinned her veil and dropped it on the coffee table. "Mama, I bet you've been sitting here the whole afternoon rubbing his feet. Well, rub mine for a little while."

"You want your stockings on or off?"

"On, leave 'em on. I don't have the strength to pull 'em off right now."

"Did you bring Odessa back with you?" asked Luker, who now sat at the table examining his daughter's work on the graph paper.

"I'm here," said Odessa from the kitchen door.

"That's what took us so long," said Leigh. "We went back to the church, took care of everything there—though when there's only seven people attending and just one coffin, there's not a whole lot to do."

"What'd you do with the extra flowers?"

"We took 'em over to Odessa's church. Old man died there last night, family didn't have anything so we carried the flowers over and put 'em in the church. We're all invited to the funeral, but I told 'em no, I didn't think we'd come after all, one funeral a week was enough for just about anybody."

"Can I get y'all anything?" asked Odessa.

"Iced tea," said Leigh, "please, Odessa."

"Scotch and lots of ice," said Big Barbara.

"Better let me get that," said Luker to Odessa. "I think I'll start to catch up myself. You want anything, India?"

India, who didn't approve of family retainers, had shaken her head to Odessa's offer; but to her father she said, "Maybe some sherry . . ."

"Dauphin has Punt e Mes," said Luker.

"Oh, great! With an ice cube."

Big Barbara twisted around. "Luker, does that child *drink?*"

"Only since we got her off speed," said Luker, and winked at Odessa.

"You are too *young* to drink!" cried Big Barbara to her grand-daughter.

"No I'm not," replied India calmly.

"Well you are certainly too young to drink in front of me!"

"Then turn around."

"I will!" said Big Barbara, and did. She looked at Leigh. "Do you know that that child sees dead people all the time in New York—*on the street.* Dead people on the street, did you ever hear of such a thing? People dying where you can see 'em and poke 'em with a stick!"

"India's much more grown up than I was at her age, Mama," said Leigh. "I don't think you have to be particularly worried about her."

"Luker would be a terrible man to have for a father, if you ask me. He's the meanest man in the world, you ask anybody."

"Is that why you love him more than you love me?" asked Leigh.

Big Barbara didn't answer, but India laughed. "Luker's not bad," she said.

Luker appeared with a tray of drinks. He went to India first. "Barbara, watch," he said, "see how well I've got her trained. What do you say, India?"

India stood from the table, dropped a curtsy, and said in a simpering voice, "Thank you very much, Father, for bringing me the glass of Punt e Mes with ice."

India sat down again, but Big Barbara was unconvinced. "She's got manners, but what has she got in the way of morals?"

"Oh," said Luker blithely, "she and I don't have any morals. We have to get along with a scruple or two."

"I thought so," said Big Barbara. "Nothing's ever going to come of either one of you."

India turned to her grandmother. "We're different from you," she said simply.

Big Barbara shook her head. "Were truer words ever spoken within your hearing, Leigh?"

"No," said Leigh as she accidentally cascaded half her iced tea down the front of her black dress. Shaking her head at her own clumsiness, she rose and went in to change. When she returned a few minutes later, Luker had grabbed his place again on the couch; he made an insincere offer to give it up to her.

"Well, y'all," said Leigh, sitting in a chair that faced them, "are y'all dying to hear about the knife or not?"

"You know!" cried Big Barbara.

"Odessa told me on the way back to the church."

"How come Odessa knew and you didn't?" asked Luker.

"Because it's a Savage family secret, that's why, and there's nothing about the Savages that Odessa doesn't know."

"Marian Savage told me *everything*," said Big Barbara, "but she never mentioned a word about sticking knives in dead people. I would have remembered something like that."

"Go on and tell us," Luker demanded, impatient despite his languorous posture. The light in the room was now entirely green.

"Get me a drink, Luker, and I'll tell y'all what Odessa told me. And after y'all know all about it, y'all are not gone mention it to Dauphin, understand? He didn't like doing it, he didn't want to stick that knife in Marian's chest."

"He should have asked me to do it!" said Luker.

Nails screamed in his cage.

"I despise that bird," said Leigh wearily.

Luker got up to get the drink, and when he returned, Odessa

came along behind him. "You're going to make sure she tells it right?" asked Luker over his shoulder, and she nodded. With her bony black fingers running up and down the sides of a glass of iced tea, she sat at the far corner of the long table where India bent low over the pad of graph paper.

Leigh faced them all, and her expression was serious. "Odessa, you're gone interrupt me if I get anything wrong, aren't you?"

"Yes, ma'am, I sure will," said Odessa, and bargain-sealed with a swallow of tea.

"Well," began Leigh, "we all know 'bout how long the Savages have been in Mobile—"

"Since before there *was* a Mobile," said Big Barbara. "They were French. The French were the first ones to come here—after the Spanish, I mean. They were originally the *Sauvages.*" The little speech was directed to India, who nodded over her sketchbook.

"Well, about that time—about two hundred and fifty years ago—Mobile was owned by the French, and the Savages were real important even then. The governor of the whole French territory around here was a Savage, and he had a daughter—I don't know her name, do you Odessa?"

Odessa shook her head.

"Well, this daughter died in giving birth. The baby died too, and they were buried together in the family mausoleum. It's not the one where we buried Marian today, it was one that came before that one—it's gone now. Anyway, the next year, this woman's husband died too—of cholera or something—and they opened the mausoleum again." She paused.

"And you know what they found?" Odessa prompted from behind.

No one had any idea.

"They found out they had buried that girl alive," Leigh said. "She waked up in her coffin, and she pushed off the lid and she screamed and screamed and nobody heard her and she tore her hands all up trying to get the door open and she couldn't and she didn't have anything to eat—*so she ate the dead baby.* And when she was through eating the baby, she piled up the bones in the corner and put the baby's clothes on top of them. Then she starved to death, and that's what they found when they opened the mausoleum."

"It wouldn't have happened if they had embalmed her," said Big Barbara. "A lot of times people turn black for a minute on the embalming table, and that means there was a little bit of life left in 'em, but after the embalming fluid goes in, nobody wakes up again. Whoever's around when I die, I want 'em to make sure I get embalmed."

"I don't think that was the end of the story, Barbara," said Luker, reproving her for the interruption.

"Well," said Big Barbara defensively, "it's just a terrible story already, I don't see how there could be a whole lot more to it."

"Well, when they found the dead woman on the floor of the mausoleum and the little pile of bones, everybody was so upset that they figured they had to do something to prevent it from ever happening again. So at every funeral after that, the head of the family stuck a knife through the heart of the dead person just to make sure he was really dead. They always did it at the funeral so everybody could see that it had been done and wouldn't worry about the corpse waking up in the mausoleum. It wasn't a bad idea, considering that they probably didn't know about embalming fluid."

India had looked up from the graph paper and was listening attentively to Leigh. However, her pencil moved unceasingly and purposefully across the page, and now and then she glanced down as if surprised by the picture that was forming there.

"So after that, every person that was born into the Savage family got a knife presented to him at his christening, and that knife went with him for the rest of his life. And then when he died, that knife was stuck in his chest, and then got buried in the coffin with him."

"And then it became ritual," said Luker. "I mean, Dauphin didn't push the knife all the way in, did he? He just sort of nicked her."

"That's right," said Odessa, "but it's still not ever'thing."

"I cain't believe there's more!" cried Big Barbara.

"Sometime before the Civil War," said Leigh, "there was a girl who married a Savage boy and she had two children, both of 'em girls, and the third baby would have been a boy, but he died at birth. And she died right after. They had the funeral with the mother and the baby in the coffin, just like the first time."

"Did they stick the knife in the dead baby too?" asked India. Her pencil did minute cross-hatching on the pad without her looking at it.

"Yes," said Odessa.

"Yes," said Leigh, "they certainly did. The boy's father stuck the knife in the baby first, and then pulled it out—it must have been a terrible thing to have to do. So the church was full, and the father pulled the knife out of his little baby. He was crying, but he was brave and he raised it up high and brought it down and stuck it in his wife's chest . . ."

"And?" prompted Luker when she paused.

"And she woke up screaming," said Leigh softly. "She woke up from the shock of the knife going in her. Blood went everywhere, all over the burial dress, all over the coffin, all over the baby, and all over her husband. She grabbed him around the neck, and pulled him down in the coffin with her, and then the coffin tipped over and all three of 'em rolled out in the middle aisle. She kept her arms around his neck, and she died that way. Then they had the *real* funeral . . ."

"What happened to the husband?" asked India, curious.

"He married again," said Leigh. "That was Dauphin's great-great-grandfather, and he was the one who built Beldame."

Big Barbara began to weep, affected not only by the story but by the declining afternoon, the scotch she had consumed, and her growing sense of loss. Luker, who saw this, kneaded his mother's thigh with the soles of his feet in comfort.

"So that's why they don't push the knife all the way in any more?" said Luker softly.

"That's right," said Odessa.

"They just touch the chest with the point of the knife—that's the symbolic part," said Leigh. "But then they bury the knife in the dead person's hands, and that part's *not* symbolic. They figure that if they wake up in the coffin, then they can kill themselves with the knife."

"But wasn't Marian Savage embalmed?" asked Luker.

"No," said Big Barbara, "she wasn't. Bothwell wasn't embalmed, and so she said she wasn't going to get it either."

"Well," said Luker practically, "if the Savages would all just get themselves embalmed, they wouldn't have to bother about the knife."

"You're a Savage now," said India to Leigh. "Do *you* have a knife?"

"No," said Leigh, surprised—for she had not considered this before. "I don't have one, I don't know what they'll do—"

"Yes, ma'am," said Odessa, "you do have one."

Leigh looked up. "I do? Where is it, Odessa, I didn't know . . ."

"Miz Savage give it to you on your wedding, but Mr. Dauphin wouldn't let you see it. He hid it. He knows where it is and I know where it is. I can show it to you if you want to see it." She got up to get the knife.

"No," cried Big Barbara, "leave it be, Odessa." Odessa sat.

"That's creepy," said Leigh, with a little shudder, "I didn't know, I—"

"I don't want them to do that to you," said Big Barbara.

"She's a Savage now, Big Barbara," said India. "It's got to be done —when she's dead, I mean." India's pencil moved rapidly and at a great angle against the paper. Still she did not look at what she drew.

"No!" cried Big Barbara. "Dauphin's not gone stick a knife in you, he—"

"Barbara," said Luker, "don't get wrought up. If she's dead, it can't hurt her. Leigh's not dead yet, and besides you probably won't be around when it happens anyway."

"I still don't like it!"

"Well, Mama, don't worry about it. I just wanted you all to know about the knife so that you wouldn't say anything about it to Dauphin when he comes in. He was being real good to us just by letting us go to the service. The Savage family funerals have always been completely private because of the knives, but he was showing us how much he trusted us. He knew that we wouldn't go spreading it all over creation that he and Mary-Scot stuck a dagger in Marian's chest after she was dead—"

"Of course we wouldn't!" cried Big Barbara, and swilled the last of her melted ice.

"Does Dauphin know we know?" asked Luker.

"He told me to tell Miz Leigh so she could tell y'all," said Odessa, "so he knows."

"Good," said Luker, looking hard at his mother, "then we won't ever mention this again. Dauphin is the sweetest man on the face of the earth, and not one of us is going to say *anything* that might make him the least bit uncomfortable, are we, Barbara?"

"Of course not!"

"I'm gone start supper for y'all," said Odessa, rising to go into the kitchen.

Leigh and her mother went into the bedroom to find something more comfortable for Big Barbara to put on. Mother and daughter McCray's intimacy subsisted principally on helping one another dress and undress.

Luker went into the kitchen to replenish his own and his daughter's glasses. When he returned, he sat on the bench next to India and said, "Let me see what you've done."

She withheld the drawing. "I didn't do it," she said.

"What do you mean?"

"I mean," said India, "that I wasn't doing the drawing. I was just holding the pencil."

Luker looked at her blankly. "Show me the drawing."

She handed it to him. "I didn't even look at it. I started to draw something else, then I stopped to listen to the story, but the pencil kept on going. Look," she said, pointing to several stray lines, "that's where I started to draw, but it got covered up."

"This isn't your style," said Luker curiously. The drawing was in red pencil on the back of a sheet of graph paper—an oddly formal construction, a picture of a fat woman with a saturnine face sitting stiffly in a chair that was invisible beneath her great bulk. She wore a dress with a tight bodice and an enormously wide skirt. Her arms were outstretched before her. "What is she holding, India?"

"I didn't draw it," said India. "I guess they're dolls. They're hideous, aren't they? They look like wax dolls that were left out in the sun too long—all melted and deformed. You know in the Museum of the City of New York, those awful German dolls that were modeled on real babies—you said they were the ugliest things you had ever seen? That's probably what they are—that's probably what I was remembering when . . ."

"When what?"

"When I drew this," she said in a low puzzled voice. "Except I didn't really draw it—it drew itself."

Luker looked at his daughter closely. "I don't think you really *did* draw it—it *isn't* your style."

India shook her head and took a sip of her sherry.

"This dress the woman's wearing, India, can you date it?"

"Ah . . ." She hesitated. "The 1920s?"

"Bad guess," said Luker, "it's about 1875. As a matter of fact, it's perfect 1875, and you really didn't know that, did you?"

"No," said India. "I was sitting here, listening to Leigh's story, and the drawing did itself." She glanced down at it with distaste. "And I don't like it either."

"No," said Luker, "neither do I."

CHAPTER 3

That evening, when Dauphin had returned from driving Sister Mary-Scot to the convent in Pensacola, no one spoke either of the funeral or the knife, and Leigh hid the stack of letters of condolence that she had retrieved from the post office box. Supper went quietly enough, and though everyone but Dauphin had changed clothes, they all felt as if they had been starched and pressed into their chairs. Even Dauphin took too much wine, and actually called back the third bottle when Odessa disapprovingly removed it. Over that meal they made their plans for leaving Mobile the following day: choosing which cars were to be taken to the coast, who would do the shopping, what time they ought to get started, what must be done about the mail and business and Lawton McCray. Marian Savage's death was the ostensible reason for their going away, but she was not talked of. The Great House was too near, and the principal bedroom from which the dying woman had scarcely stirred in the two years of her illness now seemed to vibrate its unaccustomed emptiness through the night.

From his place at the table, Dauphin would often lean to one side to discern his mother's bedroom window, just visible from the dining room, as if he expected or feared to find it lighted—as it had been lighted every night at dinnertime since he and Leigh had returned from their honeymoon.

They lingered over dessert and coffee, and it was getting on when at last they rose from the table. Leigh went immediately to bed, and Big Barbara went into the kitchen to help Odessa load the dishwashers. Following her father and Dauphin on to the porch, India stretched out on the couch with her head in Luker's lap and fell asleep without disturbing the saucer and cup of cooling coffee that rested on her belly.

Not much later, Big Barbara appeared in the kitchen doorway and said wearily, "Dauphin, Luker, I'm gone drive Odessa home now, and then I'm going back to the house. I'll see y'all early in the morning."

"Big Barbara," said Dauphin, "let me drive Odessa. You stay here with Luker, you stay here tonight. No reason your going out."

"I'll see you two in the morning, bright and early," said Big Barbara. "I suspect Lawton's home by now, and he's gone want to hear"—she refused to speak of the funeral—"he's gone want to tell me all about his day."

"All right," said Dauphin, "you sure you don't want me to drive you?"

"I'm sure," said Big Barbara. "Luker, your father is gone want to see you and India before we get off to Beldame tomorrow. What do you want me to say?"

"Tell him I'll drop by in the morning before we get started."

"He said he wanted to talk to you about something."

"He probably wants me to change my last name," said Luker in a low voice to Dauphin, and stroked India's hair. "Good night, Barbara," he said loudly, "see you in the morning."

India was asleep and the two men sat silent. Through the windows the night was utterly black. Clouds blotted the moon and stars; foliage obscured the streetlamps. Somehow, from just the degree of air conditioning in the house, they could tell that it was still warm and damply uncomfortable outside. In the corner, away from Dauphin's chair, a single lamp burned. Luker carefully pried India's fingers from the saucer and removed it to the coffee table; with a nod he accepted the port that his brother-in-law brought to him.

"I sure am glad you decided to come down, Luker," said Dauphin softly, seating himself.

"It's been a bad time, I take it."

Dauphin nodded. "Mama'd been sick for about two years, but for the last eight months she was really dying. You could see it. She got worse and worse every day. She might have lasted who knows how long if she hadn't gone down to Beldame. I wanted to tell her no—actually I did tell her no, but she went on anyway. And it killed her."

"I'm sorry it was so hard on you," said Luker. His sympathy for Dauphin did not extend to fabricating a hypocritical kind word for the dead woman, and he knew that Dauphin did not expect to hear it. "But are you sure that going to Beldame is the right thing to do now? There must be a hundred thousand things to take care of— the will and so forth. And when there's so much money involved, so much money and property, it's got to be a lot of work—and you're the only one to do it."

"I knew this was coming." Dauphin shrugged. "And I've already taken care of what I could. I know what's in the will, and they'll have it read in a few weeks—I'll come back up for that. But you're right, there's a lot to be done."

"Even if you *have* taken care of everything, are you sure the right thing to do is go off on a vacation? God knows there's nothing to do at Beldame—what are you going to do but sit around all day and think about Marian? Wouldn't it be better if you stayed here, doing a little business every day, getting used to seeing the Great House empty? Getting used to Marian not being around?"

"Probably," agreed Dauphin, "but, Luker, I tell you, I've been through this for two years, and Mama was never the easiest person to get along with in the world, even when she was well. It was too bad—of us three children, she loved Darnley best, but one day Darnley went sailing and he never came back. You know, Mama always looked for Darnley's sail whenever she came within sight of the water. I don't think she ever got over the feeling that one day he was just gone pull up on the beach at Beldame and say, 'Hey, y'all, when's supper gone be ready?' And after Darnley, she loved Mary-Scot. Then Mary-Scot went and joined the convent—they had a big fight about that, you remember. And so then there was just me left, and Mama never loved me like she loved Darnley and Mary-Scot. I'm not complaining, of course. Mama couldn't help who she loved. I was just always sorry it wasn't one of the others who stayed behind to take care of her. Taking care of Mama wasn't easy, but I did everything I could. I think I'd feel a lot better now if she had died over at the Great House instead of at Beldame. People in town say I ought not to have let her go down there, but I'd like to see anybody try to stop Mama from doing something that Mama got it in her head to do! Odessa says there wasn't anything we could have done—that it was Mama's turn to die, and she just plopped out of the swing onto the verandah, and that was that! Luker, I *need* to get away, and I'm glad we're all going down to Beldame together. I didn't want to drag Leigh away all by herself—I know I'd get on her nerves if we were all by ourselves, so I asked Big Barbara to go with us, except I didn't think she would because of Lawton's campaign—"

"Wait," said Luker, "let me ask you something—"

"What?"

"Are you giving Lawton any money for that campaign?"

"A little," said Dauphin.

"What's a little? More than ten thousand?"

"Yes."

"More than fifty?"

"No."

"You're still a fool, Dauphin," said Luker.

"I don't know why you say that," said Dauphin, but not defensively. "He's running for Congress, and he can use the money. It's not like I'm throwing it away. Lawton's never lost a campaign yet. He got city councillor the first time he ran, and then he got state rep first time he ran, and state senator—I don't see any reason to believe that he won't be going up to Washington next year. Leigh didn't say I should give him any money, and Big Barbara didn't say it either. *Lawton* didn't even say it. It was my idea, and I'm not gone feel bad about giving it to him, no matter what you say."

"Well, I hope at least you're getting big deductions on this."

Dauphin shifted uncomfortably. "On some of it yes—the part that comes under campaign laws. You have to be careful."

"You mean you're giving more than the legal limit?"

Dauphin nodded. "It's complicated. Actually, it's Leigh who gives the money to him. I give it to her and she gives it to Big Barbara and Big Barbara puts it in a joint account and Lawton draws on it. They're real sticky about campaign funds. So the fact is, I don't take a deduction on more than a few thousand. But"—he smiled—"I'm happy to do it. It'd be nice to have my father-in-law in Congress. Wouldn't you be proud to tell your friends that your father is in the House of Representatives?"

"Lawton's career has never been a particular source of pride for me," said Luker dryly. "I just wish *I* had been born with your money. You wouldn't catch me providing Lawton McCray's campaign funds." He gathered India in his arms and took her into the nearer of the two adjoining bedrooms they had been given. When he returned, he found Dauphin placing the cover over Nails's cage.

"You don't want to go to sleep yet, do you?" asked Luker.

"I should," said Dauphin. "Today was a long day, a bad day. Tomorrow's gone be long too, I should go to bed now—but I'm not. Stay up and talk to me, if you will. You don't come back here near often enough, Luker."

"Why don't you and Leigh come see me in New York? I can put you up—or you can stay in a hotel. Leigh could see what it was like to shop in a real store instead of out of a catalog."

"She'd like that, I bet," said Dauphin mildly. "I would have come to see you, but Mama . . ."

Luker nodded.

". . . Mama wasn't doing so hot," Dauphin finished bravely. "It wasn't easy to get away. I told Leigh she ought to go up there and see you, but she decided to stay with me. She didn't have to, but I was glad she did. She was a lot of help, even though she was always pretending that she was just in the way, and that she didn't really like Mama at all . . ."

Kindly, Luker encouraged Dauphin to talk on, about Marian Savage, about her illness, about her death. The bereaved son detailed the minutiae of Marian Savage's physical deterioration, but told nothing of his own feelings. Luker suspected that Dauphin, in his self-effacing manner, felt that these were of no importance against the tremendous, stifling fact of the woman's death. But Dauphin's genuine love for his hardhearted, bristling mother was a trailing whisper at the end of every sentence he spoke.

In the night, the house settled. Creaks sounded in the hallways like errant footsteps, windows popped in their frames, china rattled in the cupboards, and pictures suddenly slipped awry on the walls. As the two men drank their port, Dauphin talked and Luker listened. Luker knew very well that Dauphin had no male friends, only business associates; and those who toadied for his friendship were after his money or the benefits of his position. Luker was fond of Dauphin, and knew it would help the man if he only sat still and let him talk. Poor Dauphin had no one to whom he might unburden himself; for though he trusted and loved both Leigh and Big Barbara, Dauphin's diffidence could never stand against their crushing volubility.

By half past two Dauphin had spun out his little store of grief for that terrible day—though Luker was certain it would be renewed fully on the next, and for many days after that. Luker had shifted their conversation onto less distressing topics: the progress of Lawton McCray's congressional campaign, the probable infestation of sand flies at Beldame, and Luker's recent photographic assignment in Costa Rica. Soon he would be able to suggest that they go to bed: Luker was already curled in a corner of the sofa and playing stupidly with his empty, sticky glass.

"More?" said Dauphin, standing with his own glass out-raised.

"Take it away," said Luker. Dauphin carried both glasses into the darkened kitchen and Luker closed his eyes against his brother-in-law's return—he hoped Dauphin would see that he was ready for sleep.

"What's this?" said Dauphin in a tone of voice that made Luker open his eyes quickly. Dauphin stood by the long table holding up the stack of India's graph paper and turning it toward the light.

"It's what India was drawing this afternoon, just before you got back from Pensacola. It was strange, she—"

"Why was she drawing *this*?" said Dauphin, with obvious—if inexplicable—pain.

"I don't know," said Luker, bewildered. "She was drawing it while—"

"While what?"

"While Leigh was telling us a story."

"What story?"

"A story that Odessa told her," said Luker evasively. Dauphin
nodded, understanding. "And she said that she didn't draw it, she
said it was the pencil that drew it. And the odd thing is that it's not
India's style at all. She never does anything this finished. I actually
saw her—she was drawing on the pad and the pencil was going
ninety to nothing, but she didn't even look down at it. I thought
she was just making scribbles. If I didn't know India, I'd say she
was lying, that somebody else did the drawing and she just made
scribbles on another page . . ."

Dauphin leafed quickly through the other sheets. "All the other
pages are blank."

"I know. She did the drawing, but I really don't think she knew
what she was doing. I mean, those dolls—"

"Those aren't dolls," said Dauphin with something like harsh-
ness.

"They *look* like dolls, not even Irish babies are that ugly, I've—"

"Listen," said Dauphin, "why don't you go get ready for bed?
Take this with you"—he handed the sketch to Luker—"and I'll be
in your room in about five minutes."

That much later, Luker was sitting on the edge of the bed with
India's sketch at his side. He studied the drawing of the saturnine
fat woman holding the two dolls—that Dauphin said were not
dolls—in the massive palms of her outstretched hands.

Still in the suit that he had worn at the funeral, and with the
black tourniquet still around his arm, Dauphin entered the room.
From his breast pocket, he drew a small photograph mounted on
stiff cardboard and handed it to Luker.

It was a *carte de visite*, which Luker, who was knowledgeable
of the history of photography, instinctively dated as Civil War or
perhaps a year or so later. He studied the back, with the photographer's logo and claims, before he allowed the meaning of the
image to break in on him.

The picture, faded but still clear, was of a great fat woman with a
crimped fringe of hair, wearing a hooped dress widely bordered in
black along the skirt and sleeves. She was seated in a chair that was
invisible beneath her great bulk. In her outstretched hands she held
two little heaps of misshapen flesh that were not, after all, dolls.

"It's my great-great-grandmother," said Dauphin. "The babies were twins, and they were stillborn. She had the picture taken before they were buried. They were both boys, and their names were Darnley and Dauphin."

"Why would she want to have a picture taken of stillborn children?" asked Luker.

"Ever since they started taking pictures, the Savages have had photographs taken of their corpses. I've got a whole box of 'em in there. These babies were buried in the cemetery, and I guess if they rated tombstones, they rated a picture."

Luker turned the photograph over, studied the back again without knowing what he thought. "India must have seen this . . ." he said at last, lying full length upon the bed and holding up the *carte de visite* at arm's length, directly above his face. He turned it so that reflected light obscured the image.

Dauphin took the photograph back. "No, she couldn't have. The old family pictures are kept locked in the file cabinet in my study. I had to use my key to get it out."

"Somebody must have described it to her," Luker persisted.

"Nobody knows about that picture, nobody except Odessa and me. I hadn't seen it for years. I just remembered it because it used to give me nightmares. When I was little, Darnley and I used to take out all the pictures of the dead Savages and look at 'em, and this was the one that scared me the most. This was my great-great-grandmother, and she was the first one to live in the house at Beldame. And this picture and the picture that India drew are just alike."

"No they're not," said Luker. "The dresses are different. The dress in the photograph is obviously earlier than the one India drew. The photograph is about 1865, India's picture is about ten years later."

"How can you tell?"

Luker shrugged. "I know something about American costume, that's all, and it's obvious. And if India were just copying the picture, then she'd copy the dress that was in the photograph. She wouldn't think up another dress that came along about ten years later—India, I'm sorry to say, knows nothing of the history of fashion."

"But what does that mean—that the dresses are different?" asked Dauphin, perplexed.

"I have no idea," replied Luker, "I don't understand any of it."

Luker kept India's drawing and promised Dauphin that he would next day question her more carefully about it—what its meaning could be, neither of them had any idea. Luker expressed the hope that it was only the port that had befuddled them, and that morning would solve the mystery in some simple and satisfactory manner.

Dauphin took the photograph back to his study and placed it in the box that contained photographs of the corpses of all the Savages who had died in the past hundred and thirty years. His mother's would be added in a week's time, for the photographer had visited the Church of St. Jude Thaddeus an hour before the funeral. He turned the key in the lock of this box, hid that key in another drawer of the file cabinet, then locked both the file cabinet and the door of the study. He walked slowly and thoughtfully through the darkened hallways of the house and back onto the glassed-in porch. He turned out the light, but then, in the darkness and his slight inebriation, he knocked his head against the parrot's cage.

"Oh," he whispered, "sorry, Nails, you all right?" He smiled, remembering in what affection his mother had held the shrill bird —despite its disappointing speechlessness. He raised the cover to peer inside.

The parrot flapped its iridescent, blood-red wings and stuck its beak between the bars. Its flat black eye reflected light that was not in the room. For the first time in its eight-year life, the parrot spoke. In cold imitation of Luker McCray's voice, the parrot cried: *"Savage mothers eat their children up!"*

CHAPTER 4

While the next morning was frittered away in preparations for the journey to Beldame, the unsettling coincidence of the century-old photograph and India's unconscious drawing was forgotten. Daylight had not brought a solution, but it had accorded indifference.

Having arrived in Alabama only the day before, Luker and India had never really unpacked, so it was no difficulty for them to prepare for this secondary journey. And Odessa had little to carry: she brought her wicker suitcase with her to the Small House when Leigh picked her up. But Dauphin had unavoidable early morning calls and these precipitated further errands; and Leigh and Big Barbara had to scuttle among their friends for a time, saying good-byes, returning borrowed items, and begging that certain small but consequential matters be accomplished in their possibly protracted absence. It seemed impossible to Leigh that Marian Savage had been alive not four days before. At times, in this round of visits, she was brought up short, remembering that she must assume a face of grief, and respond that *yes*, they really did need to get away from it all for a while, and where better to go than Beldame, a place so remote you might as well be at the end of the world?

India roused Luker at nine, went to the kitchen and prepared him coffee—she didn't trust the maids for this—then took it to his room and roused him again. "Oh, God," he whispered, "thanks." He sipped it, set it aside, rose and stumbled naked around the room for a few minutes.

"If you want the bathroom," said India from where she sat in a deep chair with her coffee carefully balanced on the narrow arm, "it's there." She pointed.

When Luker emerged, India had laid out his clothes. "Are we going to see your father today?" she asked. India preferred not to distinguish the man either by his Christian name or the sickening, loaded appellation of *grandfather*.

"Yes," said Luker. "Do you mind *very* much?"

"Even if I did, we'd still have to go, wouldn't we?"

"I suppose I could tell him that you were vomiting blood or something and you could stay out in the car."

"It's all right," said India, "I'll go in and speak to him, if you promise that we're not going to have to stay very long."

"Of course not," said Luker, buttoning his jeans.

"If he gets elected to Congress, would Big Barbara move to Washington? She'd be a lot nearer us then."

"I don't know," said Luker, "that depends. Do you want her to be nearer us?" Luker unbuttoned his jeans in order to tuck in his shirt.

"Yes," said India, "I'm actually very fond of Big Barbara."

"Well," said Luker, "little girls are *supposed* to be fond of their grandmothers."

India looked away sourly. "Depends on what?" she asked.

"It depends on how Big Barbara is getting along. It depends on how she and Lawton are getting along together."

"Big Barbara is an alkie, isn't she?"

"Yes," replied Luker. "And unfortunately, there's no methadone for alkies."

A few minutes later Big Barbara called to tell them that Lawton had gone out to the farm early that morning. If they did not catch him there in the next couple of hours they would have to wait until the middle of the afternoon, when he had returned from his lunchtime speech to the Mothers of the Rainbow Girls. The careful plans of the previous night were then scrapped, and India and Luker—not wishing to postpone the onerous visit—took off toward the farm. Odessa, having packed the trunk with numerous boxes of food for Beldame, rode with them. They went in the Fairlane that Dauphin had bought a year or so back solely for the use of houseguests or acquaintances who, for one reason or another, found themselves temporarily without transportation.

The Alabama panhandle, which consists only of Mobile and Baldwin counties, is shaped rather like a heavily abscessed tooth. Mobile Bay represents the large element of decay that separates the halves, and at their northern extremities the counties are further divided by a complex system of meandering rivers and marsh. The McCrays' land was situated along the Fish River about twenty miles from Mobile, but on the other side of Mobile Bay in Baldwin County. It was rich loamy flat acreage, excellent for cattle and fruit trees and just about any sort of cash crop one cared to plant. In addition to his agricultural activities, which were entirely supervised by a family of farmers named Dwight whom he had long ago bought out of bankruptcy, Lawton McCray had a fertilizer supply business situated in the nearby and scarcely discernible town of Belforest. Despite recent steep increases in the price of phosphorus, the fertilizer business had continued to make the McCrays a great deal of money.

The concern was set in a cleared space about a hundred yards square near the tracks of the railroad that no longer stopped at Belforest. There were three large storage sheds, a couple of old barns converted to the same purpose, and a paved area on which rested a number of trucks and trailers and spreading equipment. Set to one side was the office, a small, low concrete-block building with aquamarine walls and grimy windows. A barking dog of ignoble breed was tied to a sagging porch support. Luker would have driven right past the place and gone on to the farm, had he not recognized his father's pink Continental drawn up before the office. When Luker lowered his window, they heard Lawton McCray's vituperative voice inside the air-conditioned office, arguing with the impoverished distant relative who ran the operation so profitably for him. As soon as Luker got out of the Fairlane his father spied him through the dirt-streaked window. Lawton McCray came out to greet his son. He was a large man with beautiful white hair, but enough extra flesh—in the form of pendulous cheeks, a large nose, and several chins—to make up another face altogether. His clothes were expensive, fit him ill, and might have done with a cleaning. He and Luker hugged perfunctorily, then Lawton surged around the Fairlane and rapped sharply on the window through which his only grandchild peered up at him mistrustfully. India hesitantly lowered the window, and stiffened when Lawton McCray plunged his head and shoulders through to kiss her.

"How you, India?" the man bellowed. His mouth widened and his eyes narrowed to a fearful extent. India didn't know whether she liked him less as a relative or a politician.

"Very well, thank you," she replied.

"Odessa," twisting his large head on his thick neck, he yelled into the back seat, "how you?"

"I'm fine, Mr. Lawton."

"Odessa," he demanded, "you ever seen a girl pretty as this one?"

"I never have," said Odessa calmly.

"I never have either! This is a girl to be reckoned with. She is my only grandchild, and I love her like I love my soul! She is the delight of my old age!"

"You not old, Mr. Lawton," said Odessa obediently.

"You gone vote for me?" he laughed.

"Oh, sure."

"You gone get Johnny Red to vote for me, that no-account?"

"Mr. Lawton, I tried to get Johnny to register, but he talks to me 'bout poll tax. I tell him there ain't no such thing no more, but he still won't go down and sign up. You got to go talk to him, you want him to vote for you!"

"You tell him I'm not never gone get him out of jail any more if he don't go down and register."

"I'll tell him," said Odessa.

Lawton McCray smiled grimly, then turned back to India, who was cowering against the violence and vulgarity of her grandfather's voice.

"How'd you like the funeral yesterday? Big Barbara said it was your first time. I never saw a dead man 'fore I went in the service, but kids grow up quick these days, I s'pose. D'you find it interesting? You gone tell your friends 'bout a Southern funeral? You gone make a report on it in the schoolroom, India?"

"It was very interesting," said India. She cautiously reached toward him with one slender arm. "Do you mind if I raise the window?" she said with an icy smile. "All the cool air is getting out." And she hardly let him withdraw his head and shoulders before she vigorously spun the handle.

"Luker!" yelled Lawton McCray at his son, who wasn't two feet away, "that child has sprung up! That child has grown a head since I last saw her! She is a doll! Glad she didn't inherit your looks. She's already 'most as big as you are now, isn't she! Looks more and more like her mother every day, I s'pose."

"Yes," said Luker expressionlessly, "I suppose she does."

"Come on over here, I want to talk to you for a minute."

Lawton McCray pulled his son into the shadow of a yellow Caterpillar—though in this place that stank of chemicals, diesel fuel, and phosphorus dust, there could be no real relief from the Alabama sun. Standing with one foot on the serrated maw of the tractor, as if daring it to start up and shovel him high into the air, Lawton McCray held Luker in reluctant conversation for nearly ten minutes.

Each time that India looked out at her father and grandfather she was more surprised that Luker remained so long. On the viable pretense that all the cold air in the car had dissipated, India lowered her window. But even with that, she could hear nothing of what the two men said. Lawton's voice was uncharacteristically moderated. "What are they talking about?" she asked Odessa. Her curiosity overcame her indisposition to speak to the black woman.

"What else those two got to talk about?" replied Odessa rhetorically. "They talking about Miz Barbara."

India nodded: that made sense. In another few moments, the two men—one beefy, red-faced, corpulent, and slow-moving, and the other small, quick, dark-skinned, but unburnt, as much like father and son as India and Odessa appeared mother and daughter —moved back toward the car. Lawton McCray thrust his thick arm through the window and grabbed India by the chin. He pulled her halfway out.

"I just cain't get over how much you look like your mother. Your mother was the prettiest woman I ever saw in my life."

"I don't look a bit like her!"

Lawton McCray laughed loudly in her face. "And you talk like her too! I was sorry when your daddy got a divorce. But law, India, he don't need her when he's got you!"

India was too ashamed to speak.

"How's she doing, your mama?"

"I don't know," replied India, lying. "I haven't seen her in seven years. I don't even remember what she looks like any more."

"Look in the mirror, India, look in the damn mirror!"

"Lawton," said Luker, "we got to get going if we're going to reach Beldame before the tide comes in."

"You get going then!" yelled his father. "And listen, Luker, you let me know how things are going, you understand me? I'm depending on you!"

Luker nodded significantly. *How things were going* appeared to possess a specific and weighty meaning for both men.

As Luker drove away from the compound of the McCray Fertilizer Company, Lawton McCray raised his arm and held it high in the dust-filled air.

"Listen," said India to her father, "I don't have to tell any of my friends, do I, if he's elected . . . ?"

CHAPTER 5

Their way lay south through the interior of Baldwin County, down a narrow unshaded secondary road that was bordered by shallow ditches filled with grass and some ugly yellow flower. Beyond the low ramshackle fences of post or wire lay vast fields of leguminous crops that hugged the ground and seemed very cheap and dusty and to have been planted for some reason other than an ultimate ingestion by either man or cattle. The sky was washed out almost to whiteness, and wispy clouds hovered timorously at the horizon on every side, but hadn't the courage to hang directly above. Now and then they passed some sort of house, and whether that house was five or a hundred years old, its front porch sagged, its sides had been blistered by the sun, its chimney leaned precariously. Dilapidation was consistent, as was the apparent absence of all life. Even India, who had little enough expectation of the excitement of the rural existence, found it remarkable that she had seen not a living thing for fifteen miles: not man, woman, child, dog, or carrion crow.

"It's dinnertime," said Odessa. "Ever'body's inside at the table. That's why you don't see nobody. Nobody's outside at twelve o'clock."

Even Foley, a town that advertised a population of three thousand souls, appeared deserted when they drove through. Certainly there were cars parked downtown, and Odessa claimed to have seen faces in the bank window, and a police cruiser turned a corner two blocks ahead—but the town was unaccountably empty.

"Would you be out on a day like this?" said Odessa. "You got sense you stay inside where it's air-conditioned."

Experimentally, India rolled down her window a little: heat bellowed inside and seared her cheek. The thermometer on the Foley bank had read 103 degrees.

"Good God!" said India. "I hope it's air-conditioned where we're going."

"It's not," said Luker. "India, when I was little, and we were coming to Beldame every summer, we didn't even have electricity, isn't that right, Odessa?"

"That's right, and it don't even work *all* the time now. You cain't depend on that generator. We got candles at Beldame. We got kerosene lamps. That generator—I don't trust it. But child, we got a whole drawerful of paper fans."

India glanced ruefully at her father: to what sort of place was he taking her? What advantages could Beldame have over the Upper West Side, even the Upper West Side in the most miserably hot summer imaginable? Luker had told India that Beldame was every bit as beautiful as Fire Island—a place that India loved—but Fire Island's inconveniences were only picturesque and quaint. India suspected that Beldame wasn't civilized, and she feared that she would be not only bored but actually uncomfortable. "What's the hot water situation?" she asked, thinking that a fair standard by which to judge the place.

"Oh, it don't hardly take no time to heat up on the stove," said Odessa. "Got high flames on the stoves at Beldame!"

India asked no more questions. From Foley to the coast was little more than ten miles. The fields gave out and were replaced by a weak-willed stubby forest of diseased pine and scrub oak. In places the undergrowth, thick and brownish and uninteresting, was plotted in white sand. White sand now and then blew across the road, and dunes of white sand rose in the distance. Over a little rise the Gulf of Mexico became visible. It was opalescent blue, the color that the sky ought to have been. The foam that broke at the top of the nearer waves was gray in comparison to the white sand that shouldered the road.

Gulf Shores hove suddenly into sight: a vacation community

with a couple of hundred houses and a dozen small stores and conveniences. All the buildings were green shingled and gray roofed, and all the screens on all the windows were rusted. Even if there were few persons actually in residence there now, in the middle of the week, the place at least maintained the illusion of being crowded, and India allowed her hope a little space to rise. Then, as if on purpose to deflate that meager hope, Luker remarked that this stretch of Gulf coastline was known as the Redneck Riviera. He turned off at a sign that read Dixie Graves Parkway, on to a ribbon of asphalt that was sometimes lost beneath a film of white blowing sand. Gulf Shores was put quickly behind them.

On both sides of the road rolled soft white dunes, with here and there a handful of tall stiff grass or a clump of sea roses. Beyond on both sides was blue water; but only on the left side were there breakers. Odessa pointed to the right. "That's the bay. That's Mobile Bay. Mobile's up there—'bout how far would you say, Mr. Luker?"

"About fifty miles."

"So you cain't see it," said Odessa, "but it's there. And"—pointing to the left—"that's the Gulf. There's nothing out there, nothing at all."

India felt certain of it.

They came to another community, this one with only a couple of dozen houses and no stores at all. Tons of crushed oyster shells that had been laid out over the sand formed the driveways and yards of the houses. Only a few houses were not boarded up, and the place seemed to India the last stage of desolation.

"Is this Beldame?" she asked uneasily.

"Law, no!" laughed Odessa. "This is *Gasque!*"—this said as if India had mistaken the World Trade Center for the Flatiron Building.

Luker pulled into the lot of a gasoline station that had evidently been closed a number of years. The pumps were of a type that India had never even seen before, slender and round with red glass caps that made them look like bishops on a chess board. "This place is closed," she said to her father. "Are we out of gas?" she asked miserably, wishing all the while that she were standing on the corner of Seventy-fourth Street and Broadway. (How clearly she could see it in her mind!)

"No, we're fine," said Luker, pulling around behind the station. "We've just got to change cars, that's all."

"Change cars!"

Behind the station and attached to it was a small garage. Luker got out of the Fairlane and pulled open the unlocked door. Inside were a jeep and an International Scout. Both vehicles had Alabama plates. Luker took a key that was hanging from a hook just inside, climbed into the Scout, and backed it out. "I want you to help transfer everything, India," said Luker, and reluctantly, sullenly, India stepped out of the air-conditioned car. In a few minutes all their bags and the boxes of food that had been packed in the trunk and back seat of the Fairlane were piled in the back of the Scout. The Fairlane was put inside the garage, and the door closed again.

"Well," said India, when Luker and Odessa had climbed into the front of the Scout, "where am I supposed to sit?"

"You get your choice," said Luker. "You can stand on the running board or you can sit on Odessa's lap. *Or*—you can ride on the hood."

"What!"

"But if you ride on the hood, you'll have to hold on tight."

"I'll fall off!" cried India.

"We'll stop for you," laughed Luker.

"Goddamn you, Luker, I'd rather walk, I'd—"

"Child!" cried Odessa. "What was that word?"

"It's too far to walk," laughed Luker. "Come on, here's a towel. Put it up on the hood and sit on it. We won't be going fast, and if you slide off, just be sure you don't get caught under the back wheels. I used to *love* to ride on the hood! Leigh and I used to *fight* to see who got to ride on the hood!"

India was fearful of scraping her feet if she stood on the running board and sitting in Odessa's lap was an unthinkable indignity. When Luker refused to leave her there and make a return trip to pick her up, she leaped angrily on to the hood of the Scout. After she had arranged herself on the towel Odessa handed her, Luker drove away from the gas station onto the Gulf beach.

The sensation of riding on the hood of the Scout was not, after all, unpleasant, despite the blowing white sand that crept beneath India's clothes and lodged beneath her eyelids. Even behind her sunglasses she squinted in the glare. Luker drove slowly, just along the high tide line, and now and then broad arcs of foamy water crept under the tires. Gulls and pipers and four other kinds of birds India couldn't identify fled at their approach. Crabs scuttled away, and when she peered over the fender she could see a thousand tiny sinkholes in the wet sand, where shelled creatures breathed. Fish leaped in the nearer waves, and Luker, whose voice she could not hear over the heavy surf, pointed away in the distance where, beyond a light green line that must have been a sandbar, a school of porpoises frolicked. In comparison to this, the shore of Fire Island was dead.

They rode on toward the west for perhaps four miles. After Gasque was behind them they saw no more houses. The thread of the Dixie Graves Parkway was occasionally visible, but no cars traveled on it. India turned and shouted through the windshield: "How far is it?" Neither Luker nor Odessa answered her. Her hand touched the hood of the Scout and she jerked it away, burned.

Luker turned the Scout sharply, and India had to scramble not to slide off. A wave larger than the rest broke against the front fender, dousing the hood and India. "Feel better?" shouted Luker and laughed at her evident discomfort.

With the inside of her sleeve, which was the only part of her clothing that had escaped wetting, India wiped her pouting face. She wouldn't turn around again. In only a few minutes, the sun had dried her. The sound of the waves, the delicate rocking of the Scout, the rumble of the engine beneath the hood, and most of all the heat that engorged all creation in that lonely place hypnotized the girl until she had almost forgot her anger. Luker blew the horn, and she jerked around.

He pointed ahead, and mouthed the word *Beldame*. India leaned back against the windshield, not caring if she blocked his vision, and stared ahead. They crossed a small damp depression of wet sand and clay, shell-littered, that looked rather like a dried river-bed, and proceeded onto a long spit of land, no more than fifty yards wide. On the left-hand side there was the Gulf, with gulls and flying fish, and porpoises in the distance; but on the right was a narrow lagoon of green motionless water and beyond it the much wider peninsula that was traversed by the Dixie Graves Parkway.

On this narrow spit they traveled another quarter of a mile, and the little lagoon on the right grew wider and seemingly deeper. And now before her, she saw a group of houses: but not houses such as had been built at Gulf Shores and Gasque—those little shingled shoe boxes raised on concrete blocks with rusting screens and dried-out roofs. These were large, eccentric, old houses such as appeared in coffee table books on *outré* American architecture.

There were three of them she saw now; three solitary houses arranged at the very end of the spit. They were large, tall, Victorian structures weathered a uniform gray, with angular verticalities and hundreds of scraps of unexpected wooden ornamentation. As they drove closer, India saw that the three houses were identical, with identical windows placed identically in their façades and identical cupolaed verandahs running around three identical sides. Each faced a different way. The house on the left looked toward the Gulf, the house on the right toward the lagoon and the peninsula of land that snaked out from Gulf Shores. The third house, in the middle, looked toward the end of the spit, but its western view was evidently blocked by the high dunes that had formed there.

The houses were placed at right angles and backed onto an open square of shelled walks and low shrubs. Except for this vegetation, all was white sand, and the houses stood foursquare on the undulating surface of the shifting beach.

India was entranced. What mattered intermittent electricity, what mattered washing her hair in cold water, when three such splendid houses composed the whole and entirety of Beldame?

Luker pulled the Scout up to the shrubbery shared by the three houses. India jumped off the hood. "Which one is ours?" she demanded, and her father laughed at the excitement she could not hide.

He pointed to the house on the Gulf. "That's ours," he said. He pointed to the house directly opposite it, on the little lagoon, "That's Leigh and Dauphin's place. The water is called Elmo's Lagoon. At high tide, you know, the Gulf flows into St. Elmo's and we're completely cut off here. At high tide, Beldame is an island."

India pointed to the third house. "And whose is that?"

"Nobody's," replied Odessa, as she lifted one of the boxes of food out of the Scout.

"Nobody's?" asked India. "It's a wonderful house—they're all wonderful! Why doesn't anybody live there?"

"They can't," said Luker, with a smile.

"Why not?"

"Go round the front and see," he said, pulling the first of the bags out of the Scout. "Go round and take a look, and then come back and help Odessa and me unpack."

India stepped quickly along the paths in the common ground, what Luker called the yard, and now she saw how closely the sand dunes at the end of the spit had encroached upon the third house. Something made her hesitate to mount the steps up to the verandah, and she skipped around the side. She stopped short.

The dune of white sand—blinding now that the sun shone glancingly off it directly into her eyes—did not merely encroach upon the house, it had actually begun to swallow it. The back of the house was intact but sand had covered the entire front of the house to a line well above the verandah roof. The dune slid gracefully along the verandah, and had trapped an oaken swing that hung in chains from the ceiling.

India crept around to the other side of the house. It was the same there, though the sand began at not so high a point, and its slope to the bare ground was gentler. She longed to go inside the third house to see whether the dune continued within the rooms in the same gentle curves, or whether the walls and windows had held against the sand. Would she be able to stand before a window and look through the glass into the interior of the dune?

She hesitated at the corner of the verandah. Her curiosity was intense: she had forgot all her animosity toward her father for bringing her to this godforsaken place.

Yet something kept India from mounting the steps of the verandah; something told her not to peer into the windows of that house where no one came to stay; something held her even from pushing her toe into the last grains of white sand that had spilled from the top of the dune onto the bare ground at her feet. Luker called her name, and she ran back to help him unload the Scout.

CHAPTER 6

After the Scout was unpacked, India went room by room through the house that belonged to the McCrays. Thinking of the frigid decorator-opulence of Big Barbara's house in Mobile, she was surprised by its homely but well-grounded taste. Luker explained that the vacation house had been refurnished when they bought it in 1950 and, except for replacing upholstery, cushions, and draperies, which quickly rotted in the salt air, it had been untouched since then. All that was lacking to India's mind was carpets on the wooden floors, but Luker said that it was impossible to keep carpets clean when sand was being tracked through the house all day.

The first floor of each of the houses of Beldame consisted of three large rooms: a living room that ran the length of the house along one side, and, opposite this, a dining room at the front and a kitchen at the back. The single bathroom had been made out of a corner of the kitchen. On the second floor four bedrooms were set into the corners, each with two windows and a single door opening onto a central hallway. A narrow staircase descended to the first floor, and an even narrower set of stairs led up to the third. This top part of each house was a single narrow room, with a window at either end, which had always been made over to servants.

India was given the second floor bedroom that at the front looked out over the Gulf and from the side provided an entrancing view of the destructive dune that was devouring the third house. It contained a double bed of iron with brass insets, a painted vanity, a chifforobe, a wicker writing desk, and a large standing cupboard.

While India was unpacking, her father wandered into the room; he sat on the edge of the bed and loaded film into his Nikon.

"Which room did you take?" asked India.

"That one," he said, pointing at the wall she shared with the other bedroom at the front of the house. "That's been my room since '53. Big Barbara has the one catercorner from this, next to me.

"So," he said, lifting the camera and quickly taking a couple of photographs of his daughter as she stood before the open suitcase, "how do you like Beldame?"

"I like it very much," she said quietly, and meant him to understand more than that.

"I thought so. Even if it is the end of the world." She nodded. "That's very New York of you, you know."

"What is?" she asked.

"Unpacking your suitcase first thing."

"Why is that such a New York thing to do?" she asked defensively, pausing between the suitcase and the dresser.

"Because when you're finished you'll snap it shut and stick it under the bed—these houses don't have any closets, I suppose you've noticed—and you'll say to yourself, 'Well now we can get down to business!'"

India laughed. "That's right. I guess I'm thinking of Fire Island."

"Yes," said Luker, "but we'd be at the Island for only two or three days at a time—turn to the right a little, you're in shadow. God only knows how long we're going to be *here*. And in case you haven't noticed, I should point out that there's not much in the way of diversion at Beldame."

"It'll be worse for you than for me"—she shrugged—"at least I'm not old enough to get horny . . ."

"I'll be all right," said Luker. "I've been coming here all my life, at least up until you were born. *That woman*—as Barbara calls her—*that woman* and I came here once, part of our honeymoon, and she hated the place and said she would never come here again. We only stayed long enough to conceive you."

"What? You think that happened here?"

Luker shrugged. "I think so. *That woman* and I screwed around a lot before we were married, of course, but then she was on the pill. On our honeymoon she went off it—she didn't tell me that, of course. And when I found out, we had this huge fight and then didn't have sex again for like two months—so the timing's about right for you to have been conceived here."

"You're also saying I was a mistake, aren't you?"

"Of course, you don't really think that I *wanted* a child . . ."

"But it's so weird then," said India.

"What is?"

"That I might have been conceived here and this is the first time I've been back since."

"I don't imagine that you remember a whole lot about it."

"No," replied India, "but the place doesn't seem entirely strange to me, either."

"When your mother said she hated Beldame, I guess I knew there was something wrong with the marriage. Anyway, what with one thing and another, *I* haven't been back since either—it's strange to be here."

"Lots of memories?"

"Of course," he said, and waved her toward the window. India, who had had many thousands of photographs taken of her by her father and her father's friends, complied without self-consciousness and assumed the poses and the expressions that she knew pleased him. "*But*," he said, fiddling with the exposure, "I just wanted to warn you that you would pretty much have to entertain yourself."

"I know."

"And if it gets too bad, just give me the high sign and I'll slip you a down."

India frowned. "I get twisted on downs."

"I was joking. You're not going to need anything here." The Gulf broke loudly against the shore, and they must speak carefully above the noise. The wind blew off the water, and the thin curtains wrapped themselves delicately around India.

"The pictures on the wall are mine," said Luker. "I used to paint when I came here. I used to think I was going to be a painter."

"The pictures stink," said India mildly. "But you're a *good* photographer. Why don't you take these down and put up some prints?"

"Maybe I will. Maybe that's going to be this year's project, if I can get up the energy. I ought to warn you—Beldame's a pretty low-energy place. You can figure on getting about two things done a day, and one of 'em is getting out of bed."

"Luker, I can take care of myself. You don't have to worry about me. I brought that panel with me that I want to hang over my bed at home, and that'll take me forever. As long as I've got a needle and thread I'll be all right."

"All right," said Luker then, relieved. "I promise I won't worry about you."

"How long are we going to be here?"

He shrugged. "I don't know. It depends. Don't get antsy."

"I'm not. But what does it depend on?"

"On Big Barbara."

India nodded; she understood from Luker's reluctance to elaborate that this was a matter not yet to be discussed between them. Having finished her unpacking, India shut the suitcase and slid it beneath the bed. She sat before the vanity, and Luker took photographs of her and her mirrored reflection.

"Stand by the window," said Luker after a few moments, "I want the Gulf in the background." Instead of moving to the window that looked directly out on to the water, she placed herself at the other casement, and gazed at the third house, fifty feet away. There was nothing but a square of undisturbed sand between the two houses.

"I just can't get over that house," said India. "Who owns it? Does it belong to the Savages?"

"I think . . ." said Luker hesitantly.

"That's crazy. There are only three houses at Beldame, and you've been coming here for thirty years—but you're not sure who owns the third house?"

"No."

He was taking her picture, moving about quickly to get her from different angles and, it seemed to India, from angles that would not include the third house in the background.

"Let's go downstairs," said India, "and sit outside. I want you to tell me about Beldame. You know, you've practically kept this place a *secret* from me. You never told me it was anything as wonderful as this!"

Luker nodded; and in a few minutes they were seated in the swing that was hung beneath the southeastern cupola of the verandah. From here they could see only the Gulf before them; if they turned they could see the Savage house directly behind, but the third house lay out of sight around the corner of the verandah. India clapped her hands upon a mosquito, and asked, "When was Beldame built?"

"Dauphin's great-great-grandfather built all three houses in 1875. He built one for himself and his second wife, one for his sister and her husband, and one for his oldest daughter and *her* husband. And they all had children. Probably he decided to use just one set of plans to avoid arguments about who had gotten the best deal—or maybe he was just cheap. Of course, it couldn't have been cheap to get labor and materials out here in 1875. It would have all come by boat from Mobile, I guess, or Pensacola. I wish I knew more of the details about the construction—that would be the really interesting part. Maybe Dauphin knows where the records are—the Savages never get rid of *anything*." Luker glanced at his daughter to see if she appeared still interested in the story. She understood, and nodded her desire for him to continue.

"Anyway," he went on, "all three families used to stay out here from the middle of May until the middle of September. That must have been about twenty people, not including servants and guests. It wasn't that it was so much cooler here in the summer, it's just that Mobile wasn't healthy. A lot of people died of swamp fever. And the houses passed on down through the Savage family. During the Depression, two of 'em got sold, this house and the third house—though if you ask me the Savages were fools not to keep this one, the one that faces the Gulf. Lawton and Big Barbara got it in 1950 from some people named Hightower who owed them money, and Lawton accepted the house as payment—or part payment. We started coming down every year, and Big Barbara and I would stay almost the whole summer. That's when Big Barbara and Marian Savage got to be such good friends. And they were pregnant with Leigh and Mary-Scot at the same time. And of course Dauphin and Darnley and I played together all day long. Darnley was my age."

"So no one stayed in the third house then either?"

Luker shook his head. "Not since I've been coming here. It wasn't always covered with sand, of course. I don't think that even started much more than twenty years ago. Before that, the place was just closed up, and nobody came. I can't remember exactly what the story was. The house was sold in the Depression, like I said, and people came to stay here. But they didn't stay long—I think that was it. They bought the house but they'd never use it, and when the Savages made some of their money back in World War II, I think they bought the house back. It's something like that—Dauphin could tell you for sure."

"Why did the people who bought the third house stop coming here? Did something happen?"

"I don't know," said Luker with a shrug. "I don't remember what the story was. It's strange to think about all this again, there's a lot I've really forgotten. After we had been coming a few years, Leigh and Mary-Scot were born, and a few years after that Darnley started spending his summers at this sailing camp in North Carolina. That was when Dauphin and I became really close. I'm three years older than he is. It's funny you should call it *the third house*, because that's what we always called it. It used to scare me, and Leigh too. That's why my bedroom is where it is—because from there, you can't see the third house. I was scared to get up at night and look at it, I was scared there was something that lived inside it."

"But you put me in a room that looks out on it," said India.

"But you're not scared," said Luker. "I've raised you not to be scared of things like that."

"Is there a lot more sand now than when you were here last time?"

Luker hesitated before answering. He slapped at a sand fly on his arm. "I don't know," he said, "I'd have to go look at it."

"Let's go look," said India. "I want to see what it's like. Get your camera, and you can take pictures. Maybe if we could get inside, you could take pictures of me in a room that's half filled with sand—that'd be hot!"

"Oh," said Luker softly, "don't get so fired up, India. We've got all the time in the world. There's so little to do at Beldame, maybe you ought to save a little of the excitement for when you're *really* bored." He pushed his foot against the floorboards, and propelled the swing into a wide sideways arc. Through the open window of the Savage house they heard Odessa putting up groceries in the kitchen cabinets.

CHAPTER 7

India, who had her mother's delicate skin, wore long sleeves and a coolie hat when Luker toured her around the spit. They started at a point just in front of their own house and walked to the wide shallow depression that looked like a dry riverbed. Through this channel, at high tide, St. Elmo's Lagoon flowed into the Gulf, and cut off Beldame entirely from the peninsular mainland. They walked along St. Elmo's Lagoon—India marveling at the beauty of the placid green water.

"I don't know why you haven't told all your friends in New York about Beldame," said India. "I mean, it's the perfect place for a house party. Your friends have money, they could afford to fly down for a weekend. There's nothing like this on Long Island—there's nothing that's this remote."

Luker didn't like the question, and that was apparent to India. "Beldame is a very private place," he said to her finally. "It's a family place. It belongs to us—the McCrays and the Savages. We've never invited a whole lot of people to come down."

"Ever?" demanded India. "Have there ever been guests at Beldame?"

"Oh, sure!" replied Luker. "Lots of times—but not recently, I guess."

"Not since when?"

Luker shrugged. "Not since Dauphin got out of high school."

"Why did you stop inviting people?"

"Oh, we just realized that guests—that people not in the family —didn't really take to Beldame."

"I love it," said India.

"You're family, dummy."

"To have a family is real strange," said India thoughtfully. "All these people you wouldn't have anything to do with except that they're related to you. It's easier for you because you grew up with a whole bunch of people. I've only had you."

"Better just me than your mother and me together."

"That's the truth!" exclaimed India. "But what made you all of a sudden decide not to invite any more people to Beldame?"

"Oh, I'm not exactly sure . . ."

"Yes you are," said India. "Tell, tell."

"Well, Dauphin had a party down here. It was right after his graduation, and he invited a bunch of his friends down for the weekend—"

"Were you here?"

"I was taking extra courses at Columbia that summer. I couldn't come. But Big Barbara and Leigh were here, and they had all the girls stay over at our house. The boys stayed at the Savages'. Odessa and Marian Savage were down too, of course, keeping an eye on things."

"And something happened?"

Luker nodded.

"What?" demanded India.

"I'm not sure . . ."

"What does that mean?"

"It means I'm not really sure if anything happened. Probably nothing happened. But all the girls were sleeping in our house, and they had the two bedrooms on the western side—the one you're in now and the one next to it, that also looks out on the third house. So they were up late on Saturday night, talking and gossiping and putting their hair up and whatever else high school girls do when they go to the beach, and they saw something outside."

"What'd they see?"

"Well, they thought they saw a woman . . ."

"A woman? What sort of woman?"

"They couldn't see very clearly. It was just a woman—she was fat and had on a long dress, that's all they could tell."

"What was she doing? Was she just walking around the yard or something? Maybe it was Marian Savage."

"Marian Savage was very thin, even before she got cancer. No, this was a big fat woman—and she was walking on the roof of the third house."

"What?"

"She was up on the roof over the verandah, just walking around and looking in all the windows and trying to raise them from the outside. They couldn't see very well because it was so dark. They—"

"Did the woman get inside the third house?"

"There wasn't any woman," said Luker. "They imagined it. It was a collective hallucination or something. There wasn't anybody there. You saw how hard it is to get out to Beldame—nobody's going to come in the middle of the night. Especially not a fat woman in a long dress. And there's no way to get up to that roof without a ladder and there weren't any ladders around the next morning. They imagined it all."

"Maybe she was a burglar or something."

"Fat women make terrible burglars, India. And besides, why would a burglar come out here when there were lots of other people around, when most of the time the place is completely deserted? And those girls were screaming, too—and the woman never even turned around to look at them."

"Where'd she go then? What happened to her?"

"The girls said she just went around the corner and disappeared and they didn't see her again."

"Maybe she got through a window on the other side of the house. Did anybody go in the house the next day?"

"Of course not. There was no woman. But the girls were scared. They got Big Barbara up, and Odessa and Marian Savage, and they all went back to Mobile that night. And since then, we haven't asked anybody to come back to Beldame. And I get the feeling from what Big Barbara has said, that most people wouldn't come even if they got asked."

This exchange had brought them to the front of the Savage house. Luker stopped and pointed at the slight movement of darkness visible through the second-floor window. "Odessa is getting ready for the others. She's been coming here as long as anybody else. They offered her one of the bedrooms on the second floor— the one, in fact, that looks out over the third house—but she wouldn't take it. She took the third floor instead. She has it all to herself and she claims that the heat doesn't bother her. After spending about thirty summers up there, I guess it really doesn't."

Luker had paused before the house, and to India it appeared that he would much rather continue to talk of Odessa than to complete their circumambulation of Beldame. She pulled him past the Savage house to the very tip of the spit. Here the lowering sun sparkled on the cross-hatching patterns of colliding waves.

"I don't know anything about marine geology, or whatever it's called," said Luker, "so I'm not exactly sure what's happening here. But when I was your age there was a lot more beach here, but that's all underwater now, and it's not much more than a sandbar—and not a very safe sandbar at that. It *looks* safe but I wouldn't trust it. When I was little the dune was just starting to build up, and Marian Savage would complain about all the sand that blew up on the porch of the third house. We didn't know then that the entire house was going to be covered. Every time we'd come back we'd find the dune a little higher. Now look," he said, standing with his back to the water, "from here you can barely see over the top of the sand."

What India could see of the third house was most of the second floor and the single window at the top. The sun reflecting in the unbroken glass of these windows blinded her.

She jumped forward and placed her foot on the base of the dune; the texture of the sand there was sufficiently different from that of the beach that one might speak of "the base of the dune."

"What are you doing?" demanded Luker sharply.

"I'm going to climb to the top and look in the windows. Come on!" She trudged a couple of steps upward.

"No!" cried Luker. India turned and smiled: she was testing him. His reluctance to talk of the house except at her prompting had been obvious.

"You're still scared of it," she said. "You were scared of it when you were a little boy, and you're still scared of it now, aren't you?" She stood several feet higher than he, and her feet sank slowly in the loose fine sand.

"Yes," he replied, "of course I am. Ask Leigh, and she'll tell you that she's scared of it too."

"What about Dauphin? Is he scared of the third house?"

Luker nodded.

"And what about Big Barbara and Odessa?"

"Why should they be scared?" asked Luker. "When they started coming to Beldame, they were already grown up. I think the house probably just works on children. There's nothing wrong with it, there aren't any stories about ghosts or anything like that. It's probably just that the house was empty, and that the sand was creeping up on it, and it was so boring here that there wasn't anything better to do than get scared, that's all."

"Then climb up here with me and let's look in the windows. I want to see if the sand has gotten inside the house."

"It's not safe, India."

"Goddamn it, Luker, it's a goddamn sand dune, and you've been on enough of 'em on Fire Island, haven't you?" she demanded with sarcasm.

"Yes," he replied. "But those were permanent dunes on the Island, they—"

"Dunes aren't permanent," said India sententiously, "that's what makes them dunes, and besides, this one's only about fifteen feet high." Without waiting for her father's permission, she turned and strode quickly toward the top. Her sandaled feet sank deep in the fine white sand, and were difficult to raise. She paused, removed the sandals, and tossed them down to Luker. He picked them up, knocked them against his thigh, and swung them impatiently by their straps.

India headed for the window on the left, in order to see into the room that corresponded to her own. Sand reached up to the second of four rows of panes in the casement.

Barefoot, India attained the top of the dune. She would have slid down again but that she grabbed hold of one of the carved fleurs-de-lis that friezed the second floor of the house. She pulled herself up straight before the casement and stared down through the window into a room that was structurally identical to her own.

She was never sure afterward what she had expected, but whatever that expectation had been, it was not fulfilled by what she saw.

The chamber, which perfectly resembled her own in the matter of proportion, woodwork, and ornamentation, was furnished in a style she recognized as late Victorian. There was a mahogany bedstead with four high posts with carved pineapples for finials; a wardrobe, dresser, and dressing table of the same wood were carved in the same style. Rush matting had been laid over the floor and the walls were covered in a striped paper of green and black.

From a picture molding hung a number of dark-framed prints, only slightly askew on their triangled wires. On a table beside the bed was a ruby-glass carafe with a ruby-glass tumbler inverted over the mouth. India could see that it still held water. On the dressing table was a jumble of brushes, and an opened box with a mirror that she suspected was a shaving kit.

The sun shone directly through the window, illuminating a portion of the room brilliantly, and leaving the rest obscure. India's own black shadow of curiosity stretched across the floor, like a startled residue of the room's last inhabitant.

Through the open doorway into the hall, she could discern faintly the banister of the staircase leading down to the first floor.

India was fascinated. Peering now into the room's obscurities, she saw the marks of passing time's casual violence. The mirror in the shaving box had cracked, and a sliver that had fallen onto the dresser reflected a spot of sunlight onto the side wall. One of the picture wires had snapped, and a corner of the broken frame lay just within her sight on the far side of the bed. A severe line of red dust lay upon the matting just underneath the hanging spread where the fringe had rotted. But the room was marvelously intact. It was with a look of bewilderment that she turned back to her father.

"India, what is it?" he asked, disturbed and displeased.

"Luker, you've *got* to come up here and look, it's—"

The fleur-de-lis by which she still held herself upright in the shifting, sinking sand snapped off in her grasp. Gasping, she fell forward into the dune. Her hands and knees sank into the sand, and she stared surprised down at her father, who had not moved upward to help her. "See what I mean?" he said. "Come down."

She tried to stand, but on the incline she could not get firm footing. Her feet had disappeared beneath the sand, and when she struggled to lift them out, she accidentally shoved her right foot through one of the lower panes of the window.

The notion that part of her was now actually inside that miraculously preserved bedroom frightened India. Something that had hid along the wall, just out of her sight, would now grab her leg and pull her through the window. Something that—

She jerked her foot back through and scrambled away.

"India, what happened?" hissed Luker.

"I'm sorry," she whispered, sitting back in the sand and sliding downward a few inches. She straightened the coolie hat, which had been knocked askew. "I broke one of the panes in the window, I didn't mean to, I—"

"It's all right," said Luker. "But did you cut yourself?"

She drew out her bare foot and turned it this way and that. "No," she said, herself surprised to find no blood. The window-pane must already have been loose, and the slight pressure of her foot added to that exerted by the sand had simply imploded it into the bedchamber.

"Come down," said Luker. "Come down now, there's no point in getting tetanus on your first day here. I have no—"

He stopped suddenly at some sound that India had not heard.

"It's the jeep," he said, "the others are here. Come on down now." He tossed her sandals back up to her and jogged away around the dune and back to the other houses.

India picked up her sandals out of the sand, carefully maintaining her balance on the slope. But instead of going back down directly, she turned and walked up to the casement again. She declined to take to herself Luker's unreasoning fear of the third house.

With a little tremor, she looked through the window again, and simply seeing that the room was unchanged was a reassuring comfort. The pane had broken into several large pieces on the matting, and even as she watched these were covered up in a little mound of sand that poured through the aperture. When she moved her foot no more than an inch, the sand spilled faster. She felt guilty that it was by her clumsiness that the room had been violated at last by the sand, which heretofore had been confined to the first floor. Who knew?—if it had not been for her stupid foot, the sand might have raised itself inch by inch outside the window and completely covered it over without ever finding substantial entrance. The room which before had been perfect was now on its way to destruction—and by her carelessness. Her temptation now was actually to kick in a second pane, and had she not feared injury, might well have done so.

She looked over the room again. If it was going to fill with sand, why shouldn't they get the things out of it? She suspected that it was fear and not respect for private property that had kept Luker from appropriating the marvelous things that were in this room—and probably in the others too. Turning away, she resolved to suggest that they get everything valuable out of the house before it was entirely taken over by the dune. That ruby-glass carafe and tumbler on the night table would do very well by *her* bed on Seventy-fourth Street.

Through the window, she stared at the carafe, thinking of home, and wondering how long it would be before she returned there. The sand hissed through the opening in the window and piled higher on the floor. A little funnel appeared in the sand between India's feet; experimentally she took the ribbon from the brim of her hat, untied it, and dangled it above the hole. She dropped it lower, and it was sucked into the funnel. The draw was surprisingly strong, and the silk slipped out of her fingers. She stared through the window, and saw the ribbon spill onto the top of the mound that was forming on the rush matting. It was as if the room had become an enormous hourglass, slowly to be filled with sand; she watched fascinated as the ribbon was covered. So close was her attention to the hiss of sand on silk that she did not attend to the other slight noise in the room but when she looked up suddenly, it was to see the door to the center hallway being drawn carefully shut.

CHAPTER 8

Luker lay at full length upon his mother's great mahogany bed, and would have fallen asleep if Big Barbara had not talked at him ceaselessly as she unpacked her bags. Small piles of her under-clothes were stacked on his chest and thighs awaiting distribution into their proper drawers. Big Barbara's bedroom had no view to speak of: a triangle of the Gulf out the side window and the Savage house to the back. It got the morning sun.

Luker said, "You made it just in time. The tide had started to come in. I thought maybe you were going to have to hold off until tomorrow." The light outside was beginning to change color and intensify.

"No," said Big Barbara, "there wasn't more than a foot of water cutting us off, and I believe Leigh would have built a raft to get over here tonight."

"I didn't know she was so anxious."

"She's anxious on Dauphin's account. She's hoping that being out here will help him get over poor Marian's dying. *And* that business at the funeral. Mary-Scot's got the nuns for consolation, but Dauphin's just got us. Now, Luker," she said, leaning against the dresser to push two drawers closed at once, "I know why *Dauphin* decided to come to Beldame, but what I want to know is what made *you* rise up and come down to Alabama. I know Marian Savage wasn't one of your favorite people in the world, and truth to tell, darling, you weren't one of hers."

"I used the funeral as an excuse to come to Beldame."

"You didn't need an excuse to come to Beldame. I've been begging you for years to come back down here and stay with me, and bring India. And Dauphin and Leigh have been begging too. Luker, you haven't been to Beldame since you were here with *that woman* in '68. And you know what she said to me then? She said—"

"I don't want to know. I don't want to talk about her."

"I just wish I could believe that woman was dead! A photograph of her headstone would make your mother a happy woman, Luker! A happy woman!"

"No, she's not dead, she . . ." Luker turned his face against the pillow in a yawn.

Big Barbara rolled him back over. "Luker! Don't you tell me that you've seen her!"

"No. I don't know where she is."

"Good," said Big Barbara, "there aren't enough days in hell for that woman . . ." She vindictively snatched her brassieres off Luker's chest and pushed them into the top drawer of the dresser. "Good!" she said again, "that's all done. Now, why don't you run down and make me a drink and we'll go over and see how Dauphin and Leigh are doing."

"No," said Luker.

"No what?"

"No, I'm not going to get you a drink." For this he opened his eyes and looked at her.

"Well," she said cautiously, sensing that something was up, "I'll have to get it myself. Do you want anything?"

"No."

"Luker—"

"Barbara, there's no liquor in the house. I didn't bring any down."

"Luker, I set out the box, it was right in the laundry room, ready to go in the trunk. How you could have missed it, I *don't* know."

"I did see it. But I didn't pack it—on purpose."

"Well," said Big Barbara, "then I just hope that Dauphin had the good sense to put it in the Mercedes, I—"

"Dauphin didn't bring it either," said Luker. "Barbara, Beldame just went dry, by vote of the populace."

"I didn't vote!"

"It didn't matter. Majority would have gone prohibition anyway."

Big Barbara had seated herself at the vanity and now talked to her son's reflection in the mirror. Luker had sat up on the bed.

"*That's* why you're here," said Big Barbara softly. "*That's* why you've come to Beldame, isn't it—to be my keeper."

"That's right."

"You could have had the decency to tell me, Luker."

"You would have tried to wiggle out of it."

"Of course I would have, and you should have given me the chance!"

"No," said Luker quietly. "Barbara, you're an alcoholic. And you won't get help. I know Leigh's already talked to you and Lawton's talked to you, and if Dauphin weren't so goddamned polite, he would have talked to you too. But you wouldn't do anything about it and every night you'd come in and fill yourself up to the dotted line with booze—"

Big Barbara turned away from the mirror. "Luker," she pleaded, "I wish you wouldn't—"

"I tell you, Barbara," said her son, "of all the problems that you can make your friends and your family deal with, alcoholism is the most boring. It's got nothing to recommend it. And *you're* particularly bad. When you drink you start talking, and there's nothing that's going to shut you up. You tell things that ought not be told, you tell them to *anyone* and you embarrass everybody. And I tell you, Barbara, when you're full of booze, it's hard to love you."

"And *so*," said Big Barbara, "you've brought me down here to work the miracle cure. You're going to take the leather straps off your bags and tie me to the bed, and then you and India are going to run over to the next house hoping that you can't hear me screaming!"

"If that's what it takes." Luker shrugged. "Barbara, if you go on drinking, you're going to be alive for about five more years, and most of that time you're going to be sicker than Marian Savage was. You're a fool to drink the way you do. I don't know why you do it."

"I do," snapped Big Barbara. "I drink because I like it."

"I like to drink too," said Luker, "but sometimes I put the bottle down before it's empty. Barbara, you didn't drink this way when Leigh and I were little."

"That's when I started though," said Big Barbara, "when you and Leigh were little."

"Why? Why did you start?"

"Luker, when I got married, I was just a sweet little Southern girl, and I had never even been north of the Mason-Dixon line. I had two children and a happy marriage. Lawton used to like to go fishing, and I liked to drink. I had three reasons for drinking. Two children were the first two reasons, and the third reason was I liked to *go off*. About six o'clock every evening, I'd be sitting out on the patio among the magnolias and the gardenias—gardenias all in bloom and stinking to high heaven!—and I'd be thinking, 'I won't have a drink' and then you or Leigh would come up and say 'Mama—' and I'd say, 'Oh, Lord, got to get me a drink' and I'd run in the house. Then by seven-thirty, I'd be off somewhere else, I'd have gone away . . .'"

"But I grew up," said Luker, "and Leigh grew up. And Lawton stopped fishing ten years ago."

"Oh, but Luker—I still like to go off . . ."

"Going off's great," said Luker. "It's a lot of laughs, but Barbara, you don't have control over it any more!"

For a minute, Big Barbara McCray sat very still and tried to control the anger she felt against her family for their high-handedness in this matter. Giving up drink had become, since her daughter and husband had begun to speak of it, an itching responsibility;

but Luker, by tricking her out to Beldame without an ounce of spirits, had deprived her of the glory attendant upon voluntary renunciation.

She could not in fact be angry with Luker, for she knew how little he liked to be away from New York—and how much of an effort it must have been to coax India down to Alabama for some indefinite period. He came then entirely for love of her; but Big Barbara's frustration and dread of the coming days and weeks— when she was already nervous because it was six o'clock and she hadn't tasted scotch since noon—necessitated some outlet for her resentment.

"It was Lawton," she said at last, "who asked you to come."

"Yes, he did. But I came because of you, not because of him. You know that."

"I do," said Big Barbara grimly, "but I am furious with Lawton for going about it like this. You know why he did it, don't you?"

Luker didn't answer.

"I'll tell you why he did it. He did it because he didn't want me embarrassing him during the campaign. He didn't want me passing out with my face in a plate of chicken salad at a church picnic. He didn't want to see me carried out of a bar on a stretcher—"

"Barbara, that's exactly what happened last week. How do you think I felt when Leigh called me up—in the middle of a dinner party—to say that you were in the Mobile General detox? That didn't make any of us happy."

"That wasn't because I was drinking. That was because I had just heard that Marian had died. Lawton doesn't care about me. It'd be fine with him if I would just lock myself in the closet and tilt a bottle down my gullet. He'd say, 'Oh, sure, that's fine. She's having a great time in there, don't nobody go in and disturb her when she's having such a great time!' That's what he thinks. He thinks I'm a liability to his campaign. Like that representative from Kansas whose wife beat their two-year-old to death a week before the last election. She was a liability to him and he lost. Lawton makes me furious. That man wouldn't be anything if I hadn't pushed him! I *still* have to watch him! I was the one who taught him not to talk about hog butchering in front of the vice-president's wife! That man wouldn't be *anything* without me today, Luker. We wouldn't have doodlum-squat in the bank! On the day you were born I said to Lawton, 'Lawton,' I said, *'fertilizer is the wave of the future.'* And he listened to me then! Oh, back then, on the day you were born, he would still listen to what I had to say! He went out and bought a fertilizer company, and *it has just rolled in.* If it weren't for that fertilizer company, he couldn't run for Congress. Without that fertilizer company he couldn't run to catch a bus!"

Breathing heavily, she jerked away and mopped her eyes with a tissue. When she spoke again to Luker, it was in a quieter, controlled voice. "Luker, this morning before I came over to the house Lawton told me that if I didn't dry out he was gone file for a divorce directly after the election and it didn't make a damn bit of difference if he won or lost, he wasn't gone be saddled with a wife who could drink more than a barnful of Irishmen."

"Would a divorce be so bad? If you got divorced from Lawton, you could live with Leigh and Dauphin. They'd love to have you. I think you should have filed for one yourself on the day Leigh became a Savage."

"A divorce would kill me, Luker. I know you don't get along with Lawton the best in the world, and I know you don't love him the same way you love me . . ."

Luker laughed harshly.

". . . but I love Lawton and I always have. I know he's cheap, and I know he lies, and it was Marian Savage herself—never tell Dauphin this—who told me about this grass widow in Fairhope your father has been going to see since 1962, and she's got kinky red hair and a rear end you could lean a baseball team up against—"

"Barbara, you never told me about this!"

"Why should I? There was no reason for you to know."

"Were you upset when you found out?"

"Of course! But I never said a word. But when it hurt most was when he started talking about a divorce—this morning wasn't the first time he's brought it up. Luker, listen, I'm gone give in to you, and I'm gone try this thing—"

She turned away for several moments, contemplating what difficulties lay before her. Then turning to her son, she cried: "Oh, God, get me a glass to hold. I got to curl my fingers around something!"

Luker slipped down from the enormous mahogany bed and stretched. "You'll be all right," he said off-handedly.

CHAPTER 9

On his way down from Mobile, Dauphin had picked up half a dozen lobsters, and these Odessa boiled for their dinner—with potatoes and cole slaw on the side. They all ate in the dining room of the Savage house, and Luker kindly forbore to complain to Big Barbara that her alcoholic infirmity would keep the rest of them from enjoying beer or wine with their dinners. The meal was not a happy one, for no one was entirely easy in his mind; but at least they were all hungry. It was only when they had finished their lobsters, and the cracking of the shells and the noise of the sweet lobster meat being sucked from the shattered carcasses no longer covered their silence, that speechlessness became oppressive.

Dauphin, ever dutiful, took it upon himself to rescue them. Scorning superficialities, he said to India without preface: "Luker told me that I shouldn't have come out here to Beldame after Mama died, that I'd do better staying in Mobile—"

"Yes," said India, not understanding why this remark should have been directed to her. "I know that's what he said. But you don't think so."

"No, I don't. Beldame is the place where I've been the happiest in my life. I'm twenty-nine years old and I've been coming to Beldame every summer since I was born. I've never wanted to go anywhere else. The summers I spent here with Luker, you just cain't imagine how happy I was then—and how miserable I was when it was time to go back to Mobile! Luker wouldn't speak to me when we got back home. We were best friends at Beldame, but in Mobile he wouldn't give me the time of day."

"You were three years younger than me," shrugged Luker. "And I had an image to maintain."

"It made me *very* unhappy," said Dauphin, smiling. "Anyway, I still came out here even after Luker got married and didn't come any more. Mama and Odessa and I would come out, and I was pretty happy then too. And all that time Leigh was growing up, and she was so smart—she was valedictorian of her class in high school and she made the dean's list at Vanderbilt and she was winning beauty contests right and left—"

"I was Fire Queen of Mozart," said Leigh with self-deprecation. "And one time I won an electric toothbrush in a poetry contest."

"Anyway," said Dauphin to India, "I thought that the most wonderful thing in the world was that when we were at Beldame together she'd walk down the beach with me."

"That's because I knew you had about eighteen million dollars in your checking account," said Leigh to her husband.

He paid her no mind. "And one day we were sitting here at this table, just her and me—"

"I was upstairs telling Marian what was gone happen," said Big Barbara.

"And Odessa was in the kitchen trying to smack a wasp," laughed Leigh, "and all the time that Dauphin was trying to propose, we'd hear this *thwack thwack thwack* on the walls, and all the pans would rattle."

"—and I said, 'Hey, Leigh, I know you're smart, and I know you're beautiful and there're about eighteen million men who would jump off the back of a moving truck just to get the chance to say something nice to you, but I've got a lot of money and if we get married you sure will have a good time spending it . . .'"

"And I said, 'Dauphin, I sure will!'" said Leigh. "And I sure do!"

"Well, Barbara," said Luker, "now that Leigh has been taken care of, I hope that you and Lawton have changed your will to leave me sole beneficiary of the McCray Fertilizer Company."

"That will depend on how you treat me in future," said Big Barbara.

Odessa came out of the kitchen to pour more coffee and remove the dishes. India's question was almost lost under the clatter of the plates. "Dauphin, are you frightened of the third house too?"

"Yes," he answered, without hesitation.

"What makes you ask such a question, child?" demanded Big Barbara.

"Because Luker's afraid of it."

"Luker," said his mother, "have you been telling that child tales?"

Luker didn't answer.

"India," said Leigh, "there's nothing in the third house. People just think there is because it's been abandoned so long, and it's getting covered up with sand and so forth. I mean, the place looks . . ." She didn't want to finish that sentence.

"It looks as if something were wrong with it," said Luker. "That's all. India asked me why we never invited anybody down here but family, and I told her about Dauphin's graduation party."

"Oh, that was nothing!" said Big Barbara. "India, that was nothing! That was ten little girls sitting up late and telling each other ghost stories and all of 'em getting scared together, because Beldame *is* a lonely place at night if you're not used to it. They made it all up. I was in the house that night and I didn't see anything. There were about ten boys staying here in the Savage house, and they didn't see anything. There wasn't anything to see."

"But you still don't invite anybody down," said India.

"People like excitement and bright lights these days," said Big Barbara, "they don't want to come to poky old Beldame, where there's nothing to do but memorize the tide tables."

"Anyway," said Leigh, "there's no point in *you* being afraid of the third house, India. The only reason Dauphin and Luker and I are afraid is that we grew up with it. We were always making up stories about it, saying there was somebody who lived inside—somebody who was always hiding in the rooms where we couldn't see him. We'd dare each other to look through the windows, and when we looked through the windows whoever was inside would be hiding under the bed or behind the couch or something."

"Today," said India, "this afternoon, I—"

"India was very foolish today," interrupted her father, "and she climbed to the top of the dune at the front of the third house. She looked in one of the windows."

Dauphin appeared horrified by this, and Big Barbara spluttered her alarm. Leigh said, "India, you ought not to have done that. Luker, you ought not to have let her. That sand isn't firm, she could have slipped right under! The sand at that end of Beldame is treacherous, just treacherous!"

"I looked in the window, and—"

"No!" said Big Barbara. "We are going to stop talking about

all this—because it's just nonsense. Isn't it, Odessa?" Odessa had come in with more coffee.

"Sure is," said Odessa. "Nothing in the third house 'cept sand and dust."

"India," said her grandmother, "we wouldn't let you play on an abandoned roller coaster, and we're not gone let you play around the third house either. It's rotted and it's dangerous."

India placed her hand over her coffee cup and wouldn't take any more.

Dauphin had admitted to India his fear, but refused to elaborate upon it. However, it was certain that he had taken the bedroom at the northeastern corner of the house for Leigh and himself. From its two windows, you could see nothing but St. Elmo's Lagoon, which shone with a sickly green phosphorescence. It was the loneliest and saddest vista that Beldame afforded, and this especially at night. Nowhere were nights blacker than at Beldame; there wasn't a streetlight within thirty miles of the place. Just offshore the Gulf was deep and had no need of buoys. When everyone had gone to bed and the lights in the houses were extinguished, there were only the stars overhead and the wide rippling ribbon of St. Elmo's Lagoon. The new moon was a black patch stitched onto a blacker quilt.

After supper, when Luker, India, and Big Barbara had crossed the yard together and gone into their own house, Dauphin stood at the window of his and Leigh's room and looked out at the lagoon. Above, he heard the footsteps of Odessa and Leigh on the third floor. When Leigh came down he begged her to read in bed until he had fallen asleep.

"All right," she said, "why?"

"Because," he replied simply, "I'm afraid to be the last one asleep at Beldame."

"Even when I'm in bed right next to you?"

He nodded.

"What did you used to do when you had to sleep all by yourself?" Leigh asked.

"I made Odessa sit up with me. I've never been the last one to go to sleep at Beldame."

"Dauphin, why haven't you ever told me this before?"

"I was afraid you would think I was being stupid."

Leigh laughed. "Why are you telling me now?"

"Oh, because of what India was talking about tonight."

"The third house?"

"Yes. I don't like talking about it. It's not that I'm still afraid—"

"But you are," said his wife. "You are still afraid of it."

He nodded. "I guess I am. It's funny to be back now. And it's odd, I thought I'd be thinking the whole time about Mama, but I got here, and I was out sitting in the swing, and it wasn't till just now that I remembered that Mama died in that swing. I wasn't thinking about her, I was just thinking about the third house . . ."

"Dauphin, I don't think you're foolish. Mama and Marian, they were the foolish ones, raising us to be superstitious, raising us to be scared of things. If we have any children, I'm gone raise 'em different. They're not gone hear a word about the third house."

"That'd probably be best," said Dauphin. "It's not good, I can tell you, to grow up all the time scared of things."

Leigh turned on the bedside light and read a *Cosmopolitan* that was dated fifteen months back. Dauphin fell asleep with his head buried in her side, and his arm reaching across her breast. Even his feet were tangled in her legs—for protection against the third house.

When he felt the warmth of the rising sun on the sheet that lay across his body, he tried to avoid waking. Leigh lay within his arms but did not rouse when he squeezed her. Still he did not open his eyes, hoping that despite the increased warmth—which already was making him sweat—and despite the light that burned carmine against the inside of his lids, he would be overtaken by sleep again.

Experimentally, he pushed away from Leigh, and turned his back to her. But sleep would not come again, and Leigh did not wake. The effort of keeping his eyes closed became at last too great, and he allowed them to open. A large rectangle of red light—carefully outlined and divided like the window—was focused on the door into the hallway; as he stared it shifted a little, dropping toward the knob. It was probably not later than five.

He waited for Odessa's step on the floor above. He knew in

which of the half-dozen beds she slept, and that it lay directly above the dresser. As soon as she put her foot upon the floor, he would know it. And when she had dressed herself and he heard her footsteps on the stairs, he would allow himself to rise. He had not minded admitting to his wife that he was fearful of being the last to go to sleep at Beldame; but he would have been ashamed to have it known that he was also frightened of being the first to rise. Anyone could understand night terror, but what could one say of a man whose fears persisted through the dawn?

Dauphin jerked: the footfall had come, but in an unexpected place, just above the chifforobe in the opposite corner. Dauphin wondered what could have induced Odessa to change a habit of thirty-five years, and this season sleep in a different bed. He stared at the spot where her foot had sounded. Why had Odessa . . .

Why had he heard no more footsteps? he wondered suddenly, lifting his head from the pillow for the first time.

Then more footsteps sounded: Odessa moving carefully about the room, knowing she could be heard in the rooms below. For the duration of thirty summers at Beldame (he had first come to the place in Marian Savage's pregnant belly), Dauphin had risen within minutes of Odessa. He had always been the first for whom Odessa prepared breakfast, at the same time that she fixed her own; and it was only this meal, in this place, and only with Dauphin that Odessa broke her own rule against eating with her employers. At Beldame, at six-fifteen every morning, Odessa and Dauphin Savage shared breakfast at the kitchen table.

Dauphin also knew that the staircase to the third floor emerged directly into the middle of the room above him, just at the foot of the fourth bed. There was no door to open, and presently Dauphin heard Odessa descending the stairs.

He had risen from the bed and slipped on his pajamas, intending to follow her downstairs. Unwilling to risk waking Leigh, Odessa would not speak to him until they were together in the kitchen. The square of red morning sunlight burnished the brass knob of the door; Dauphin turned the key in the lock, and pulled the door open.

Marian Savage stood there. In her hands she held a large red vase that he had never seen before. "Dauphin," she said.

Dauphin smiled, then remembered that his mother was dead.

PART II

THE THIRD HOUSE

CHAPTER 10

While Dauphin Savage dreamed that his dead mother had come to the door of his bedroom, India McCray stood at her window and stared at the third house. In the black hour before dawn when the prickled stars were cloud-obscured, and St. Elmo's Lagoon provided only a scant spectral glow, she could see almost nothing of the building that so intrigued her. With a little shudder, she realized that she had never been in a place so dark as this. All her life she had lived in the city, where night was characterized not by blackness but only by a relative diminution of light. There were streetlamps and neon signs and uncurtained windows, car headlamps and a haze of red reflected light that covered New York from sundown until dawn. At Beldame, in the night, light was extinguished, and India was as if stricken blind.

The silence of the place oppressed her. The waves that broke on the shore, a few dozen yards distant, were an irritating reverberation in her ears and seemed unconnected to any physical source. India felt that the unpredictable and ever-changing pattern of the noise—which was all the more static and monotonous for its undeviating inconstancy—covered a real silence in the place, a sinister waiting silence. Things might move and things might shift themselves without her being able to hear them over the powerful thunder of the waves.

She had been awakened by some jarring noise beneath the regular surf and, knowing that whatever had spoken had spoken in the third house, she had gone immediately to the window. She stood fingering the curtain and cocked her ear. Perhaps the noises she heard after that, creaking doors and breaking glass, were but her imagination. In the waves one could hear anything: the sirens' call or the scraping tread of the dead on the sand.

The windows of the third house began to reflect the lightening sky in the east. The panes of glass burned a cold gray while the rest of the house remained the same undifferentiated black as the sky beyond it.

India returned to her bed and slept dreamlessly until ten o'clock. When she awakened, she did not remember that she had risen in the hour before dawn.

She did not have breakfast, for everyone else had already eaten and the idea of being specially waited on by Odessa appalled her. She poured herself a cup of coffee from the pot that was keeping warm on the stove and then wandered into the living room of the Savage house. Big Barbara was there alone.

"India," she said, "come and sit by me."

India did so, and asked, "How do you feel this morning?"

"Oh, law! This morning I look one day older than God and a year younger than water! Last night I didn't close my eyes. At five o'clock this morning I was still awake in my bed, turning and tossing and thinking about Big D."

"Dallas?"

"Dying, precious—Big D is death."

"Is that because you didn't have anything to drink last night?"

"Child, that is a rude thing to say to me! I wonder why Luker didn't feed you a spoonful of manners when you were little!"

India shrugged. "Alcoholism is a disease," she said. "Like athlete's foot. Or herpes. It's nothing to be ashamed of. Luker and I have lots of friends who are alcoholics. And speed freaks too."

"Well, it's still not what I choose to talk about with my own family. But I tell you what I *do* want to talk about . . ."

"What?"

"I want you to tell me about your life in New York City. I want to know how you spend your days. I want you to tell me about all your little friends, and what you and Luker do when you're alone together. India, you're my one and only grandchild and I hardly *ever* get to see you."

"All right," said India hesitantly. "You ask me questions and I'll answer them." She took a bolstering sip of her black coffee. There were things about her father India knew very well but could not possibly reveal to her grandmother; she must be on her guard to say nothing that would dismay or too much astonish Big Barbara.

"Oh, I'm so happy!" cried Big Barbara. "India, you bring that cup and we'll go out on our verandah and look at the Gulf. You and I will get the benefit of the breeze."

Big Barbara and India crossed the yard and seated themselves in the swing on the McCray verandah. If they stood at the porch rail they could see the single blanket on which Luker, Leigh, and Dauphin lay sunning. From her room India retrieved a morsel of sewing, the blue work shirt she was embroidering.

"All right," she said to her grandmother, snapping the hoop shut around the front pocket, "what did you want to know?"

"I want to know *everything*! You tell me what you want me to hear."

India thought, then smiled. "I'll tell you about my mother, how's that?"

Big Barbara pulled back so quickly that the swing rocked on its chains and India broke a needle against her thimble. "Not a word, child! Don't mention that woman! That sloozy! I'd like to grind her soul into a blacktopped road! That's what would make *me* happy!"

"What's a *sloozy*?" asked India.

"That's something between a slut and a floozy—and that was your mother!"

"I'm sorry I mentioned her, then. Let's see. What else can I tell you? I'll tell you—"

"What do you know about her?" demanded Big Barbara. "You haven't seen her, have you? Child, that woman left you high and dry. Right now I hope she's selling encyclopedias door to door, I hope she's picking potatoes in Louisiana, I hope she's at the end of the earth, I hope—"

"She lives about two blocks away from us," said India placidly. "I go to school with this kid who lives in the same building, but he's on the floor above and I won't—"

"What!" cried Big Barbara. "Do you mean to tell me you have *seen* her!"

"Of course. I pass her on the street all the time. Not 'all the time,' I guess, but once a week maybe. I—"

"Luker told me he had no idea what had become of that woman!"

"Probably he didn't want to upset you," said India after a moment.

"He's not thinking of . . . of a reconciliation? I mean, he's not *seeing* her, is he?"

"God, no!" India laughed. "He won't even speak to her. He cuts her dead on the street."

"You are not to trust that woman, India, do you hear me?" said Big Barbara sternly. "You are to stick your fingers in your ears when she talks to you, and if you see her coming down the street, I want you to turn right around and run the other way as fast as you can. Before you go away I'm going to give you a roll of quarters. I want you to have that money with you at all times, so when you see that woman coming you can jump in the first bus you see and get away from her!"

"She can't do anything to me," said India. She rode over what looked to be another interruption from Big Barbara: "Let me tell you about what happened with her, and then you won't be upset."

"India, tell me everything! I'd *love* to be alone with that woman and a bathtubful of boiling water!"

India pulled her green-threaded needle through the blue cloth and began, "When Mother ran off, Luker didn't make up any stories or anything, he just said to me, 'Your mother has run off, I don't know where and I don't know why and to tell you the truth I'm pretty glad about it.' And so everything was fine for about eight years, and then one day we were on our way to a movie or something, and she came right up to us on the street—I recognized her from her photographs. So she came up to us, and she said 'Hello,' and Luker said, 'Fuck off, bitch'—"

"India!" cried Big Barbara, stunned by the profanity, even if it was only quoted.

"—and we walked off. I didn't say anything to her. Then one day I was by myself and she saw me on the street and said she wanted to talk to me for a few minutes. So I said okay."

"Oh, India, what a mistake!"

"So it turned out she lived about two blocks away. She was living with this psychiatrist whose name was Orr, and he was real rich and she had this ditsy job doing PR for an auction gallery."

"I can't believe you just let her talk to you like that!"

"Well, it wasn't so bad. I just sat there and she gave me all this bullshit about how she'd like to have the chance to form some kind of relationship, that the time would come when I needed a mother—"

"You *always* have me!"

"—and I listened to what she had to say, and I said, 'We'll see.'"

"And was that all that happened?"

"No," replied India. "Something else happened. One day I was home alone. Luker was shooting in the Poconos and I knew he wouldn't be back before late. There was a knock at the door, and I went and opened it. She was standing there—I don't know how she got in the building. If she had rung the buzzer, I wouldn't have let her in. She had this little bag from Zabar's and she said, 'Can I come in and talk to you for a while—I brought you some lox.' I didn't want to let her in, but I go apeshit over lox. I don't know *how* she knew that."

"The devil knows everything!"

"Anyway, I let her in, and she was very polite and we talked for a few minutes and then she said, 'Let me go in the kitchen and fix everything.' She said she had forgotten to get anything to drink, and she gave me a five-dollar bill and told me to go out and buy some Perrier and limes. So I did—"

"You left her alone in Luker's apartment!"

"Yes," said India. "It was an asshole thing to do, all right. When I came back with the Perrier, she was already gone—and she even took the lox with her!"

"And what else? She must have done something else!"

"She did. She went to the refrigerator and took a bite out of everything that was in there. I had just made three dozen chocolate chip cookies, and there was a bite taken out of every one of 'em. She punched teeny-tiny holes in all the eggs and turned 'em upside down. She peeled all the bananas, and squeezed out all the almond paste. There was this new loaf of bread, and she opened it and she took a cookie cutter and cut out the middle of every slice.

She punched holes in the bottom of the canister set, and she mixed all the spices together in the Cuisinart. And she got out the punch bowl and poured in every bottle of wine and liquor in the house!"

"Oh, no!" groaned Big Barbara. "You poor child! What did you do?"

"I was upset, because I didn't know how I was going to explain to Luker what had happened. I sat down and cried and cried, and when Luker came home all he said was that I was a real asshole for letting her in. He said I should have poked her eyes out and ripped her tits off and slammed the door in her face."

"That's what I would have done," said Big Barbara complacently. "But did Luker have her arrested?"

"No, we just called her up. He was on one extension and I was on the other, and when she answered it we both blew police whistles as loud as we could. He said we probably broke her eardrum and there must have been blood all over her phone. And now when we see each other on the street we don't even speak. One time Dr. Orr—the psychiatrist she lives with—called me up and said he wanted to talk to me about mother-daughter relationships in general, but I told him to drop dead in a shed, Fred."

"Oh, child!" cried Big Barbara, embracing her granddaughter. "If it weren't for your language, I would say that Luker had raised you as a child for us all to be proud of!"

CHAPTER 11

Big Barbara had exaggerated when she told India that she had not closed her eyes all night. Nothing could keep that woman from sleep, but a very little could prevent her from sleeping well. After Odessa had served up a lunch of hamburgers and potato chips, Big Barbara put on her bathing suit and commandeered the blanket that had been laid on the Gulf beach. A few minutes later Luker came over and draped a large towel over his mother's sleeping body so that she would not burn. In deference to Big Barbara's modesty, Luker carried another blanket farther down the beach out of sight of the three houses before he took off his bathing suit and lay naked in the sun.

"You're disgusting," said India, waking him an hour or so later.

He opened his eyes, shaded them and looked up at her; but in the glare he could make out only her colorless outline against the sky. "Why?" he whispered; for the sun had leached out not only his energy and his intellect but his voice as well.

"The way you tan," she replied. "You haven't been in the sun in six months, but you're out here one day, and already you're starting to go dark brown." India wore long pants, a long-sleeved shirt, and her coolie hat. She seated herself in the sand beside him. "And look at me. The only part of me that's uncovered is my feet, and they're already starting to burn."

"Tough shit," said Luker.

"Can I borrow your camera?"

"Sure. But you have to be careful. It's very easy to get sand in it out here. What are you going to take pictures of?"

"The third house, of course. What else?"

Luker said nothing for a moment. "I thought you wanted *me* to take pictures of it," he said carefully.

"No, I decided that I would do it. You're not going to, that's obvious."

"Why do you say that?"

"I know you. You won't go near the place. If I asked you to do it, you'd put me off and put me off. So I decided I'd do it myself."

"India," said Luker, "I don't want you climbing that dune again. It's dangerous. You nearly cut your foot off up there yesterday. Let that be a lesson. And don't go up on the verandah either. I don't think those boards are safe. You could fall through. Those splinters would eat you alive."

"Whenever you come back to Alabama, you start acting like a father. India, do this; India, don't do that. Listen, the third house is just as safe as the other two, and you know it. Lend me your camera and let me take a few pictures. I'm not going to make a big deal of it, and I'm certainly not going inside—at least not today. I just want to get some shots of what it looks like from different angles, how the sand is taking over. I can't believe that you've never taken any pictures of it—you could have sold about a million prints."

"Listen, India. Nobody knows about Beldame, and if people find out there are these three perfect Victorian houses down here, they're going to be out here in droves. Beldame has never been robbed, and I don't intend to give people any ideas."

"That's bullshit," said India contemptuously. "You're scared shitless of the third house, that's all."

"Of course I am," said Luke, rolling over with something like anger. "It's a fucking childhood trauma, and we've all got childhood traumas . . ."

"I don't."

"Your whole life is a fucking trauma," said Luker. "You just don't know it yet. Wait'll you grow up, then you'll see how fucked-up you were . . ."

"Can I borrow your camera?" India persisted.

"I told you yes," said Luker. As she walked off back toward the houses, he called after her: "India, *be careful!*"

From his room, India took her father's second-best Nikon and his light meter and carried them out into the yard. Odessa sat on the back steps of the Savage house, shelling peas in a wide pan and tossing the pods into a newspaper laid open at her feet. India measured the available light, and snapped on the wide-angle lens and a sunlight filter. Odessa rose from the steps and came to her side. She pointed to the second floor of the house. "Mr. Dauphin and Miz Leigh sleeping," she said in a whisper. "You gone take some pictures?"

"Of the third house," replied India.

"Why? Nobody lives there. Why you want pictures of that old place?" Odessa frowned—and there was warning, not curiosity, in her voice.

"Because it's very strange looking. It'll make good photographs. Have you ever been inside?"

"No!"

"I'd like to take some pictures inside the house," mused India.

"There's no air inside that house," said Odessa. "You'd suffocate."

India raised the camera, framed the house quickly, and took a picture. She half expected Odessa to object, but the black woman said nothing. India moved a couple of steps away and took another photograph.

"Luker says the place is dangerous—"

"It is," said Odessa quickly, "you just don't know what—"

"He says it's structurally unsafe."

"What?" said Odessa, not understanding.

"Luker says the boards will give way. I think he's just scared. I—"

"Don't stand there," said Odessa. "Cain't see anything from there, move over there." She pointed to a spot on the broken-shell walk a yard closer to the house. Puzzled, India moved there and took another photograph.

Odessa nodded, satisfied, then pointed out another spot, several places to the left, but inconveniently close to a thorny bush, so that India's ankles were scratched.

India could not imagine what knowledge this black woman had of photographic setups, that she could dictate these positions. But Odessa pushed India all around that yard, told her on which windows and architectural details to focus, and whether the camera should be held horizontally or vertically. And all this in a whisper, so as not to disturb the sleepers on the second floor. India obeyed her mechanically.

In the camera the compositions seemed to frame themselves perfectly, and often India had no more to do than check the lighting and trip the shutter. She anticipated happily showing her father a set of splendid photographs of the third house and the dune that was slowly burying it.

After fifteen or so changes of positions, and perhaps two dozen photographs—Odessa sometimes demanded that a particular picture be taken twice—the black woman said, "All right. That's enough, child. You'll get what you want out of that. And once you see those pictures, you'll have had enough of the third house, I can tell you."

"Thank you," said India, who now thought that Odessa's directions had been merely to keep her from mounting the back steps of the place or going too near the windows. "But I still have the other side of the house to do."

"Child," said Odessa softly, "don't . . ."

India looked Odessa in the eye. "I think you're all crazy," she said, then went around to the other side of the dune to photograph what little was visible of the front of the house.

She had intended to regard her father's commands to the letter, but as she stood alone at the base of the dune with the shallow Gulf waters breaking in low waves directly behind her, she understood that she must, at all costs, keep at bay the fear of the third house that was fast rising in her. It was necessary that she conquer it, as all the others evidently had not.

It was not the entire house that frightened her, but only that single room that corresponded to the one in which she slept in the McCray house—the door of which had been slowly pulled shut as she watched through the window. India wondered now why she had said nothing of what she had seen to any of the others. Partly, she considered, she had been afraid, afraid to describe an experience that smacked of the supernatural. Partly, Luker's reluctance to talk of the house had infected her as well. Too, India had never been an obvious child, and to speak of what was uppermost in her mind seemed a crass superficiality. At the last, the occurrence, the vision—whatever it had been, had seemed meant for India alone. And India wasn't one to betray a confidence.

The sun was almost directly overhead. India knew that she could not go away without looking into that room once more. She snapped the cap over the camera lens and quickly climbed to the top of the dune. On the way she tossed aside her coolie hat, fearful that it would flaw her balance. Her foot unearthed the fleur-de-lis that she had broken off the frieze; she picked it up and flung it into the sea. She grabbed hold of another, and stood before the window once more.

She wasn't certain whether she had hoped to find the door closed or open; whatever her preference might have been, the door remained closed. Probably, it occurred to her now with considerable relief, the shutting of the door had been the result merely of the atmospheric change in the room occasioned by the breaking of the pane. But whatever the case, the fact was that now the room looked quite different. She realized quickly however that this was only on account of the difference in light. An entirely new set of objects in the room was delineated, it seemed; and those she distinctly remembered were now hidden in obscurity. Above the door was a plate painted with a proverb she could not at such a distance decipher. Two slats had fallen out of the bed frame. On the shelf of the dresser she saw a chipped cup piled high with silver coins: half-dollars and dimes.

But she could no longer see the line of red dust on the rush matting. The broken picture frame behind the bed was only a shadow. The shaving implements atop the dressing table appeared an indistinguishable jumble.

On the floor beneath the window was a mound of sand as high as the window and fanning gently out from the broken pane, at greatest to a distance of about four feet. It replicated in miniature the dune that crouched outside the house. The pressure of her weight sent more sand through the aperture, and at a place on the left-hand arc of the fan, the delta buried several more knots of the rush matting.

The destruction was not so bad as it might have been, India supposed, but she didn't recall pleasurably that her agency had begun it. How easily the sand had got in, she knew; and how difficult it would be to clear the room of it now, she could scarcely imagine.

She took half a dozen photographs of the room, with the regular lens, attempting to record everything that could be seen through that window. She must hold the camera with only one hand, for with the other she maintained her balance and position. With the slow shutter speed required to capture the dim interior, she feared that the slight trembling of her hand might blur the image. She smiled to think that her indiscretion would be discovered by Luker only when he saw the developed prints—but that might not be for weeks, and by then, who knew? she might actually have gone inside the third house. Luker's fear was obviously groundless—as he had said, a childhood trauma and nothing more. She herself had been frightened by the third house, but only momentarily; she had returned and proved both that she was not afraid and that there was nothing to fear.

One shot more would finish the second roll of film. She held the camera up to the window and peered through the viewer, focusing on the mirrored door of the opened chifforobe. It reflected a portion of the front wall otherwise invisible to India. Looking through the camera at this mirrored door, she caught sight of a slight but agitated movement in the sand—as if something burrowed beneath. She quickly lowered the camera, and peered through the window; though she twisted and leaned far to the right, she could not see directly that portion of the sand heap figured in the mirror. She returned her gaze to the mirror, and watched mystified as the sand slowly bulged and twisted.

She looked down at the broken window. Sand spilled through still, but at only a slow rate, and it now accumulated to the right side of the window, not the left.

Now she could see the shape of whatever was beneath the sand—yet that was not it precisely. The shape rather seemed to form out of the sand itself. It was human, but small, about India's own size.

The sand twisted and spilled over itself in ropes and nobs, sculpting the form and image of a child. In a few seconds, it became obvious the child was female.

When the figure was complete the sand was still again, breathlessly still. Amazed, India raised her camera and focused it on the mirror in the chifforobe; she even remembered to adjust for the discrepancy of reflected distance.

She looked through the viewer and framed the shot.

As she pressed the shutter, the prone figure of sand sat suddenly up. The sand on her breast and head fell quickly away. It was a little grinning black girl whose short hair had been carefully divided into eight squares, braided and ribboned. Her dress was red, ill-made, and coarsely textured—the cloth seemed exactly the same as that of the bedspread, even to a fringed hem around the bottom.

India stood at the window, the camera dangling against her beating breast. The heat of the sun tore at her uncovered head.

The black child crawled toward the window and the sand spilled off her as she came, every second revealing more blackness of her skin, more redness of her stiff red dress. India made herself look down through the panes.

The Negro child pawed up the dune to the window and lifted her black face to stare into India's. Sand welled in the corners of her white-pupilled black eyes. She opened her mouth to laugh, but no sound, only a long ribbon of white dry sand spilled out of it.

CHAPTER 12

India never told what she had seen. She scrambled and slid down the dune, raced around to the front of the McCray house, and fled upstairs to her own room. A stultifying weariness overcame her, and she fell immediately asleep crossways on the bed, her father's Nikon still hanging around her neck. Grain by grain two small mounds of sand were formed beneath her dangling feet.

When Luker awakened her hours later, he declared that she had suffered sunstroke. Long-sleeved clothing and hats were not going to be enough until she could get used to the Alabama sun: she must stay in-of-doors during the worst of the day's heat. Early morning and late afternoon she might walk about or swim in the Gulf, though for no more than fifteen minutes at the time. "Too much sun," he warned her, "is a kind of poison, especially for someone who's as fair-skinned as you."

"Does it cause hallucinations?" India wanted to know.

Luker, pointedly not demanding why she should ask so leading a question, replied merely, "Sometimes . . ." and told her she ought to get ready for supper.

And in the days that followed, the overwhelming stately routine of Beldame buried everything, even fear. At the end of her first week there, India understood how Luker and Dauphin and Odessa could contemplate returning to the place, when they were evidently very much afraid of the third house and whatever inhabited it. Days at Beldame were so exquisitely dull and stuffy, so brightly illumined and so hot to the touch, that the quivers and fretwork of emotion were quite burned away.

India had previously entertained no sympathy for the Southern way of life, with its pervasive friendliness, its offhanded viciousness, its overwhelming lassitude. She had always wanted to punch it into shape, to make it sit up straight and say what it meant—but Beldame proved too much for her. She was bewitched, as surely as Merlin by Nimue. By afternoon her physical indolence was such that she could scarcely raise her arm, and ten minutes' consideration was hardly enough to decide whether to move from the swing on the McCray verandah to the glider on the Savage porch. It was probably a good thing that she had unpacked in the first minutes of her arrival at Beldame, for had she put it off, it might not have been accomplished yet. The very air was soporific, the food swung in the belly like ballast from meal to meal, the furniture seemed specifically designed to accommodate the human form in sleep. There was nothing sharp at Beldame, even the corners of the houses seemed rounded off. There were no sudden or shrill noises, for the surf never left off its masking roar. Worry, clever thought, conversation all were crushed by the weight of the atmosphere.

Days and nights were dull, but they were never tedious. The autumn before, India and Luker had gone to England together, and ridden the train from London to Glasgow. The Midlands were stupidly industrial, the Lake Country magnificent, but it was the unending monotonous barren hills of southwestern Scotland that most intrigued India and her father. There was grandeur in a vista that was wholly and even aggressively uninteresting. So it was with Beldame: nothing happened there, nothing *could* happen there. Days were entirely characterized by the weather: it was a hot day, or it was a day that wasn't so very hot; it rained, or it looked as if it might rain; or it had rained yesterday but would probably be only hot today. India had quickly lost the flow of the days of the week: time divided itself into brief arbitrary runs of hot days and rainy days. The words *yesterday* and *tomorrow* might have been excised from their vocabulary: for yesterday had entertained nothing that was worth today's speech, and tomorrow could promise no change from today. Transfixed, as out of a train window, India stared at life at Beldame.

The Savage house rose early, and the McCray house rose late; and the time of everyone's rising, that never varied more than a quarter of an hour, constituted the length and breadth of the morning's conversation. Odessa stood in the kitchen and prepared a succession of breakfasts. Late in the morning, everyone but India and Odessa lay upon the beach for an hour or so, and it was rare that they did not all fall directly asleep again. At noontime when the sun was so strong that not even Luker could abide it, everyone came inside and worked crossword puzzles, or read paperback books someone had bought in Mobile fifteen years before, or worked one of the great jigsaw puzzles that was always laid out on the McCrays' dining room table. At one o'clock, by which time breakfast had been sufficiently digested, they sat down to lunch; and after lunch, they returned to their frivolous occupations for half an hour before they began to yawn, stretching out on gliders or climbing unsteadily into hammocks to sleep. During all the long afternoon, Odessa sat and worked at the jigsaw. It infuriated India that the black woman's proficiency was never augmented by her long hours at the puzzle; she remained abysmally slow at it always.

If food or other supplies were wanted or laundry needed to be done, Luker or Leigh or Dauphin drove over to Gulf Shores at low tide, when the channel was clear. India, not having completely excised the notion that Beldame was a place to escape from, had gone along on the first couple of these small expeditions; but she found that after Beldame, Gulf Shores was but a tawdry, cramped place. The people she saw there were not the kind to excite her imagination: in fact they were of the sort actually to depress her, possessing money certainly but not enough taste to hang around their necks on a string. It was the Redneck Riviera indeed. So after those first two trips India let the others go to Gulf Shores alone, and herself treasured an even more deserted Beldame.

In the late afternoon when the sun had abated its strength, everyone went back out onto the beach, and even India allowed herself a little time in the waves. The water on the Gulf side was always bright and clean, and even the scant seaweed there looked as if it had been fresh-washed. India, not used to swimming in the sea, had asked if she might not go in the calmer St. Elmo's Lagoon, but Leigh had told her that no one swam there since Odessa's little girl Martha-Ann had drowned eleven years before.

"Oh," cried India, "I didn't even know that Odessa was married!"

"She isn't," said Big Barbara, "and it's a good thing too, considering what Martha-Ann's father is like. Johnny Red gardened for us one year, and he stole my best azaleas!"

India's favorite spot was the little course through which St. Elmo's Lagoon and the Gulf were connected twice a day. It was about thirty feet wide, dry at low tide, and about three feet deep at high. Despite this shallowness, Luker warned her not to wade across it when it was full, and when she asked the reason for the caution, he was annoyingly vague. But at high tide, when the water of the Gulf rushed across and made of Beldame an island, India and Big Barbara sat at the edge of the channel and fished for crab with cane poles and minnows that India had captured with a large strainer. It was a homely occupation that brought grandmother and granddaughter closer than a hundred intimate conversations could have done.

These attenuated afternoons were an exquisite time, warm but not hot, with golden, lambent light, lasting always a little longer than they imagined it would, slipping suddenly into night. When the sun touched the horizon, they came in off the beach—waving and snapping their towels in the air, as if in ritualized farewell to the day—rolled out of the hammock and wandered inside the house, or trekked slowly back along St. Elmo's Lagoon to watch the evening phosphorescence rise.

Supper was usually no more than a potful of boiled crab; and the taste was so sweet and fresh that they never grew tired of it. Evenings at Beldame passed with surprising swiftness. There was no television, and the single transistor radio was reserved for emergencies or terrible weather. They worked on the puzzle or played cards or word games or Scrabble and Parcheesi. India did her needlework and Odessa, sitting in the most distant corner, read the Bible. At ten o'clock, or a little later, everyone went to bed and immediately fell asleep, as if exhausted by a day of emotional frenzy or unceasing labor.

India, rather to Luker's surprise, had taken immediately to Beldame, rarely spoke of New York, and never expressed the wish to return there speedily. She said, in fact, that she would be content to remain on the Gulf until Labor Day, the Wednesday after which she must begin school. Luker himself, who had long subsisted on late evenings and a wide acquaintance, had expected to chafe in the solitude of Beldame as much as his daughter. But he adapted as readily, reconstructing other indolent summers spent there. He did nothing, he thought of nothing; he didn't even bother to feel guilty that he was not working. When Big Barbara asked him if he could afford to take so long a time off, he replied: "Oh, hell, the day before I leave, I'll take a couple of rolls of pictures; and then the whole trip can come off of my taxes."

"But you're not earning anything while you're here."

"I could stand to be in a lower bracket this year." He shrugged. "Don't worry about me, Barbara. If I lack in September, I'll come begging."

Leigh had always been happy at Beldame—Leigh was happy anywhere, and under all circumstances. But this for her was one of the most pleasant interludes, following so closely as it did on the death of her mother-in-law. Against Marian Savage, Leigh spoke not a word now; after all, the woman was dead and could never defeat her again.

Dauphin perhaps benefited most from the seclusion of Beldame: away from his business, away from the Great House, away from friends' clumsy ministrations to his grief. Marian Savage was truly mourned by only one person: her son, although he had little cause to love her as he did. Sister Mary-Scot had never made a pretense of affection for Marian Savage, and had at thirteen made a vow to God that if she were not married by the time she finished college, she would go into a convent. She refused two proposals in her junior year, and took her final vows on her twenty-third birthday.

Luker wondered that Beldame didn't remind Dauphin as much of Marian Savage as had the Great House in Mobile, but to this Leigh replied, "There were times that Dauphin came here without her, and I have the feeling that he believes she's still alive back in Mobile and that he's just enjoying a little vacation away from her. You'll notice that he didn't bring Nails. Nails would have been too much of a reminder that Marian was dead." But whatever Dauphin's thoughts and motives, his spirit improved markedly over the weeks and something like cheer was added to his equable temperament and gentleness.

It was only Big Barbara who suffered in any degree, and that was because of the alcohol deprivation. She did not go into fits, but sometimes in the late afternoon she had urges to spin right down into the sand like a dervish or to scrape her skin with broken shells because of the impossibility of getting a drink. In her rare moments of anger she was more sullen and louder than was usual with her. She was irritable, impatient, restless, and always hungry.

And it was only grudgingly she admitted that she felt a good deal better than she had in some months. In a particularly weak moment she promised that when they opened the cage and let her fly back to Mobile, she would continue her abstinence, "Though I know everybody in town is gone be saying I went to Houston to get Dr. DeBakey to remove that glass from my hand . . ."

Odessa was Odessa, and day in and day out voiced neither wish nor complaint but was at all times content and placid.

CHAPTER 13

In fact, Beldame as a whole for these weeks was content and placid, but the inhabitants realized this only when it abruptly ceased to be so, one Thursday morning late in June. It was then, just at the time that India was having her first cup of coffee, that Lawton McCray appeared in their midst, having arrived not in a jeep or a Scout, but in a small boat that he had rented in Gulf Shores. With him he brought a tall fat man who wore large glasses and a rumpled seersucker suit. Lawton was greeted with mild surprise, for his visit had not been at all anticipated; and his companion was treated with offhanded politeness, except by Dauphin, who was sincerely cordial to everyone.

And it was Dauphin whom they had come to see; and Dauphin, Lawton and the man in the rumpled suit—whose name was Sonny Joe Black—forthwith closeted themselves in the Savage living room.

"Lawton's funds must be running low," said Luker to his mother on the verandah of the McCray house. "Leigh," he said, talking over his shoulder to his sister, "you ought to tell Dauphin not to give Lawton a penny. It'll be down the tubes if he does."

"But what if Lawton wins!" cried Big Barbara.

"Then Dauphin will just have to learn to live with the guilt of having helped to elect such a man to national office," replied Luker.

Half an hour later, Lawton McCray ambled across the yard alone. A light rain was falling so that even the bristling white sand, pockmarked and shelled, seemed to take on the grayness of the sky. He sat on the swing next to his wife.

"Lawton," remarked Big Barbara, "we had no idea to expect you today!"

"If y'all would get a telephone put in here I could have called. They got phones in Gasque, they could have 'em out here."

"Dauphin doesn't want to ruin the view with telephone poles," said Leigh, "and I agree with him. We've never had a telephone out here, and we can get along all right a while longer I guess."

"Barbara," said her husband, "how you doing?"

"I'm fine."

"How's she doing?" asked Lawton of his son.

"She's just fine," replied Luker sullenly. Lawton always spoiled Luker's day.

"She's just fine!" cried Leigh and India together, before they had to be asked.

"Who's that man you brought out here?" demanded Luker. "What's he want with Dauphin?"

"Oh, you know," said Lawton McCray, "talking business—just talking business."

"What kind of business, Daddy?" asked Leigh.

Lawton McCray slowly shrugged his wide soft shoulders, and instead of answering his daughter's question, he said, "I wanted to talk to y'all 'bout something for a few minutes. Now I can pretty much tell that all of you are having just about the time of your lives down here"—he glanced around the gray rainy vista that Beldame afforded that afternoon—"but it sure would be a favor to me if y'all would just think about coming back to Mobile for a few days around the Fourth. There's gone be meetings and parties and all like that and it wouldn't do me a bit of harm in the world, Barbara, if you went to a couple of 'em with me."

"You sure you trust me to get through it all right? You not afraid I'm gone throw up on the after-dinner speaker?"

"I can tell, Barbara, you're doing just real good down here. Luker and Leigh—they've been taking good care of you. It's made a difference. If you would, I'd appreciate it if you'd come back for a few days—Fourth's on Tuesday, I could use you 'bout Saturday to Wednesday, I s'pose. Some of those things you can go to with me, and some of 'em you can go to by yourself."

"Oh, Lawton," smiled Big Barbara, with shy gratitude creeping into her voice, "'course I'll come up. You want Leigh and Dauphin too?"

"Wouldn't hurt. Never hurts to have Dauphin round—everybody thinks so high of Dauphin. And Leigh too. Nobody in Mobile got as much money and respect as Dauphin. You two doing all right since Marian died, aren't you?" he asked his daughter.

"We're okay," said Leigh.

"When's the money coming through?"

"Don't know yet," replied Leigh. "Dauphin's got to go up in a few days and see about the will."

"Don't you want Luker and me to represent you too?" asked India blandly.

"Yeah," laughed Luker, "India and I'll give your campaign a little New York class. How's that?"

"Thank you, Luker," replied Lawton heavily. "'Preciate it, India. I'm glad to get *anybody's* support, but I tell you, if y'all had rather just hang on here at Beldame, I'm not gone beg you away. I know y'all don't get down here too often, and there's no reason for y'all to have to mix in an election that y'all don't really have much to do with . . ."

"I tell you what, Lawton," said Luker, "one afternoon we'll ride over to Belforest, and I'll take a publicity photo of you standing on a pile of fertilizer."

"Really do 'preciate it, Luker," said Lawton gravely. "We'll see about it." He pulled at the sleeve of his shirt, which was damp with water that had fallen from the roof and splashed on the porch railing. "Well, y'all, I am about to be drowned out here. I am going inside and wait for Sonny Joe to get finished talking to Dauphin. Barbara, you want to come inside and talk to me for a couple of minutes?"

A little nervously, Big Barbara assented and followed her husband into the house.

"That man pisses me off," said Luker to his sister and daughter.

"You ought not let him bother you like that," said Leigh. "He's always been just like that."

"India, look through the window and see if you can see where they've gone."

"They went upstairs," said India, who had already been watching.

"He doesn't want us to hear," sighed Leigh. "Mama's been doing so well—I hope he doesn't say anything to upset her."

"His just coming here upset her," said Luker. "Didn't you see how nervous she was?"

Leigh nodded. "Sometimes Daddy upsets her without intending to, I think."

"Daddy is an asshole," said Luker finally. He remembered how many times as a child he had seen Lawton escort Big Barbara to their bedroom; the two would remain there for an hour, and Luker could hear their voices, mysterious and low and earnest, through the walls. Big Barbara would emerge tearful and wanting a drink—no matter the time of day. Things hadn't changed, it seemed; but now that he was thirty-three, Luker had some idea of what was being said in the bedroom upstairs.

Luker and India and Leigh sat silent on the porch; the swing chains creaked in the damp air. The Gulf was a silvering gray; pristine and cold, with a tide much higher than was usual. Now and then, when the wind was just right, they heard a word or two that was spoken upstairs in the house, by Lawton or by Big Barbara.

"I hate it when they go upstairs like that," said Leigh, and Luker knew that she too had those memories.

With a newspaper to shield her head, Odessa strode across the yard from the Savage house and came up onto the porch. She seated herself in a chair a little removed from the others, drew her Bible out of a paper sack, and remarked: "Nothing much to do today but read . . ."

"They still talking over there, Dauphin and that man?" asked Leigh.

Odessa nodded.

"What are they talking about? Did you hear anything?" asked Luker.

Odessa nodded. "I heard. I was cleaning upstairs, and I heard what they were saying. I heard what Mr. Lawton said, and I heard what that other man said too."

"What'd they say?" asked Luker again, his interest aroused by Odessa's hesitant manner.

"Mr. Lawton trying to get Mr. Dauphin to sell Beldame . . ." said Odessa with pursed lips.

"What!" cried Leigh.

"Oh, shit!" breathed Luker in disgust.

"Oil," said Odessa. "They say they got oil out there"—she pointed vaguely over the gray water—"and they want all this place for setting things up on. They want to tear the houses down."

"Goddamn that fucker to hell," Luker said in a low voice to his daughter, and she nodded her acquiescence in this anathema.

"Dauphin's not gone sell," said Leigh to her brother. "He's not gone let Lawton talk him into it."

India stood and pointed across St. Elmo's Lagoon. "Why don't they buy land over there? Farther down the coast? Wouldn't that be the same thing? Then they wouldn't have to tear the houses down."

Luker answered this: "Water's shallow along this part of the coast. It's only right here, just along Beldame, that the Gulf has any depth near the shore."

"They said only this place would do," Odessa concurred.

"So that's why that man came," said Luker. "Leigh, if Dauphin sells, you're going to have enough shekels to pave the Dixie Graves Parkway."

"I hope he doesn't sell," shrugged Leigh. "We've got so much money now I think I ought to have me twenty-seven maids instead of just three."

"So," said Luker to Odessa, "what'd Dauphin say to the man?"

"Said he'd think about it, that's all, said he'd think about it. And when I come downstairs, they had all these maps spread out over the table and the man was showing Mr. Dauphin stuff."

"That was Dauphin being polite," said Leigh.

"India," said Luker, "why don't you run get an ice pick and punch some holes in that boat out there?"

A few minutes later Lawton came downstairs from his conference with Big Barbara and went out without speaking to his family again. India from her post at the corner of the verandah reported that he had gone in the back door of the Savage house. Ten minutes later he returned through the rain with Sonny Joe Black and Dauphin close behind him. Both Sonny Joe and Lawton took hearty leave of Dauphin, cautioned him to think things over carefully, and promised they'd all talk again when Dauphin was back in Mobile on the first of July.

Luker, Leigh, and India received the parting politenesses of the two men with reserve that bordered on rudeness. Big Barbara did not come down to see her husband off; she remained in the bedroom upstairs.

As their boat sputtered away in the direction of Gulf Shores, Luker remarked: "Maybe if the rain keeps up, it'll wash away the stink."

Dauphin reassured them that he had not committed himself in any way to Mr. Black, who was a very nice man, and that he had no intention of selling or leasing any of the land that he owned along the Gulf; he agreed with his wife that he had plenty of money without that addition.

"But, oh, Lord," said Dauphin, "Lawton was all for it, and said I'd be dealing a death blow to the entire Arab world if I sold off Beldame. He pulled me over and he told me that with what the oil companies would pay me for Beldame I could afford to buy me five counties in South Carolina."

"You're a fool to listen to that man," said Luker. "He'd lick your balls if it put another dollar in his pocket. I hope you told him to fuck off."

"Oh, Luker," said Dauphin, dismayed that he should talk so before three women, "I couldn't say any such thing. I like Lawton. And I don't want to 'tagonize him. See, I've got to keep him on my good side so that I can convince him it's a good idea for me not to sell or lease Beldame. And then I've got to convince him that it's also a good idea for *him* not to sell either."

"What!" cried Luker. "He couldn't sell unless you did, he—"

"But he could," said Dauphin. "Lawton owns this house free and clear, and if he sold it to the oil companies, I couldn't stop him. They'd tear down your house and put up a dock, and then the place would be just ruined, and I'd end up selling too . . ."

It was feared that Lawton had left Big Barbara in a bad way. Those on the porch downstairs delegated India to go up to her room and ascertain her condition. India knocked on the door and from within Big Barbara called, "Who is it?"

"India!"

"Oh, child, come on in!" Big Barbara sat up on the bed, leaning against the headboard, studying her tear-stained face in a hand mirror.

"Are you all right?" India asked politely. "They sent me to find out."

"Child," smiled Big Barbara, "I'm just so fine you wouldn't hardly believe it!"

"Really?"

"Really and truly."

"What did Lawton say to you?"

"He said that he thought I was making wonderful progress and that he was sure I was gone be just fine and if I was gone be just fine then there wasn't any need for a divorce and everything between us was gone be just fine from now on, forever and ever. That's what Lawton said to me. I tell you—I'll admit it—when he said he wanted to talk to me, I was sure he was gone set a date for me to come up and sign divorce papers. But instead he made me feel so good, I volunteered to go back with him today. I said I'd ride all the way to Gulf Shores in that teeny-tiny boat, even if I had to sit in his lap—but he said no, I ought to stay here and get to feeling real, real good before I came back to help him with his campaign. All you children underestimate Lawton. You don't accord him his true worth."

"I suppose we don't," remarked India drily.

"I *know* you don't. And I suppose everybody's sitting down there out on the porch waiting to hear how I am, aren't they?"

India nodded.

"Well you go tell them I'm just fine—"

"Why don't you come down?"

"Looking like I do, when I've been crying? Luker sees I've been crying, he won't believe I'm happy. You tell them I'm up here strumming a harp, and then you come back up and talk to me."

India did as she was told, and as his mother had predicted, Luker could not believe that it was good news that Big Barbara had received at Lawton's hands. "She's just putting on a brave front," he said to the others.

"I don't think she is," said India. "She seems real happy, and she wants me to go back up and talk to her."

"I'll go back up and talk to her," said Luker. "That man didn't speak a word of truth the entire time he was here today, he—"

"Don't go," said Leigh when her brother stood from the swing.

"Leave her alone for a while," said Dauphin.

Odessa nodded her agreement with this advice.

Luker shook his head ruefully. "You know that whatever it was he said to her, he was lying. And she took it for gospel, the way she always does. Why she—"

"If she's happy about it right now," said Leigh, "then don't spoil it. She's got enough to think about, just climbing up on the wagon. When you're coming down off liquor, you don't need to be told that your husband's lying to you—and Luker, you don't know for sure that he was!"

"Go on back up then, India. Go talk to her, if that's what she wants," suggested Dauphin.

India returned to Big Barbara and sat at the foot of the bed.

"Child," she cried, "you have brought in all kinds of sand, and now you have got it all over my sheets! Stand up and brush it off!" But this without anger.

India climbed down from the bed and carefully brushed the sand off the sheets. Then she emptied her shoes of it, turned out her cuffs, and flapped the tails of her shirt. A little circle of sand was scattered around her at the side of the bed.

"India, I never saw anybody that attracted sand like you do!"

India had not left the house all morning. How had sand found its way into her cuffs and shoes? Of this, however, she said nothing to her grandmother, but rather began to tell Big Barbara somewhat of life as it is lived on the Upper West Side.

CHAPTER 14

They were not happy at Beldame in the hours that followed Lawton McCray's visit with Sonny Joe Black. It was not simply the prospect of change for themselves that distressed them, the returning to Mobile solely for Lawton's benefit and convenience when they were entirely happy at Beldame, but that Beldame itself—Beldame considered as a place or a thing—might be doomed was almost more than they could bear. Luker told his sister he might still live in perfect contentment if he went away tomorrow and never returned—as long as he was assured that Beldame remained as it was; but if he learned that the place had been substantially altered or destroyed, his life would be considerably diminished. To them all, Beldame represented the fair and possible reward for distress, misfortune, and labor in this world—it was to them a heaven on earth, and resembled the other, preached-of heaven in that it was bright, remote, timeless, and empty. And that in so imperfect a world such a perfection as Beldame should be endangered by Lawton McCray, that crass conniving son of a bitch, was an affront to every man that had some vision to treasure.

The very perfection of Beldame wore down their anger and alarm. The rain continued the afternoon and the night; but the next morning was bright and hot, and steam rose in a thousand funnels off St. Elmo's Lagoon even as early as seven o'clock. Dauphin vowed that no harm would ever come to Beldame as long as he was alive, and the others comfortably allowed themselves to believe him. By the afternoon, when Big Barbara complained that it was hotter than a boiled owl, no one thought any more of Lawton McCray; and if anything distressed them, it was the thought of returning to Mobile in a week's time. They might well come back to Beldame after the Fourth, but they all knew that the real charm of a vacation was broken by such an hiatus.

Of them all, Lawton McCray's visit affected India the most. She was young and didn't understand the subtle language of threat and persuasion and inference among Southern businessmen and was certain that Lawton McCray could override the objections of weak-willed Dauphin, and Beldame—on which she now projected a yearly visit for her father and herself forever and ever—would be razed. Her photographs of the houses would then be found on the pages of the new edition of *Lost American Architecture*. It was a little comfort to think that Luker would eventually be made rich by the transaction with the oil companies, but then she began to fear that her grandfather would find a way to deprive his son of his just share of the proceeds. By the others, Lawton McCray was cheerfully damned to hell; but to India he rose from that place with black skin and red wings and his malodorous shadow covered all Beldame.

India McCray liked to have an enemy. At school she usually had one child in her class whom she half despised and half feared; whom she treated at once with contempt and respect; whom she alternately spat upon and cringed before. This pattern of behavior became so apparent to her teachers that they called in Luker, explained the situation and advised him to put India into therapy. Luker that evening told India that she was an uncomplex little fool, and that if she wanted to hate anybody she should hate her mother (whom they had seen on the street the week before). India accepted this advice, and when that woman appeared no longer to pose any threat, she gave the place to the superintendent of the building next door who maltreated small animals; but he was forgotten in Alabama, when there wasn't yelping and screeching to remind India of his reprehensible pastime.

At Beldame, the enemy had been Odessa, not because Odessa had done anything bad to her—or even because India instinctively disliked her—but only because it was inconvenient to dislike any of the others: Luker, Big Barbara, Leigh, or Dauphin.

India had always thought of herself as politically liberal—as Luker was—and with that liberalism came a discomfort with servants. Other appurtenances of the rich didn't bother her, and she had often benefited from the largesse of some of Luker's friends: weekends in large houses, rides in limousines and private planes, Beluga and Dom Perignon, private screenings and empty beaches—and had enjoyed them all without guilt. But servants walked and talked and had feelings and yet weren't equal, and India thought that to deal with them was a practical impossibility. She asked nothing of Odessa, and would have prepared all her own food rather than be waited on by the black woman—except that Odessa insisted that she have the kitchen entirely to herself. India could not use the kitchen at the McCray house, for there the gas and the refrigerator had not even been turned on.

But Lawton McCray succeeded in triumph to the place that Odessa had held but tenuously in India's imagination. The man was a perfect enemy, in fact, as perfect as her own mother had been:

contemptible, cruel, powerful, and directly threatening. Thus, on the very evening of Lawton's visit, the others noticed a difference in India's treatment of Odessa: a smile that had never been displayed before, a willingness to work at the jigsaw puzzle with her, a special and cordial good-night.

One rainy night, India lay in bed waiting for her father; it was their custom to speak for a few minutes at the last of the day, after all Beldame was still. The lights in the McCray house had been extinguished, and none were to be seen across the way in the Savage house either. The Gulf at low tide was rough and distant. For the first time since her arrival, India needed not only a sheet but the chenille bedspread, and still she shivered once or twice. Rain blew through the open windows and spattered on the floor of the room.

India had moved her bed after her first night there, and now, if she sat up, she could see the bedroom windows of the third house. But that was in good weather and on nights when the moon shone; now beyond the window all was blackness.

Luker wandered in, and stood by the window that faced the water. "Goddamn!" he said, "I cain't even see the fucking Gulf!"

India, whose eyes had become accustomed to the darkness, could just see that her father had moved away from the window, and leaned against the wall with his arms folded across his chest. "Did you know that your accent comes back when you come down here?" she asked.

"No!" he laughed, "does it really?"

"Can't you tell?"

"No, I cain't."

"Well," said India, "for one thing, you say *cain't* instead of *can't*. And you start to talk the way Big Barbara does. In New York, you don't have an accent at all, nobody can tell you're from Alabama. The only time you have an accent in New York is when you're talking to somebody from Alabama on the telephone. Then it comes back."

"When I went to Columbia," said Luker, "everybody thought I was dumb because I had a Southern accent, and it took so much time proving to people that I wasn't an asshole that I decided to get rid of the accent, and I did."

"How did you do it? Get rid of the accent I mean?"

"I just said to myself: 'I'm not gone talk that way any more . . .' And I didn't."

"I sort of like it," said India.

"Um-hmm," said Luker from the darkness.

"Tell me about Odessa," said India.

"What do you mean? What do you want to know?"

"I don't know. Just tell me about her. Tell me about her daughter that drowned."

"I wasn't here then, but Leigh was. That was ten, eleven years ago or something—I was married by then. Odessa and her common-law husband Johnny Red had one child, a little girl called Martha-Ann. Big Barbara was right, Johnny Red is no good. The Savages sort of take care of him, for Odessa's sake. They live together off and on, mostly off. Anyway, Martha-Ann used to come out to Beldame with Odessa and she'd help out around the house, but mostly she came out here to play. Well, you've got to remember that ten, fifteen years ago, things weren't as loose in the South as they are now—"

"Loose?"

"I'm talking about black people. The lines were still there then. It wasn't considered right to have Martha-Ann on the Gulf side where all the white people were. Martha-Ann had to swim in St. Elmo's Lagoon."

"That's just bullshit!" cried India, offended.

"I know," said Luker, "and it wasn't that anybody actually *said* anything to the girl. It was just one of those things that was understood. You still see it in Odessa. Odessa would never eat at the table with us, and when she does sit with us, she always sits as far away as possible. It's not that we wouldn't have her or anything like that—you know how much Dauphin loves her—it's just that *she's* not comfortable. So one afternoon Martha-Ann was out playing, right in front of the Savage house on the lagoon, where she always played, and she was chasing these birds up and down the beach, trying to feed them or something. And she chased them around to the other side of the third house. Odessa was upstairs working, and sort of watching Martha-Ann out the window, and she called out the window and told her not to go around that way."

"Why not?" demanded India.

"Odessa was afraid she'd go out in the water. Out there beyond the spit, there are lots of funny cross currents. The undertow is terrible. Nobody goes out in that water. It looks shallow, but it'll drag you right under. And that's what happened to Martha-Ann. She evidently went out in the water, and she got dragged under. Odessa was going downstairs to bring her back, and she heard Martha-Ann screaming, but by the time she got round in front of the third house, the screams had stopped and Martha-Ann had already drowned. And her body never washed up on shore."

"How did Odessa take it?"

"I don't know," said Luker. "I wasn't here."

"How do you know that Martha-Ann drowned?"

Luker paused before he replied, and India was sorry that in the darkness she could not see the expression on his face. "What do you mean?"

"How do you know that she *drowned*?" repeated India. "I mean, nobody saw her go in the water."

"What else could have happened to her?"

"The third house. What if she went inside the third house?"

"She couldn't have. The house is locked, it always has been. Besides, she was at the front of the house, and the doors and windows there were already starting to be covered up. And what if she *had* gone inside, India? She would have come out again. But we never found her body. There was nothing to bury."

"What if she's still inside? Her body, I mean. Nobody looked for her, did they? Nobody went inside the house to see if she was there, did they?"

"India, you're being stupid. I'm gone go to bed. I'm freezing my ass off in here—"

"Why does Dauphin love Odessa so much?" asked India suddenly.

"Because she's always been good to him," said Luker, stopping to give reply to a question that was reasonable. "Odessa loves Dauphin the way Marian Savage should have loved him."

"Has Odessa always worked for the Savages?"

"I don't know. For at least thirty-five years. Odessa was coming here for years before we even bought this house—Odessa remembers the Hightowers. But when Dauphin was little he came down with something, some kind of fever or something, and they all thought he was gone die. That was in the summer, and we were all here at Beldame—Darnley and Mary-Scot and Leigh and me. But Dauphin stayed in Mobile, and Odessa stayed with him. Darnley and Mary-Scot kept talking about the funeral, because they were all sure he was gone die. Bothwell Savage, Dauphin's daddy, used to go up to Mobile once a week to see if he was still alive—"

"What happened?"

"Odessa cured him. I don't know how, and he doesn't know how, but she cured him. Dauphin says she gave him things to eat and they cured him."

"Maybe he just got well—maybe the doctors cured him."

"India, it was the doctors who said he was gone die."

"Yes, but—"

"But the point is that Dauphin thinks that Odessa saved his life, and Dauphin had a pretty good idea even then—I don't think he could have been more than six or seven years old—that none of the Savages cared whether he lived or died."

"Yes, I see," said India, "but did anybody else believe that Odessa saved his life? Or is that just what Dauphin thought? What did Marian Savage think?"

"Well," said Luker, "she said she didn't believe it. She said that Dauphin was cured by penicillin, but of course Dauphin is allergic to penicillin. Now, Marian Savage never liked Odessa after that, she sort of blamed Odessa for keeping Dauphin alive. I think she wanted to fire Odessa except that Marian Savage wasn't the kind of woman to drop your acquaintance just because she hated your fucking guts. Anyway, when she got so sick, Marian wouldn't have anybody wait on her except Odessa. See, she wanted Odessa to cure her. She'd beg Odessa fifty times a day to give her something to eat that would make her well again."

"How do you know all this?"

"Dauphin told me. Odessa told him."

"She really thought Odessa could cure her?"

Luker nodded. "Marian Savage blamed Dauphin for her getting sick—she said if he hadn't married Leigh, she wouldn't have gotten cancer. That's what she told Leigh too. Half the time she'd blame

Leigh and Dauphin, and the other half the time she'd pretend that she wasn't sick at all, that there wasn't anything wrong with her."

"A real bitch, hunh?"

"Cast-iron. And then she blamed Odessa because she wasn't getting any better. She said Odessa wouldn't give her the things that would make her well again, and then she started saying that Odessa was putting things in her food that actually made her sicker."

"I don't understand why Odessa stayed on then."

Luker shrugged. "Because that's the way it is down here. Odessa wouldn't any more have thought of leaving Marian Savage than she would of leaving Dauphin and Leigh."

"Martyr complex," said India.

"No it's not," said Luker. "It's just the way things are done."

"If you had been like that, you'd have stayed with Mother."

"I know," he said, "but I'm not *entirely* like that. I got out in time —I think. Anyway," Luker went on, "Marian Savage came down here at the end as a last-ditch effort to persuade Odessa to make her well. She said to Odessa, 'Save me the way you saved Dauphin.'"

"And what did Odessa do?"

"Odessa told her that Dauphin was cured by a shot of penicillin."

"So Odessa let her die?"

"India, you just said you didn't believe that Odessa cured Dauphin . . ."

India thought this over, but in the end didn't know what she thought about it all.

CHAPTER 15

The following afternoon India left Beldame for the first time in nearly three weeks. Leigh drove her and Odessa to Gulf Shores, dropped them off at the Laundromat, and went on herself to Fairhope to buy a few clothes. When he heard of his daughter's intention of accompanying his sister and Odessa, Luker warned India: "Listen, I don't want you cornering Odessa and asking her all kinds of questions about Martha-Ann or anything."

"Martha-Ann died almost before I was born. Do you think Odessa is still upset about it?"

"I think it's none of your fucking business, is what I think," replied Luker with a grimace.

India promised to say nothing.

Once the clothes had been loaded into the washers, India and Odessa seated themselves at one end of a row of plastic chairs that was bolted into the cement in front of the Laundromat. It was unspeakably hot all over Alabama that day, but nowhere was the heat more intense than in Baldwin County; and in Baldwin County no worse than at Gulf Shores; and at Gulf Shores no more extreme than at the little green concrete building that housed the post office and the Laundromat. A thermometer on a shaded wall read 107 degrees.

"Odessa," began India, "I want to talk to you about something, if it's all right."

"What, child?"

"The third house." India watched closely for signs of perturbation, but Odessa was unmoved.

"What you want to know? You took pictures of it one day."

"You showed me which pictures to take."

Odessa nodded, and India was at a loss how to proceed.

"Luker's afraid of the third house," India said at last, "and so is Dauphin. I haven't really talked to Leigh and Big Barbara about it, but—"

"They scairt too," said Odessa.

"Do you know why?"

Odessa nodded.

"Why?"

"'Cause of what's inside."

India's shoulders contracted. "What do you mean, what's inside?"

"They's some houses that's got something inside 'em, and some houses that don't. Don't you know that?"

"You mean like a ghost?"

"No! They's no such thing. They's just some houses that got something inside 'em—a spirit like. No ghosts, no such thing as dead people coming back. Dead people go to heaven, dead people go to hell. They don't hang around. Nothing like that. They's just *something* that's maybe inside a house."

"How do you know if it's there?"

"Oh, you just feel it! How else would you know! You walk in a house, and you know right off. Don't mean it's dangerous or anything, it's just got something in it."

"You mean, like if somebody died inside, then the house gets some kind of spirit attached to it."

"No," said Odessa, "don't work that way. That's you talking and thinking about spirits. Spirits don't work that way, spirits don't work the way we want 'em to. They don't go by rules you set up for 'em. Don't matter if somebody died or got killed, or if the house is all brand-new. It's got something in it or it don't, and you can feel it and that's all there is to it."

India nodded her understanding.

"Now the third house," Odessa went on, "you don't have to go inside that one to know there's something in it, you just *know* the minute you lay eyes on it. Don't you, child? *You* know, don't you? I'm not sitting here telling you something you don't know anything about, am I?"

"No, you're not," said India. "I know there's something inside the house." She paused for a moment and she and Odessa stared out at the Gulf, visible across the way between the little square houses. The sun was blindingly reflected on the water. Heat rose in distorting waves from the blacktopped road. Someone passed with a large beach umbrella bouncing over her shoulder, and a golden retriever leaped and snapped at it.

"If there's something inside the house," asked India, "can you see it?"

Odessa glanced at India sharply, then returned her gaze to the Gulf. "Oh, I've seen things," she said slowly.

"What things?" asked India eagerly.

"Lights," she said, "lights in the house. Not lights though, just different kinds of dark. Sometimes I wake up at night and I think I'm just lying in my bed, and then I open up my eyes and I'm not in the bed any more. I'm standing at the window and I'm looking out at the third house and it's like I see things going room to room. 'Course you cain't really see anything 'cause it's all dark, but I see things going room to room, and there's different kinds of dark inside there and things get shifted around. They's doors that get shut inside the house. Sometimes things get broke."

India drew in her breath sharply, but Odessa chose to ignore this. "But it's not ghosts," she said, "they's no such things. It's just the spirit in the house, trying to make us believe in ghosts. The spirit wants you to think that the dead come back, and you can talk to 'em and they can tell you where money's buried and like that—"

"Why?" demanded India. "Why would the spirit do something like that?"

"Spirits want to fool you. *Some* spirits. 'Cause they's *bad*—they's just *bad*, that's all."

"But is it a spirit that's *inside* the house or is it the house itself? I mean, does the spirit have a body—no, not a body, I mean, does it have a shape? Can you look at it? If you saw it, would you know it? Or is just the whole house?"

"Child," said Odessa, "you saw something." She lifted her arms and pried the material away from her perspiration-soaked skin. "You saw something, didn't you?"

"I saw more than just the dark," said India. "I saw something else. I climbed to the top of the dune and I looked in the window. I did it twice, and both times I saw something."

"Don't you tell me!" cried Odessa. "I don't want to know what you saw, child!"

The black woman clutched India's arm, but India said feverishly: "Listen, Odessa, the first time I saw this room it was perfect, I mean it was like it hadn't been touched in fifty years and then I was looking in and the door shut. Somebody was out in the hall and they pushed the door shut while I was standing outside looking in the window—"

"Child, don't tell me!"

"—and then I went back the next day because I thought I had been dreaming and I looked in the window again and the sand had started to get inside the room because I had knocked out some glass in the window—"

"No," said Odessa, reaching to clap her black hand over the child's mouth.

India grabbed Odessa's wrist and pushed it away. "And there was something in the sand," she whispered. "There was something that was made out of sand. It was lying there under the window, it was part of the dune and it knew I was there. Odessa, it—"

Up flew Odessa's other hand, and stopped India's mouth.

CHAPTER 16

A couple of days after Lawton McCray's visit to Beldame, Dauphin Savage returned to Mobile for the reading of his mother's will. Leigh had offered to accompany him but he assured her that she need not bother. Since he knew the entire contents of the document, the reading would be only a formality. The will had been drawn up according to his own consultation with the family lawyer, and he had spent three months in persuading his dying mother to sign it. Dauphin told Leigh that she was welcome to go along for the ride; she could shop in town, check on the house, do whatever wanted doing in Mobile after a month's absence from the city. But Leigh and the others, to whom the invitation was also extended, declined: whatever must be done in Mobile could wait until the following week when, under Lawton's directive, they *must* return.

When, on that morning, India strolled past the jeep parked on the edge of the yard, she was surprised to find Odessa sitting inside, wearing her dark glasses and her straw sun hat.

"Why are you going?" asked India of the black woman. "Do you have shopping to do?"

Odessa shook her head.

"Why, then?" persisted India, when it appeared that Odessa had no intention of answering her question.

"Ask Mr. Dauphin," hissed Odessa, and nodded in the direction of the Savage house. Dauphin was coming out the back door.

"You ready?" he called to Odessa, and she raised a hand in acknowledgment.

When he came nearer, he said to India, "You sure you don't want to go? Aren't you getting tired of this place? Beldame's not as exciting as New York City, and I know it for a fact!"

"Why are you taking Odessa?" asked India.

Dauphin—who seemed dark and unfamiliar because of the suit that he wore—paused before climbing into the jeep. "She's gone sweep out the mausoleum. Mama was buried a month ago today."

Embarrassed that she had forced Dauphin to admit to this piece of filial piety, India asked: "You're coming back tonight, aren't you?"

"I ought to be through at the lawyer's by four," said Dauphin, "but don't ya'll count on us for supper. We're probably gone stop on the way."

Big Barbara and Luker appeared on the verandah and waved good-bye as Dauphin started the jeep. "Wait!" cried India, "can you do me a favor in Mobile?"

Dauphin smiled. "What you want me to get you, India? You want me to bring you a postcard of a traffic jam?"

"No," she said, "if you can wait a second, I'll be right back."

Dauphin nodded, and India ran into the house. A few minutes later she reappeared and handed Dauphin two small gray plastic canisters. "It's film," she said, "and I've got my name on it and everything. Could you take it somewhere and have it developed?"

"'Course," replied Dauphin, "but it probably won't be ready by the time we head back."

"That's all right, I'll pick it up next week."

He nodded, pocketed the canisters and drove off, blowing the horn in farewell.

Luker said to his daughter at lunch: "You ought not send good film out to some commercial place. They *always* scratch it. It could have waited until we got back to New York, and I would have done it right."

"Those were the pictures I took of the third house," said India. "*You're* the one I wouldn't trust with that film."

Luker laughed.

Mobile was nearly a two hours' drive from Beldame; Dauphin and Odessa pulled up into the driveway of the Small House just before noon. Odessa, who had no liking for the two maids employed by Leigh, had looked forward to disturbing them in their well-paid indolence there, but Dauphin had insisted that he call from outside the city and prepare them for his arrival. He would not even allow them to fix him lunch, but stopped at a fried chicken franchise and bought something for himself and Odessa.

The two maids declared themselves happy to see him again,

though in lackluster voices and with drooping shoulders that only a man so willingly deceived as Dauphin would have thought sincere. They turned over to him three shoe boxes filled with mail and a peach crate they had filled with catalogs that had arrived for Leigh. Dauphin and Odessa sat at opposite ends of the long table and ate their chicken. Then an inspection tour of the Great House reassured them that all was in order there.

Into the trunk of the black Mercedes the two maids put a rake, a broom, a bag of soft cloths, and a cardboard box of cleaning liquids. They did not volunteer to assist Odessa in the cleaning of the Savage family mausoleum. But when he was pulling out of the driveway, Dauphin said to Odessa, "First we're going to the drugstore and leave off India's film, then you and me are going to the lawyer's."

Odessa said, "You leave me off at the cemetery. By the time you get through I'll be done too, it's not gone—"

Dauphin interrupted her. "Odessa, I didn't tell you this 'cause I knew you wouldn't like it, but Mama mentioned you in her will. In fact you and me are the only people mentioned at all—personally I mean, so it's you and me that's got to go to the lawyer's. When we're finished there—and it won't take long—then we'll go back to the cemetery and clean up. I want to help . . ."

"Mr. Dauphin, you should have told me!" said Odessa reproachfully. "Your mama didn't have any business going and putting me in her will. I wish she hadn't done it."

"Well, I tell you, Odessa, if it makes you feel any better, she didn't want to do it, but I made her. It was all my doing. I told the lawyer what all to say, and he wrote it out and then I sat up in that room for three months until she finally signed it."

"All right then," said Odessa, "long as she didn't mean it, I guess it's all right."

At the lawyer's offices, Dauphin was greeted not only by that man, but by the president and all the fellows of the firm, making unaccustomed Saturday appearances—Dauphin was, after all, the third richest man in Mobile, and of those three he was the only one to have been born in Alabama. The reading of Marian Savage's will was perfunctory. She had left a quarter of a million dollars to the convent in which Sister Mary-Scot was resident, she had set

up a nursing scholarship at Spring Hill College, she had donated a
new Sunday school wing to the Church of St. Jude Thaddeus, and
she provided Odessa with an annuity of fifteen thousand dollars
for life, the principal to return to the family coffers after the black
woman's death. Everything else went to Dauphin. Marian Savage
had not loved her son who survived, but she was Savage to the
heart and had never entertained any thought of channeling the
family fortune away from Dauphin, Leigh, and whatever children
they might have. As she signed the will, she had given Dauphin to
understand that if Darnley had lived, or if Mary-Scot had not joined
the convent, things would have been quite different. Dauphin
would have got only a pittance. But as things were, he must have
everything.

"I thank you for what you did," said Odessa as they were driving
away again, forty-five minutes later.

"Odessa, don't—"

"You let me talk," she said sternly and Dauphin was silent.
Odessa went on: "That money'll mean I won't ever have to worry
again. I was 'ginning to worry about Social Security. I know a
woman on Social Security and after she's paid her rent, it don't buy
her a mess of black-eyed peas. When I'm not working any more, I
won't have to worry—"

"Odessa, you're gone work for Leigh and me forever, aren't
you?"

"Of course I am! I will work for you and Miz Leigh till I cain't
put one foot in front of the other!"

"You'll always have a home with us, Odessa. You know we
couldn't do without you."

"When I get old and I'm as mean as your mama was, Mr.
Dauphin, then you'll be glad enough I'm living on my own somewhere—" Dauphin looked about to make a contradictory speech
here, but Odessa rode over it: "—but now I don't need to worry.
You just got to promise me one thing, Mr. Dauphin, you *got* to
promise me—"

"I promise. What is it?"

"When I'm dead, you make sure that Johnny Red don't get a
folded dollar of that money!"

"I promise," said Dauphin, but he was already scheming charity

—trying to think of how he could take care of no-good Johnny Red in the unlikely case that that alcoholic loafer survived his common-law wife.

The Savage mausoleum was a squat square edifice of darkly veined Italian marble set in a cypress-shaded corner of Mobile's oldest cemetery. Mobile's dead had been planted here since the early part of the eighteenth century, but hurricanes and vandals and widening of the streets had obliterated all trace of the first fruits, and the Savage mausoleum was now celebrated as the oldest remaining monument. Along the three walls inside were carved the names of six generations of Savages—and this did not include infants and adolescents who, not considered worthy of the place, were relegated to a little sinking plot of earth over the way.

The bells of a nearby church were chiming four o'clock as the Mercedes pulled up before the Savage mausoleum. While Dauphin unloaded the trunk, Odessa opened the iron door of the tomb with the key that she kept with all the others of the household. She stepped inside and pushed the door shut behind her; she stood at the grating and told Dauphin to put everything down just outside.

"You let me take care of this, Mr. Dauphin," she said. "You sit in the car. You go get a ice cream cone. You come back for me in an hour, that's what I want you to do."

"Odessa, I ought to go inside and pay my respects to Mama. Mama was big on respect-paying." He smiled sadly through the grating.

"I know, but you ought not come inside, and that's the truth."

"Why not?"

"'Cause graves is no place for the living."

Dauphin shrugged and smiled, and pushed open the door. "I'm gone come on inside, Odessa, and speak to Mama for a few minutes."

The mausoleum was dim inside. The refracted light of a heavily overcast afternoon penetrated as only a filmy gray. But Dauphin immediately saw that all inside was not as he had left it on the day of the funeral. On the floor below his mother's niche was spread a small linen cloth with a jumble of objects on it.

"Odessa," he said, "somebody's been in here. What is all this stuff?"

Nervously—for no Savage could deal straightforwardly with irregularities in the matter of tombs and burials—Dauphin knelt to see what was on the cloth: an alarm clock loosely wrapped in a page torn from a calendar; a teacup whose broken handle lay inside it; two conch shells that had been smashed together; and a plastic shoe box holding the litter of a medicine chest.

Dauphin looked curiously up at Odessa, who said nothing and seemed not surprised to see those things there.

"Somebody's been playing here," said Dauphin hopefully. "Some child has got inside here, and was playing a game, and—"

Odessa shook her head.

Dauphin picked up the alarm clock. It was set for four o'clock, the time of his mother's death; the calendar page was for the month of May, and the day of her death red-circled. The teacup was of the set of dishes off which she had always had her breakfast. The conch shells were those that in summer had flanked either side of the cold hearth in her bedroom. The labels on the discarded prescription bottles at the bottom of the plastic shoe box all read, For the Use of Marian Savage.

"I put everything there," said Odessa. "Nobody broke in here. I came back early the morning after the funeral, Miz Leigh brought me over here before she carried me to the house."

Dauphin raised himself and strove to make out Odessa's eyes in the dimness of the mausoleum. "All right, but why, Odessa? Why'd you bring all this stuff here?"

"Brought it for Miz Marian."

"As an offering? That what you mean?"

Odessa shook her head. "Keep her from getting out of this place," she said, and pointed to the square of inscribed marble against which rested the foot of Marian Savage's coffin.

"Clock and calendar's gone remind her she's dead. I broke that cup—I hated to do it, but it was a extra—broken cup's gone tell her she's dead. Those shells gone speak to her of water. The dead got to cross water."

"And the pills? What about the 'scription bottles?"

"They gone remind her who she was. Dead come back, they

don't always remember who they was. Your mama reads her name there, Mr. Dauphin, and she's gone say, 'Why, I'm dead, I'm gone go right back inside and not bother nobody!'"

"Odessa, you're talking crazy. You're making me real scared. I want you to take all this junk out of here."

"You got to leave it for at least six months," said Odessa, "that's when the dead come back. They die and they start forgetting right off, but it takes six months 'fore they stop caring." She jerked her head toward Marian Savage's marble plaque. "She's back there now, and she cain't remember everything, they's things she's already forgotten, but she knows how to get out and she knows who to come after, she—"

"Odessa!" cried Dauphin, shaking all over. "Don't you say another word about this!" And he fled that dim gray place, leaving Odessa to sweep the floor and run her cloths over the marble walls. He was waiting in the car for her half an hour later, silent, nervous and morose, and they did not speak on the drive back to the Small House. But even if they had spoken, Odessa would not have told him of what she had found in the mausoleum, what had not been apparent until her eyes had grown fully accustomed to the dimness there: that the mortar around the marble plaque of his mother's monument had been chipped away in a number of places, leaving little lines of blackness all around. You could have stuck a straw through those holes and touched Marian Savage's coffin on the other side.

CHAPTER 17

Dauphin had not planned on it, but he remained that night in Mobile. His accountant found out from his lawyer that he was in town and telephoned him late in the afternoon, asking if it would be possible to talk with him that evening. Odessa assured him that it would make no difference if they did not return to Beldame until the next day, and she had just as soon spend the night in her own house. There was no way of letting those in Beldame know that they would not be coming back, but probably they would not worry unduly.

Dauphin dropped Odessa at her house, dined with Lawton McCray and Sonny Joe Black at a seafood restaurant on the municipal pier—where he heard the gratifying progress of the campaign and listened politely to the manifold reasons why he ought to sell Beldame to the oil companies. When he returned home and pressed the key into the lock of the darkened house, he realized that it was the first time he had ever spent the night alone there.

Odessa's voodoo—was there any other word for it?—with the jumbled broken artifacts of his mother's life had disturbed him. Of course the black woman had known the Savage family legends of the dead not being dead, but her accumulation of those objects on the marble floor of the tomb had seemed designed for protection against a greater evil than that. The fear had clung to Odessa like cobwebs—that Marian Savage would return from the dead. He drew the curtains in the dining room so that he would not be tempted to gaze out the window at the Great House: he feared to see lights there.

He wandered disconsolately through his home, turning on the television set loud in hope that the voices and laughter would be comforting. On a situation comedy he heard the squawk of a bird, and thought suddenly of Nails. When he went to Beldame, Nails had been deliberately left behind; he had had no wish ever to hear again the single speech the bird had uttered: *Savage mothers eat their children up!*

Dauphin went to the cage in the glassed-in porch and lifted the cover, praying that the bird would not repeat its terrible litany. The cage was empty. It had been scrubbed clean; the feeders and water trough were empty and dry.

The television set was left on all night to cover the noises in the house.

Next morning when the two maids arrived, Dauphin learned that on the day that they left for Beldame, Nails had begun to refuse his food. He pined and scraped incessantly at the newspaper at the bottom of the cage, shredding a dozen layers a day. In a week he was dead, and the gardener buried him in the bearded iris bed at the side of the Great House.

"Well, did he talk?" asked Dauphin nervously.

"Talk?" cried the maid who was thin. "That bird couldn't talk! It never said a word since the day your mama got him!"

"No," replied Dauphin to Odessa's question, "I didn't sleep well at all. I'm not used to sleeping alone, I don't like sleeping alone. And I tell you something, Odessa," he said in a tone of voice that came as near as Dauphin ever got to real annoyance, "it was all because of that business in the mausoleum yesterday, those things you put on the floor. It's not respectful to the dead, it's against religion, and I don't know what all else."

"I did it for you," said Odessa simply.

"I know you did," said Dauphin, softening already. "And I 'preciate it. I really do. But the fact is, Mama's dead. Really and truly. We got two doctors in there to say she was dead, and at the funeral—you saw me—I stuck a knife in her chest. Odessa, I hated doing it, but I checked—she didn't do any bleeding."

"Oh, she was dead," said Odessa nodding her head. The day was so cool and windy that the air conditioner wasn't wanted in the car. Both front windows were down. "And when I put those things there—when I broke that cup and emptied those pill bottles, I just wanted to make sure that your *mama* remembered that she was dead. That's all I wanted to do."

"The dead don't come back," said Dauphin flatly. They had just been through Daphne and Fairhope and were almost to Point Clear, taking the route along Mobile Bay instead of the one that went through the interior of the county. All the way down, the bay, whipped frothy, was just to their right, slate blue beneath a sky of gray slate.

"Did you have a dream?" asked Odessa, knowing that he had. "What did you dream about?"

"What else could I dream about?" said Dauphin. "I dreamed about that mausoleum. I dreamed I was dead. I dreamed I was at the funeral, and you and Leigh stood at the coffin, and Leigh touched my chest with the knife. Odessa, I could feel that metal! I could feel it in my sleep! So they took me to the mausoleum and they put me in right on top of Mama—"

"That's right where they'll put you when you *do* die," said Odessa.

"I know," said Dauphin, "and that's one reason why the dream seemed so real. They lifted me up and put me in, and suddenly I wasn't in the coffin any more. I was just lying up there in that space, and they blocked it up. It was dark and I couldn't see and I couldn't breathe and I thought I was gone die. Except I was already dead."

"What'd you do?"

"I kicked out the marker. It fell on the floor and broke all to pieces, and then I climbed down. I cut my foot but it didn't bleed. All the other markers in the place had been knocked out too. The whole place was covered with broken pieces of marble. There were all these holes in the walls where the coffins had gone, but I was the only person there. I was afraid to look in the holes, but I did, and I was the only person there."

Dauphin grew feverish telling his nightmare. Odessa must caution him to reduce the speed of the Mercedes. He did so, and when he resumed it was with a calmer voice. "The trouble was, the door was locked. I was in there all by myself, and the door was locked. I started calling for someone to come and get me. I don't remember if it was day out or night. I couldn't tell, or maybe I just don't remember now, but I called and called and nobody came. Then I heard somebody coming, and I yelled out, 'Hey, y'all, I'm in here!'"

"Who was it?"

"They came to the door and opened it."

"Who was it?" repeated Odessa.

"It was Mama and Darnley. I said, 'Oh, I'm so glad y'all came. They buried me in here, and I wasn't dead,' and then I remembered that they *were* dead. Both of 'em, and I said, 'Darnley, how'd you get here?—they never found your body.'"

"It's bad when the dead talk in dreams," said Odessa. "What'd Darnley say?"

"Darnley said, 'I came to get you, Dauphin.'"

"Were you scared in your dream?"

"No," said Dauphin, "but I started to scream anyway, and soon as I screamed, Mama jumped on me and put her mouth on my throat and she tore it out."

"Is that when you woke up?"

"No," said Dauphin. "I didn't wake up at all . . ."

In silence, they reached Point Clear and continued south toward Mullet, where the road turned inland, away from the bay. Dauphin felt better for having told the dream that had so distressed him, and now he looked forward to the return to Beldame, if for no other reason than that there he would not be sleeping alone.

The road made a sharp left, and as he took this, Mobile Bay appeared now through the rearview mirror, directly behind him. And a couple of hundred yards out in the water, seen through the mirror, was the characteristic red and orange sail of Darnley Savage's boat that had disappeared without trace thirteen years before.

Dauphin tried to will the vision away, but the sail remained in the rear-view mirror until the road curved and the entire bay was removed from his sight. Dauphin said nothing of this to Odessa: he feared that she would take it seriously, when he knew it could be no more than an hallucination, inspired by the previous night's sleeplessness, the incident in the mausoleum, the death of his mother so few weeks before. But once they had returned to Beldame, Dauphin stood nervously on the verandah of the McCray house, and nervously scanned the Gulf, watching for the sail he so very much feared to see.

CHAPTER 18

There were five days left between the return of Dauphin and Odessa and the time when they all must get back to Mobile for the July Fourth celebrations. It had occurred to them suddenly that they need not all be under Lawton's directive to go back to Mobile—though Big Barbara was certainly wanted and Dauphin too, Leigh had been invited only for her husband's sake. Odessa was useless to a congressional campaign, being only an insignificant black woman, and Luker and India were hardly the sort of family that a conservative candidate would want paraded before his future constituency. Therefore, all except Big Barbara and Dauphin might remain behind; but Leigh decided she wanted to see her doctor for a little checkup that she had postponed on account of her mother-in-law's death. Luker would like a few days on the telephone to scare up some fall assignments and India had run out of three colors of thread which wanted replacing before she could complete her embroidered panel. There was no particular reason for Odessa to remain alone, and she would return to help with the shopping. They would leave together, and they hoped, all come back together. They had been at Beldame for a month, and though happy there—seeming to find in the place respite from all the troubles that had beset them in the past year—they wondered if resumption of the vacation would be possible.

They knew how easy it was to forget Beldame, whose chief attraction was its very emptiness. In Mobile one was caught up by excitement, by the demands of friends and business and checking accounts, and one forgot how pleasant the days had been and peaceful the nights. The constant lassitude and indulgent laziness would no longer seem a thing to be desired.

Though no one dared mention it, it was also possible that in future years there would be no Beldame to return to. Dauphin had given his assurance that he would not sell the place, but not one of the family underestimated Lawton McCray's powers of persuasion or his underhandedness.

It was a sickening thought: Beldame in the hands of the oil companies. The houses demolished, St. Elmo's Lagoon slicked over in oil, the porpoises in the Gulf shredded by the propellers of motorboats—what horrors did they not imagine?

The five days were permeated with nostalgia; nostalgia for what Beldame had always been, for their scant month together, for the times there that they might now never know. And that last week of June was the hottest that anyone could remember; even Odessa was brought to say that she could not recall any time at Beldame that was more uncomfortable. These were the longest days of the year: each morning the sun rose early and bright in a cloudless sky. A thermometer was nailed outside the Savage kitchen window, and by eight o'clock each morning it read above ninety degrees. Ten o'clock was appreciably warmer, and no one could step outside between eleven and four.

In the morning they put on bathing suits and did not take them off again. Odessa's cotton print dress was stained with perspiration from breakfast on, and she must wash it out each night. No one wanted to eat for all food tasted spoiled. No one wanted to read or work puzzles or even talk. They crept into shaded corners in the interior rooms, and strung hammocks inside for maximal circulation of air around their bodies. And as much as they could, they slept through the daylight hours. Sleep at night was impossible, and they turned, sweating, on top of the sheets. There were no breezes then. Sometimes India and Luker snuck naked out of the house past midnight and swam for a hour in the Gulf, hoping for relief from the heat, but even this late the water temperature was above 80 degrees. Big Barbara stuck an oscillating fan on a straight-backed chair, and it blew over her all night long. She would try to kick off stifling covers that weren't there. Leigh and Dauphin slept at opposite edges of their double bed, fearful of touching one another, their bodies were so hot.

And through all this—the straining heat and the worrisome uneasiness over the fate of Beldame—they forgot about the third house. When nothing distracted them—and God knew there were few enough distractions at Beldame in general—the third house was a lowering, sullen, potent presence; but the sun and the sun's heat that persisted from nightfall to dawn burned away their thoughts and if there was any fear it was the fear of losing Beldame altogether.

India, invariably the last to be served breakfast, was alone with Odessa in the kitchen on the second of the five mornings left to them. She asked the black woman if she had ever known the like weather before, and Odessa replied, "No, never did. And it means something too, child."

"Means what?" asked India curiously.

"Means something's gone happen."

"Like what? A tornado you mean? Or a hurricane?"

Odessa shook her head slowly, and turned away.

"You mean," said India carefully, for she had learned that in Alabama a direct question is not always the best way of obtaining an answer, "we have to be careful."

Odessa nodded. "That's right, child. We have to be careful . . ."

"About things . . ." said India, prodding.

"That's right, child. About things."

Odessa had taken a baking pan from a cabinet next to the sink.

"Odessa, you're not going to bake anything, are you? Can you imagine what this room would be like if you turned on the oven!"

"I'm not gone bake, child." Odessa sat beside her at the kitchen table. "Ever'body's in the other house, ain't they?"

India nodded. "Just you and me here," she said. Odessa said nothing then, and India went on cautiously, "Are you going to tell me *how* to be careful?"

Odessa pushed the baking pan, old and dented and rusted, a few inches toward India.

India placed a finger in the corner of it and pulled it nearer. "What do I do with it?"

"Go outside," whispered Odessa, "and go round to the other side of the third house—don't let 'em see you, 'cause they'll stop you. Go round there and fill this up with sand and bring it back in here to me."

India's brows contracted, and something welled in her of old systems of rationality. What Odessa asked her to do made no sense.

"You sure this is—"

Odessa slapped the pan away. It slid to the edge of the table then dropped onto the floor with a clatter. "Get on out of here, child, if you're not gone believe what I say to you!"

With hands sweaty not only with the heat but her chagrin at having offended the black woman, India leaned down and picked up the pan. "Odessa," she said, "please let me go. If you say we have to be careful, then I know we do. You know what I saw in the third house, don't you? You know who's in there, don't you? And that's why *you* won't go, isn't it?" India expected Odessa to try to stop her mouth again, but Odessa only stared steadfastly into her face.

"Martha-Ann's in the third house," whispered India. "I saw her crawl out of the sand."

There was no surprise on Odessa's face. "Wasn't Martha-Ann," she said after a few moments. "Just something pretending to be Martha-Ann. Something that wanted to fool you."

"But that doesn't make sense," said India, glad that she could not see the third house from the kitchen window. "When I saw that little girl come up out of the sand—and it was horrible!—I had never even heard of Martha-Ann. I didn't even know that she had drowned in the lagoon. So it had to be the ghost of Martha-Ann in there. It couldn't have been out of my own imagination because why would I dream about somebody I never even heard of?"

"What's in that house, child, knows more than you know. What's in that house don't come out of *your* mind. It don't have to worry 'bout rules and behaving like a spirit ought to behave. It does what it does to fool you, it wants to trick you into believing what's not right. It's got no truth to it. What it did last week it's not gone be doing today. You see something in there, it wasn't there yesterday, it's not gone be there tomorrow. You stand at one of them doors thinking something's behind it—nothing's behind it. It's waiting for you upstairs, it's waiting for you downstairs. It's standing behind you. You think it's buried in the sand, why then, it's gone be standing behind that door after all! And you don't ever know *what* it is you looking for. You don't ever know what it is you gone see! Wasn't no ghost you saw, wasn't Martha-Ann."

"Then I don't understand—"

Odessa rattled the pan on the tabletop. India understood and rose immediately. "Go out the front," said Odessa, "don't let 'em see you."

India crept through the house, holding the pan behind her back, and went out the front door of the Savage house. St. Elmo's Lagoon was a blinding mirror laid in a frame of blinding white sand. After making sure no one was on the verandah of the McCray house, she ran along the edge of the lagoon and around to the end of the spit. The third house stared down at her from over the top of the dune.

She plunged the pan into the dune and buried it; then she drew it out again and leveled the heap of white sand off the top. It was pure sand and purely white: without darker grains, without impurities, without insects or the remains of plants or crushed seashells. And it was remarkably heavy.

She walked slowly back to the house, staring down at the pan all the while, careful not to spill any of what she had taken away. She felt as if she were being watched from the third house; without looking up, she could even tell from which window she was observed: the side window of the back right bedroom. She dared not look up, certain that she would see Martha-Ann there—or whatever pretended to be the drowned girl.

Odessa pointed to the table, and India put the pan down between them. From the pocket of her dress, Odessa took a letter envelope bearing a stamp that was at least twenty years old, and held open the slit top for India to look inside.

It contained seeds. She poured them out into India's cupped hands.

"You can't grow anything in sand," said India. "Nothing will grow in this. It doesn't have any nutrients. Water goes right through, that's—"

Odessa's gaze silenced her, and India sprinkled the seeds over the surface of the sand. "Should I cover them up?" India asked meekly.

Odessa shook her head. She rose and from the drawer beside the sink fetched a paring knife. Holding her left hand over the tray, Odessa deliberately sliced open her thumb. Thick red blood welled out of the top joint and dripped into the sand. Odessa ignored India's protest and methodically drenched the seeds. The blood sank quickly into the sand, leaving little more than a thin brown crust atop.

A corner of the pan she left untouched, and dapped her uninjured hand over the cut thumb to stanch the bleeding. She looked steadily at India.

"Here," said India quietly, holding her own thumb over the white corner, "but you have to do it, I'm squeamish."

Odessa nicked the girl's finger, and guided the flow of blood.

"Nothing's going to happen," said India. "We're both out of our minds for doing something like this."

"You put a Band-aid on that," said Odessa, pushing her hand away. "Then come back in here. I don't care how hot it is, you and me got to do a little baking today."

It was a simple white-bread dough that Odessa prepared, and it was with such perfect unconcern that she went about the task that India became convinced it had nothing to do with the baking pan, the sand, the seeds, and the blood. At noon Big Barbara, Luker,

Leigh and Dauphin trooped over from the McCray house for a lunch of hamburgers, and just the burners on top of the stove made the kitchen nearly unbearable.

After lunch, India declared that she would stay over and help Odessa with the dishes. When the others had gone, Odessa took out the bowl of dough, which in only an hour and a half had risen to almost triple its original bulk. She gave it to India to knead, and told her it must be a quarter-hour by the clock, and not a minute less.

"Odessa, I just don't understand how you can *think* of lighting the oven on a day like this. It's just impossible that—"

From the pantry Odessa brought out the baking pan. The seeds had sprouted and grown, flowered and fruited—all in the space of two hours. The tray supported a little field of wheatlike plants: pale green and sickly, it was true, but each stalk bore a little run of small black seeds, just like those India had seen in the envelope.

India hurried over to look but Odessa waved her back. "Don't stop!" she cried. "Keep going!"

India returned to her kneading, but repeated under her breath, "I don't believe it, I don't believe it!"

Odessa sat at the table and patiently harvested that unnatural crop, carefully stripping the plants and spilling the seeds into a bowl.

She was done before India had finished her kneading. "I want to look at those plants," said India. "What are they? What are they called?"

Odessa went to the back door, kicked it open and spilled out the pan of sand and spent plants. Returning to the table, she put a handful of seeds back into the envelope she had preserved, and the rest she scattered over a cookie sheet. She lighted the oven and toasted them for ten minutes.

The kitchen became so hot that she and India were forced out; the perspiration dripped from both to such an extent that it formed wet circles around them on the floor, where they stood silent in the dining room.

That night, with dinner—sirloin steaks grilled outside, with crab and butter beans on the side—Odessa served homemade rolls.

"Odessa," cried Big Barbara, "you and India were crazy out

of your minds to be baking in that kitchen today! But these are delicious, and I'm not gone complain too much because there is nothing in the world I like better than a poppy-seed roll."

"They's two dozen," said Odessa, with a look at India, "and that's four apiece for ever'body. India and me are gone be real upset if ever'body don't eat 'em all up."

India knew that the seeds on top of the rolls were not poppy, but she said nothing. In the failing afternoon light, when no one was looking, she stooped beside the back door of the Savage house and examined the refuse of the baking pan, where Odessa had thrown it out. The dried blood was flaked and black, and the sudden harvest was already black and rotted.

Odessa came and stood behind the screen door. India looked up at her. "Are we protected now?" she asked.

"We done all we could," said Odessa, and went away again.

CHAPTER 19

The morning of the day before they were to leave for Mobile broke hottest of all. The sun rose impossibly bright that morning. They woke—or rather rose, for no one had slept—with the certainty that this was to prove the worst of the days they had suffered through. The Gulf tide withdrew sluggishly and St. Elmo's Lagoon seemed pressed solid into its bed. The air was heavy with moisture that collected on everything but the white sand itself.

Breakfast was a hopeless formality; no one could think of food and their coffee was taken iced. They all had hoped for a pleasant last day, but the heat was so oppressive that they hadn't even the stamina to suffer disappointment. They merely suffered.

No one talked. Big Barbara and Leigh swung on the verandah of the Savage house, which was away from the sun, and fanned themselves incessantly. India languished on the windowsill in her room, sewing a couple of embroidery stitches every minute and brushing away the gauze curtains that continually blew in her face. Dauphin and Luker sat in the McCray living room, guzzling iced tea and working a jigsaw puzzle of the moon landing. Odessa took her time making the beds of the two houses. But no one said a word: the discomfort of the heat had pushed them past speech.

Toward noon, Odessa arrived at last in India's bedroom. The girl looked up and nodded to Odessa; she had come to understand that Odessa's making the beds in the morning was no chore, but a thing in which she took pride. It was indicative of their altered relationship that India now allowed the black woman, without demur, to wait on her. It showed, India considered perversely, the black woman's superiority: anyone who could perform menial tasks in a menial's capacity without loss of dignity was someone to be admired and wondered at.

When she was finished with the bed, Odessa came to the window. She looked past India's shoulder to the third house.

"Nothing is going to happen today," said India; her voice cracked on the first words she had spoken that morning. "Nothing's going to happen," she repeated, when there was no response from Odessa. "It's much too hot for anything to happen . . ."

"Spirits live in hell," said Odessa. "Spirits living in hell don't feel the heat. It's spirits living in hell that causes heat like this, that's what it is. Cain't you feel 'em, child?" she whispered, nodding toward the third house.

"Did you see something inside?" cried India, straining against the glare, for the noontime sun beat directly against the back of the third house and bleached it.

"Listen," said India, no longer annoyed by Odessa's habit of not answering questions that were put to her directly, "if something happens, will everybody see it? I mean, if everybody sees it, we'll know that it's really *real*, if you know what I mean."

When Odessa left the room India remained at the window, her embroidery laid aside. Intently she watched the third house, but knew that the changes she saw in the windows were attributable only to the movement of the sun across the sky. Nothing would happen today, she told herself. How could anything important happen, when their consciousnesses were occluded with this infernal heat?

No one could eat lunch. Odessa had prepared cold-cut sand-wiches, but only Dauphin had the stomach to take more than a few bites, and those he declared made him quite sick. But three great pitchers of iced tea were consumed, and the only reason that they didn't start on a fourth was that there was no more ice.

The heat, which had been terrible so early in the morning, had only increased with the hours. No cloud hid the sun; it was low tide and they were the hotter for the increased yardage of sand to reflect the light. Vapor steamed off St. Elmo's Lagoon in such density that it obscured the peninsular mainland. Big Barbara went to her room and lay down with the fan blowing directly in her face; but soon enough she turned her face away, because it blew only hot air. For the first time, in her weakness, she wept for wanting a drink.

Luker sat in a corner of his room on a rush mat and watched the perspiration drip from his crooked elbows and the inside of his knees. India had collapsed feverish across the foot of her bed, with her mouth gaping and contracting like that of a dying fish.

Downstairs, Dauphin lay in his bathing suit in the hammock and rocked himself by means of a cane pole that he pushed against the wall. Odessa sat nearby, holding her Bible far away from her so that her sweating hands would not stain the pages. The sounds in that house were the creaking of the hammock hardware, the occasional turning of the thin pages of Odessa's Bible, Luker and India's uneven and heavy breath, and Big Barbara's pillow-stifled weeping.

Leigh was alone in the Savage house, and Leigh was the first to whom something happened that day.

*   *   *

In her bathing suit, she lay in a hammock that was suspended across the southwestern corner of the living room. Deep sleep in such heat was impossible, and she could manage no more than a troubled slumber; but even that was restful after the previous night's sleeplessness. It might have been exhaustive collapse, she told herself, rather than sleep; but that was her last conscious thought.

When she awoke—and it was Odessa's footsteps in the bedroom directly above that roused her—the sun had appreciably lowered in the sky. She turned her head a little, and saw there was no one else in the room. Odessa, in the slight abatement of heat, had evidently come from the McCray house to work the bedrooms upstairs. Leigh began to rock the hammock, and wondered if she could fall asleep again.

There was nothing to think about—the heat precluded rational considerations—so she drowsily followed Odessa's footsteps in the room above. The vibrations shook the hammock slightly. Odessa moved from Dauphin's side of the bed over to Leigh's; evidently she was changing the sheets. A walk to the chest where the linens were kept. Leigh stared straight up and followed Odessa's feet as clearly as if they had been printed there, like beginners' dance steps. Odessa shuffled around the bed as the linens were changed, then over to the dresser. *Why to the dresser?* Leigh wondered. Then back to the head of the bed. Oh, thought Leigh then, she had left the pillowcases on the bench before the dresser. Around the bed once more, back to the dresser with linens, then to the window and pause—probably to see how low the sun now was, or whether the tide had begun to come back in. She heard the window being lowered in the sash. Leigh raised her arm to look at her watch, then remembered that she had not worn it today because in such heat even so slight an encumbrance proved uncomfortable. She had left it on the dresser, she—

Leigh sat bolt upright in the hammock so that its hardware jarred and creaked. She twisted her head up. The room directly above her was not her and Dauphin's bedroom, but one which she knew had not been occupied in twenty years—since Bothwell Savage, alone at Beldame, had had some sort of attack, and died in it. Why then had Odessa been changing the sheets on the bed?

Sweating now with a nervousness she dared not ascribe to any particular thought or fear, Leigh halted the hammock and sat very still listening for Odessa's footsteps: in that room directly overhead, in the hallway above, in another bedroom, or coming down the stairs.

The house was silent. She heard nothing but her own stertorous breathing.

The silence appalled her. The Gulf was so distant and so accustomed a voice that she did not hear it speak.

Weak-kneed, she stood out of the hammock and went to the base of the staircase. She called Odessa's name, and then repeated the call when there was no answer.

Softly calling over and over again, "Odessa! Odessa!" she mounted the stairs. She did not pause on the second floor but went all the way to the top of the house. Odessa was not in her room.

She came down to the second floor again. The doors of all four bedrooms were closed. She dreaded to open any, but determined at last to try that of her own bedroom.

The room was empty, but the bed had been made; the two other used bedrooms on the floor were empty as well, but neat, kept in readiness for the guests who were never invited to Beldame.

At last she turned to the fourth door, which opened into the room that was situated directly over that end of the living room where she had slept. It was surely in this room and no other that she had heard Odessa's footsteps. "Odessa!" she called as she turned the knob and gently kicked the door open.

What she saw first was that the window had not been lowered closed, it had been raised. *Of course*, she thought to herself, *of course these windows wouldn't have been kept open with no one living in here, they—*

Then she noticed the rest of the room—or rather, she *understood* what she ought to have realized from the first.

The room had been given over to storage. Here were superfluous dressers and broken beds, rolled-up mats, and stacks of faded curtains, extra cushions for the gliders, and trunks containing whatever there was at Beldame to be kept for long periods of time.

But the entire floor of the room was covered with this detritus of a century of habitation; one had to weave one's way carefully among the stacks and piles and rows of objects. And in the place where Leigh had listened to Odessa's steps as she made up the bed, stood a pyramid of half a dozen crates, marked variously Dishes, Glasses, and Mama's Clothes.

And over what little one could see of the floor was a glaze of white sand. No prints were visible in it—no one had walked there.

Unthinking, unable to think, for the heat was worse in this closed room than anywhere else at Beldame, Leigh moved to the window, threading her way among boxes and heaps of books. Every step kicked the sand away, leaving proof of her progress. Despite the open window, the room was stifling, the air thick and weighty and dry. She could scarcely breathe in the atmosphere which provided as little nourishment as the sand that covered Beldame. She lurched to the window, and gasped for her breath. Looking out, she saw Odessa at the corner of the McCray veran-dah; automatically she waved.

Odessa looked up, cupped her hands and shouted to her: "Get out of that room, Miz Leigh!"

In the midst of her bewilderment, she had forgot how great her fright was. Leigh slammed the window down and fled the room. There was sand even on the doorknob, and she feverishly brushed it off her hand as she clattered down the stairs.

CHAPTER 20

After what she had experienced that afternoon, Leigh was nervous being in the Savage house at all but, for Dauphin's sake and the others', she tried not to show her fear at the supper table. It was still so hot, however, that they were hard put even to remember one another's names, much less take note of stray gestures and carefully repressed emotions.

"Mr. Dauphin," said Odessa when she was clearing the dishes, "I been thinking you and Miz Leigh ought to sleep over at the McCray house tonight. Not no breeze off the lagoon, hasn't been no breeze off the lagoon all day long, you sleep over there, you gone get the breeze off the Gulf."

"All right," said Dauphin, "it doesn't much matter where we go to bed tonight, we're not gone be able to sleep anyway." This was much to the relief of Leigh, who had anticipated some trouble in getting her husband out of the house. When she had told Odessa of the spirit-invaded bedroom, Odessa had advised against spend-ing the night in the Savage house.

"You come with 'em," said Big Barbara to Odessa, "you gone sweat your eyes out up there on the third floor."

"Oh, I cain't do that," replied Odessa, "I cain't get to sleep in any bed but my own! I'll be all right," she added, with a meaningful glance at Leigh.

The heat had exhausted them altogether. It was impossible to pack even though they knew they must be off early. Easier to hope for cooler weather, for rain in the morning; and if the heat continued, why then it could be no worse than it was now. Conversation that evening was impossible; when Dauphin and Luker leaned over the jigsaw puzzle, perspiration obscured their vision and dripped saltily on to the pieces. Leigh sat in the swing a little while and pretended to feel the cooling breeze that Odessa had promised. India walked along the shore, out of sight of the houses, until she came to the course of water that ran from the lagoon to the Gulf. When the sense of being on an island suddenly overwhelmed her, she hurried back to the McCray house.

On pretense of restlessness, Big Barbara wandered the rooms of the house, skirting her eyes into corners hoping to see bottles of liquor secreted in the shadows. She was the first to go to bed. Luker followed soon after, on the threshold of his room swallowing a Quaalude that he had reserved for such an emergency. Leigh and Dauphin could have had the fourth bedroom in the house but elected instead for the hammocks in the living room. Swinging in the darkness there, unable to sleep, they talked for a long while. Wanting very much to tell her husband of the ranging footsteps in the locked, cramped room of the Savage house, but not daring to speak for Dauphin's sake, Leigh decided to divulge another secret instead. "Dauphin," she said, "you know I told you I was going in for a checkup day after tomorrow . . . ?"

"I know," whispered Dauphin, mindful of those trying to sleep upstairs. "What about it?"

"Nothing," said Leigh. "It's just that I think I'm getting pregnant . . ."

"Are you really?" He giggled, and their hammocks shook with their happiness.

*   *   *

India knew that she would not be able to sleep if she went upstairs to her room. She lay in the porch swing and with one leg pressed against the chain, gently propelled it in an easy rocking arc. A drapery of black netting kept the mosquitoes and flies off her. She listened to the slow regular creaking of the chain, the breaking of high tide's waves so close by, and now and then caught a whisper of Leigh and Dauphin's conversation through the open living room window. As long as they were awake she did not fear, though all the lights of Beldame had been extinguished, though she was alone on the porch. From where she was she could not see the third house. She would rest quietly here until sleep was irresistible and then go upstairs to her bed; in the morning she would leave for Mobile, perhaps not to return. She could not but savor this last evening alone outside. The stars, that provided light but no illumination, made lightless Beldame seem the blackest place on earth.

She fell asleep in the swing, and when she awoke the porch was no longer uniformly black, but mysteriously slanted with shadows. The waxing moon had risen over the Gulf and now shone directly overhead. What awakened her, rousing her slowly from her heat-drugged slumber, was the sound of footsteps on the porch; steps that had mounted the stairs at the back and worked their way around to where she lay. It was Odessa, obviously, who had come over from the Savage house, restless and awake—or unwilling to spend the night there alone. So familiar had India become with the tides that by the sound of the waves—how distant they were from the house—she could tell that she had slept for nearly three hours. It was past one o'clock, and what was Odessa doing up so late as that? India tugged the mosquito netting from her head, sat up in the swing, and looked down the length of the porch.

No one was there.

"Odessa!" she called softly, but her voice still cracked. "Odessa!" she called more loudly, uneasy that the black woman wasn't there —that *no* one was there.

She rose slowly from the swing, telling herself that she was quiet so as not to disturb Leigh and Dauphin sleeping inside, but knowing that her care was indicative only of her fear.

"Odessa!" she whispered. "Where are you? It's time to go to bed!"

She moved around the swing, steadying it with her hand, and

proceeded down the length of the porch. It was dark here, though the moonlight shone on the tops of the railings, rendering them brilliant as the sand beyond. The sand glowed with the moonlight, muting the whitecaps of the Gulf and the phosphorescence of the lagoon. Beyond the porch the sand was a frozen sealike whiteness, pallid and terrible.

She went to the end of the porch and looked all around. The houses of Beldame were great blocks of darkness anchored in that shining sea of moonlit sand.

The tide's not yet gone out, India thought. *We're still an island.*

She looked up at the vivid gibbous moon and hated it for its imperfection of shape. She looked where it was reflected in the second-floor window of the third house, in the casement of the room that corresponded to Big Barbara's. It quivered in that glass, but that reflected movement was the result only of India's own trembling.

The steps she had dreamed: they were the tag-end of some amorphous vision in her brain, an auditory hallucination brought on by the heat, by her cramped posture in the swing, by the insidious suggestion of Odessa's superstition.

She turned to go inside, and in that act of turning, she caught sight of the footprints that led up from the sandy yard to the verandah. The moonlight caught them in such a way to bring them full into her vision: small footprints of a deformed bare foot drawn out in sand on the wooden steps. They weren't the residue of someone who had walked barefoot across the yard either, leaving a bold print on the first pair of steps and increasingly lighter prints as he went farther on to the porch: each of the prints was as perfectly formed as if someone had sifted sand onto the boards through a delicate stencil. They were the residue of something that was *made* of sand.

The footprints came up the stairs and down the porch to where she stood; but behind her, toward the swing where she had slept, they were lost in the shadows.

India kicked off her sandals, and by sense of touch she followed the trail of sandy prints into the darkness of the verandah. The steps led up to the swing and then stopped.

India looked wildly about. She hopped to the edge of the porch, desperately brushing the sand from the soles of her feet. To the left was the lagoon and the Gulf to the right; before her the gleaming sand of Beldame stretched toward a black and amorphous horizon.

The moon was suddenly obscured by clouds, and the entire vista winked out. Beldame was so still that even the sound of the screen door of the Savage house being opened softly and closed as carefully did not escape her. She ran to the end of the porch and straining, could just make out Odessa standing on the back steps of the Savage house.

India ran out into the yard: the black woman did not seem surprised to see her.

"Odessa!" cried India in a whisper. "I'm so glad it was you that came up on the porch, I was—"

"Wasn't me, child . . ."

India was astonished, and then frightened. Odessa had turned to face the third house.

India looked up. Though the moon was still obscured, its reflection remained in that upstairs window. But it *wasn't* the moon—a face, pale and with only the barest suggestion of features, was slowly retreating from the window into the darkness of the third house.

CHAPTER 21

Odessa jangled as she walked with determination across the yard. India was afraid to accompany the black woman, but more fearful of being left behind. "What's that in your pockets?" demanded India in a whisper, seeing they were weighted down.

"Keys, child," the black woman replied. "I got the keys to the third house."

Hopping beside Odessa, India drew in her breath sharply. "Hey, where'd you get 'em?"

"Oh, had 'em all the time. Always had 'em."

"Are we going in?" cried India. "Are we actually going inside the third house?" When Odessa nodded, India tugged at her skirt. "Listen, why don't we wait till tomorrow? Why don't we wait till it's light out?"

"Be too late," said Odessa. "We got to protect ourselves."

"What about those seeds? We ate all those seeds, you said that would protect us. You said—"

"One time before I used those seeds, child, and they protected me, and they protected ever'body at Beldame. That was right after Martha-Ann got killed. They worked then, but they not working now. The spirits let 'em work the first time—they tried to fool me into thinking the seeds was always gone work, they just *let* us feel like we was protected. But the seeds ain't working, I can tell. So we got to go inside."

"I know somebody's in there," said India, actually hanging on to Odessa's skirt to prevent her from getting closer to the third house. A corner of the moon was momentarily uncovered and they were draped in its pallid glow. "There was somebody looking down at us from the window. We can't go in there when we *know* somebody's waiting inside."

"Child," said Odessa, "you don't have to go with me."

"What have you got to protect you? Have you got a gun?"

"No, but if I had, I'd have it with me right now. People say that a gun's no good against spirits, but you cain't never tell what's gone stop a spirit and what's not. They ain't going by our rules, not for a minute. I got the Bible. I'm gone read out of the Bible—and I got the keys, I'm gone see if I can lock 'em in their rooms."

"Spirits can go through walls," asserted India.

"You don't know!" exclaimed Odessa. "You been telling me from *can* to *cain't* that you don't know nothing about spirits, and now you telling me spirits cain't be locked inside a room! Well, child, you just tell me how you know they cain't!"

"I don't know," admitted India nervously. "Maybe they can. Are you actually going to go in there and try to lock 'em up?"

Odessa shrugged. "I don't know exactly what I'm gone do." She took India by the hand. "You gone hold the flashlight for me?"

Though full of fear, India nodded and took the flashlight that Odessa pulled from her dress pocket. She clicked it on and flashed it over the back porch of the third house. In dark night, illumined only in that quavering white circle, it appeared truly indistinguishable from either the McCray or the Savage house. "I'm afraid," she said.

"'Course you are," said Odessa, "and so am I, but you said you wanted to go inside, and if you don't go in now, you maybe not never gone get the chance." She took out a large ring of old-fashioned keys, similar to those that India had found in some of the doors of the McCray house. Odessa went boldly to the kitchen door, as if she were returning there after only an afternoon's grocery shopping, and tried four keys in the lock before one turned. India stood trembling on the step below Odessa, pressing her shoulder against the black woman's thigh, and trying to focus the flashlight on the keyhole. The moon had fallen behind deeper clouds and all Beldame was rendered black.

"Why can't we wait till the morning?" India asked. "Why can't we wait till it's light out?"

"Because they's in the house now, and we got to keep 'em from getting out." She placed a firm hand on India's shoulder. "They already been in Mr. Dauphin's house, got in this afternoon when Miz Leigh was 'sleep. I went up there and I read the Bible at it and I shut the window and I locked the door—but I don't know whether that got rid of it or not. I think it did. I think I done chased it out. I think it's gone back up there and we saw it in the window. I don't want to see no more traveling tonight."

The door opened, grating thickly on sand. India followed Odessa inside, convulsively grasping the woman's skirts.

India shone the feeble light around the room; she could make out little but that it was an old-fashioned kitchen, with a pump and a wood-burning stove (in Beldame, where had they gotten wood?). In the center of the room was a large table stacked with dishes and pots; but all the cupboards and doors were closed, and the long-preserved neatness of the room was unsettling.

They stood next to the table for more than a minute, motionless and scarcely breathing, listening to the sounds in the house. Beneath the dull drone of the Gulf was an insistent sizzle of falling sand. India shone her light into the corners of the ceiling and saw sand trickling there in tiny intermittent streams and piling up in the corners.

"I don't hear anything," said India. "There's nobody here. What I saw upstairs was just the reflection of the moon. I wasn't really awake when I saw it—I'm probably not really awake now."

What was the smell of a house that had been shut for decades? India hadn't anything to compare it with, but Odessa knew that it was the smell of the dessicated leaves on the floor of the Savage mausoleum.

The kitchen was hot and dry and dead. Odessa stepped quietly and quickly through a swinging door into the dining room. India followed, but what she saw on the other side startled her so that she lost her grip on the door and it swung loudly shut behind her.

In her preoccupied terror of entering the third house when she knew it to be not empty, she had forgot the encroaching dune, actually forgot it. And here it was, reproduced in the high square room just as it was outside, sloping gently from the top of the windows at the front, down to her feet. She was actually standing in it; Odessa's opening the door had leveled a large arc in the sand. Even in that lightless interior, the dune gleamed. It was smooth and dry, and when India shone the slight beam of her flashlight over it, she could see the topmost layer of grains sliding down. Perhaps, she considered thickly, they were set in motion by her and Odessa's trembling presence in a house that had known only stillness for decades.

In the middle of the room was a dining table set with chairs; though of this nothing showed but a little corner of the table, and the two chairs that were on the kitchen side. And these were already firmly anchored in the dune. The candles in the iron chandelier had entirely wilted in some severe heat of years past. On the side wall, blackened paintings had been knocked awry by the falling sand, but remained on their hooks; slowly they were being covered. The draperies on the windows had been caught by sand at the hems and dragged from the valances. The ceiling buckled noticeably toward the front of the house: the room above was that which corresponded to her own bedroom, the room into which she had allowed the sand to enter. Now it was evidently building up there to such an extent that it threatened the flooring. These details India made out but did not fully register at the time; they were seen only with the aid of the flashlight. Other bulky contours tokened something scarcely buried, but these forms she could not rightly interpret.

Her question at least was answered: the dune had got inside the

house, and the effect was more wonderful—and more terrible—
than she had imagined. The room, three-quarters filled with sand,
was intensely claustrophobic.

"Odessa," she whispered, "I don't know if it's safe—"

Odessa was no longer in the dining room. India looked frantically around, reaching out her hand hoping to catch hold of the
black woman's dress. The beam of the flashlight flew wildly over
the sand.

Odessa had not gone back through the swinging door into the
kitchen: India would have heard that. She shone the flashlight
toward the double doorway she knew opened between this and the
living room. It was almost blocked by the sand. A triangular space
remained between the wall and the dune only sufficient to sidle
through. Without thinking, India hurried over, planted her feet into
sand that was more than a foot deep here, and swung through into
the living room. "Odessa!" she called again, and Odessa answered
with a jangle of her keys from the foot of the stairs.

India shone the light in her face. "Are you going up there?" she
asked incredulously, forgetting her curiosity about the furnishings
and state of the living room.

Odessa nodded dully. "Got to," she said in a normal voice. "And
you got to come too. Cain't find the locks 'less I got some light."

India drew in her breath deeply and followed Odessa up the
steps, holding on to the hem of her dress as they proceeded.

The landing was bare and dark; a thin layer of sand grated
beneath their feet. The doors to all four bedrooms were open, but
Odessa warned her not to shine the flashlight inside the rooms.
The black woman pulled the first of the doors shut. India then
raised the light and shone it on the lock of the door. Without hurry
Odessa tried the keys until she found one that fit; she turned it,
nodded when the bolt shot, then rattled the knob to make certain
that the door would not open.

She pulled the second door shut; India shifted the light, and
the process was repeated. This was the room into which she had
peered that first day at Beldame. And whatever had shut the bedroom door that day had been standing where she stood now. The
key turned in the lock, but it was not Odessa who rattled the knob.
Whatever had been locked inside wanted to get out.

"It's Martha-Ann," said India calmly. "I saw her inside. And it was *this* room."

Odessa did not reply. She pulled the third door shut and locked it. The knob of the second door continued to rattle. Whatever was on the other side put its mouth to the keyhole and whistled at them on the landing.

The fourth room overlooked the yard; in its window India had seen a white face she had mistaken for the reflection of the moon. The door flew shut of its own accord, and some large piece of furniture was slammed against it from the inside. Calmly, Odessa pressed the last of the keys into the lock and turned it.

"Go on, child," said Odessa, and waved India toward the stairs; but the landing was so dark now that India did not see this motion. Her flashlight's beam was trained on the staircase that led upward.

"What about the third floor?" she asked. The doorknob of the second room began to rattle again—*What the hell am I doing here?* thought India—and more furniture scraped in the fourth room.

"No door up there to lock," said Odessa. "Anything up there, it's got the run of the house. Nothing we can do. Go on down, child."

India turned the flashlight beam downward and descended the stairs into the living room. The moon had emerged from the clouds and shone through the window that was at the back of the house, grayly illumining that long room. Here the dune, in a larger space, seemed not so monstrous as in the dining room.

The room was furnished with a long-preserved casualness, with fine rugs and painted wicker furniture. The fabrics, much-decayed, were small-patterned and, India suspected, had been dyed in bright colors. Now all was black and gray, except the sand, which caught and reflected the moonlight with a sickly white pallor. The dune, like a freeze-frame of a tidal wave, had swept through a third of the room.

India shone her flashlight on the dune; more sand slipped down its gentle plane. The individual falling grains caught and refracted the white light. Odessa's steps were on the stairs behind her, and India was about to turn when a square table against the outside wall was suddenly tipped over. A large lamp, with an intricate stained-glass shade made in imitation of clusters of wisteria, was smashed on the floor. Startled, India dropped the flashlight. It fell on to a bare portion of floor and the light was extinguished. On her knees India struggled soundlessly against the gritty surface; she found the flashlight again but it would not light. She became aware then that upstairs the banging of the door of the second bedroom and the scraping of furniture in the fourth bedroom had abruptly left off. Its place was taken by a furtive, shallow dry spraying noise—as if it were the breath of some creature that might exhale sand.

"Odessa," she whispered.

"Quick, child," said the black woman, her voice urgent for the first time since they had entered the house. Odessa was already in the dining room, but India could see nothing.

India scrambled toward the black triangle that would allow her into the safety of the dining room. The dry breathing had grown louder and closer; India held the flashlight as a weapon.

When she stood, a long-fingered hand closed tightly over her ankle. Hard nails punctured her skin, and she felt her blood welling to the surface. Instinctively, India brought the flashlight down hard against it—whatever it was. There was a dry gasp of breath—India felt sand sprayed lightly against her bare leg—and the grip was loosened. She leaped through the doorway into the dining room. Odessa grabbed her arm and dragged her through the kitchen and out the back door.

PART III

THE ELEMENTALS

CHAPTER 22

By the time they rose next morning, the curse of hot weather had been broken: there was a gray drizzle and the temperature was in such enormous contrast to that of the previous day that at their early breakfast, which for a change was served to them all at a single sitting, they declared themselves positively chilled. Their packing had been put off, and Luker, holding a second cup of coffee tightly in his hands for the warmth it provided, suggested that they take only what was necessary. "If we leave most of our things here," he said, "we'll *have* to come back after the holiday. India and I don't really have to get back to New York just yet, so I think we ought to try to keep it going." He glanced at his daughter, thinking that she would applaud this measure, but India—who was unaccountably wearing mirrored sunglasses at the table—glanced palely away, and would not look at him.

"Good," said Leigh, "'cause, Luker, I don't think you should leave Alabama until it's decided what's gone 'come of Beldame. You're the only one who'll really fight with Daddy, and it may come to just that."

"I'd like to rip his balls off and staple 'em to the roof of his mouth," said Luker. The others had all grown so used to his vulgarity of speech they didn't even flinch.

Thus it was decided to remain in Mobile from the first of July— that was today, Saturday—through the following Wednesday, the fifth. Anything Lawton wanted them to do, they should do without complaint and with as good a grace as could be got up for the occasion, whether it be a Rotary dinner, a speech in the park, or a tour of the shopping malls. If all went well they should be back in time for Dauphin's birthday on the sixth.

They brought down their bags, locked the houses, and had driven away by ten o'clock. Leigh, Dauphin, and Big Barbara went in the jeep; Luker, Odessa, and India in the Scout. To Luker's astonishment India sat in Odessa's lap for the entire drive back to their cars in Gasque.

"Oh, I know," said Luker to his daughter when they transferred into the Fairlane, "you're just sorry about leaving Beldame. I feel the same way. New York is one extreme, Beldame's the other. Mobile is in the middle, and you and me—we like the extremes."

"Yes," said India curtly, and Luker was puzzled.

India was still severely frightened by what had happened the night before. She had been certain, as she fled the house, that she had barely escaped with her life. The rest of that night she had spent trembling in a hammock in the Savage living room, unable at all to sleep, and keeping both eyes open and focused on the comforting presence of Odessa, who dozed in a rocking chair. Every sound had frightened her, and the steady drop in the temperature—it must have fallen thirty degrees in three hours—made her very cold.

In the dawn she ventured to wake Odessa. "Odessa," she said, "I want to know what happened."

"Nothing happened," replied Odessa. "I got you out."

"Something tried to get me. What was it?"

"I thought I got 'em locked in those rooms." She shrugged. "I didn't get 'em all, I guess."

"There was something in that second bedroom, something that rattled the doorknob, and then there was something else in the fourth bedroom, something that slammed the door. Then there was whatever tried to pull me under the sand. So there were three things in that house."

"Un-unh," said Odessa, shaking her head. "That's just what they want you to think."

"What do you mean? Why isn't that right? One, two, three. Three things in the house, we counted them!"

"See," said Odessa, "that's how they work. When we was upstairs and they let us lock 'em in those rooms, they was pretending they couldn't get out. 'Keys and locks can hold us in,' they was saying. Then we get downstairs and they're down there too, wanting to pull you under the sand."

"But that's still three! Two of 'em upstairs and one downstairs, even if two of 'em were still just pretending to be locked in!"

"No," said Odessa. "You don't know how many they was, you don't know! They might all be fifty of 'em in there, or they might be just one moving around a lot. You seeing what they want you to see—you not seeing what's really there."

"If they can do all that," said India sullenly, "then how did we manage to get away?"

Big Barbara returned to her husband's house, where he was waiting for her with a typewritten list of all the places she was to go in the next few days. They must leave almost immediately for a Junior Chamber of Commerce luncheon.

"Lawton," she said with a nervous smile, "I got to tell you what I did at Beldame."

"Barbara, all you got to do is get dressed or we gone be late. I'm speaking, and it don't do for the speaker to come in late."

"You got to listen to me though. You got to hear what I've done for you, Lawton. I got myself off the bottle, that's what I did. I don't need it now. I'm not gone be drinking any more. You don't have to worry about me. I know I've still got faults—we all still got our faults no matter *what* we do—but mine don't have anything to do with liquor any more. I got so much energy, I've been sitting on the beach all day thinking of ways to help you with this campaign. Listen," she said feverishly, unnerved by her husband's cold gaze, "I think I'd *love* to live in Washington for a few years—I know it's gone be more than a few years though, once you get up there, they're not ever gone let you out of Congress—and Lawton, I'm gone be so much help to you! I can give a good party—you know I can, even Luker says I can and Luker hates parties. I'm gone see if Dauphin and Leigh won't let me have Odessa for a while and Odessa's gone fly up and help me give the best parties you ever saw in your life. We're gone have people coming and going like our foyer was a hotel lobby! That's what I've been thinking about at Beldame, Lawton. I know you're gone win, I'm gone be right behind you too, in everything you do, I'm gone—"

"Now we gone be late for sure!" interrupted Lawton McCray angrily.

Luker and India again took the guest wing of the Small House; but Lawton McCray did not provide his son and granddaughter with any itinerary to be followed for his political benefit. They had the time free to themselves.

Luker questioned India whether anything were wrong.

"Where's Odessa?" she said.

"She went home for a while. She'll be back later in the afternoon. You know," he said to India, who still had not removed her sunglasses, "it's strange how much you've become attached to Odessa—"

"What's wrong with it?" India demanded sharply.

"Nothing," said her father. "It's just strange, since when we first went down to Beldame you wouldn't give her the time of day."

"She has inner qualities."

"Are you saying that with a straight face?"

India wouldn't reply.

They listened to the television noontime report while they were eating their lunch and discovered that for the past week Mobile had been enjoying a spate of abnormally temperate weather: cool mornings, rainy afternoons, positively chilly nights.

"Isn't that strange," said Luker. "And it was hotter than hell at Beldame, for the whole goddamn week. Fifty miles away, and we were in a-whole-nother climate."

Leigh and Dauphin were at the Junior Chamber of Commerce luncheon too, and tried not to appear too interested in Big Barbara's decisions when the waiter came around to ask if anyone wanted a cocktail before the food was served. Big Barbara flushed—not with the decision, which was an easy one, but with the consciousness that she was being watched. *Like I was the weather*, she told herself. On her way to the ladies' room, halfway through the meal, she stopped at Leigh and Dauphin's table, leaned between them and whispered: "Y'all don't need to worry about me. With everybody complimenting me on my tan, I haven't had time to raise a glass to my lips!"

While Lawton spoke, Big Barbara, whose place was on the dais next to the podium, stared up at her husband with a dizzying smile of conjugal admiration. Scarcely a man or woman in that audience but commented later how lucky the candidate was to have such a wife—and even those who liked Lawton, or professed to like him, said that they felt better about voting for him knowing that it would also be Big Barbara who would end up in Washington, D.C.

After the Junior Chamber of Commerce luncheon, as they were driving back home, Dauphin passed the drugstore where the week before he had left off India's film to be developed. He stopped and picked it up. Both he and Leigh were surprised that, when they handed it over to India, she thanked them but briefly and made no move to examine the photographs.

"Aren't you even gone look at 'em?" said Leigh.

"I'll look at 'em later," replied the girl, and took the envelope off to her room.

The action was of sufficient oddity to excite comment, and was reported to Luker a little later. Toward the end of the afternoon he came and sat in India's room; he had a tall glass in his hand. "My God, it's good to have a drink again. I think I suffered almost as much as Big Barbara."

"You had pills," said India.

"Shhh!" said her father. "I don't want you telling anybody that! But the fact is I don't think I took more than a couple of downs the whole time I was there."

"No ups?"

"What the hell for? What is there to do on speed at Beldame?"

India shrugged, dropped her chin on to her fist, and gazed out the window at the Great House. The Alabama foliage was grotesquely lush; trees seemed absolutely weighted down with leaves. The flowers in the gardens—hydrangeas, lilies, and showy annuals —drooped with blooms. Despite the absence of the family, the gardeners had been pridefully at work.

"What's wrong with you?" demanded Luker. "Are you mad because we had to leave Beldame?"

She shook her head but did not look at him.

"What then?"

"I'm"—she struggled for a word—"disoriented," she said at last.

"Oh, yeah?" said her father softly. Then after a moment: "Dauphin brought back the pictures of the third house that you took. How'd they come out?"

India glanced at him sharply and then turned away.

He waited for an answer; when none came, he went on: "Did you look at them?"

She nodded and scratched the windowsill with an unpainted fingernail.

"Let me see them," said Luker.

India shook her head slowly.

"They didn't turn out?"

India sniffed. "I'm no dummy," she said. "I can work a light meter. I've got control over my apertures. Of course they came out."

"India," said Luker, "you're being coy and I hate it. You're being like your mother, in fact. Are you going to show me the fucking pictures or not?"

"You know," she said, looking directly at him for the first time, "when I was taking those pictures, it was Odessa who told me where to stand and what to frame. She was with me the whole time—except for the last part. I didn't tell you, but for the last half-dozen frames I went to the top of the dune again and took some pictures of that bedroom, that bedroom where I broke the window."

Luker nodded slowly and crunched ice. "And they all came out?"

"A couple at the very end didn't," India replied. "There was some reflection on the windowpanes. The image isn't all there." She stood, walked to the dresser and took the envelope of photographs from one of the drawers there. "Oh, Luker," she said as she handed it to him, "I'm scared, I'm still so scared."

He took the photographs in one hand, and with the other he drew her by the wrist. He would not open the envelope until she had left off weeping.

The first nineteen of the black-and-white photographs were of India in her bedroom; forty-one more of the third house, taken from the back and the two sides. And the final ten were of the bedroom on the second floor that corresponded to India's own in the McCray house. Luker nodded as he went slowly through them, and but for India's having wept, would have pointed out where some composition might have been improved or the lighting and shutter speed adjusted to better effect. On the whole, however, he found them excellent work, and complimented India on them afterward, though with some puzzlement.

"India," he said, "these pictures are good. They're better than good, in fact, they're the best work that you've ever done. I don't understand why you were afraid to show them to me. I mean, don't you *see* that they're good?"

She nodded slowly, but still held her arm tightly wound round his.

"I look at these and I want to go back down there with a four-by-five, even an eight-by-ten. Then we could get something *really* spectacular. Maybe we could rent one when we go back on Wednesday, if there's a decent camera store in this town, we—"

"These weren't the only pictures I took," said India, interrupting him softly.

"Where are the others?"

"I pulled them."

"Why?"

After a few moments she answered: "I think Odessa should see them."

"Why Odessa? Wait a minute, India, now listen. Something upset you about these pictures, and I want to know what it is. I don't want any more of this mystery. I tell you something—mystery is real boring. Now here, I want you to take a long swallow of this drink—it's decent scotch and I know you like decent scotch—and then I want you to tell me what's bothering you. I don't intend to sit here the whole fucking afternoon, and play Twenty Fucking Questions."

India took a longer swallow than Luker expected. She rose and from the very back of another drawer of the dresser took a smaller stack of photographic prints. She handed them to her father.

"Are these from the same rolls?"

"Yes," she said. "They're not in sequence. But they're all from the second roll."

The first few photographs were of architectural details of the house: casements mostly, but one also of the turret of the verandah that protruded from the dune at the front of the house. "These are just as good as the others," said Luker wonderingly, "I don't see—"

And then he saw.

Something was leaning against the turret, on its shadowed shingles. The outline of an emaciated figure—something not much more than a skeleton wrapped in a tissue of flesh—was evidently trying to escape the camera's lens by leaning very close along the line of the turret. But the protruding ribs showed a little against the sky, as did the chin and jaw of the thrown-back head. The knees and spindly thighs could be seen, but the lower legs and feet were buried in the sand that covered the verandah roof. Whatever it was had been the same color as the slate-gray shingles. The long fingers of one withered hand protruded onto the sunlit portion of the turret. It appeared that whoever—*whatever*—this was had been caught as it scurried around the turret out of the sight of India and Odessa in the yard.

Luker looked down at India; she was crying again.

"India," he said, "when you took this picture—"

"I didn't see anything," she whispered. "There wasn't anything up there."

Luker quickly flipped through the pictures he had just gone through.

"That was the worst one of those," said India, "but look . . ." On each of the other prints she pointed out something Luker had missed: a dark bony arm laid across a windowsill, a dark withered hand fingering the rotten curtains inside the rooms of the third house. Luker shook his head in frustrated disbelief. "I hate this," he whispered. "I told you not to—"

India still held two prints in her hand, face down.

"Those are the worst?"

India nodded. "Do you want to see them?"

"No," he said, "of course I don't want to see them, but show me."

She flipped the first one over into his hand. It was a photograph of the verandah showing the handsome curve of the dune that was overtaking the lagoon side of the third house. But Luker saw at once the fat gray creature that was huddled behind the low porch railing. From its crouched position, and the fact that most of it was hidden by the railing posts, it was not possible to reconstruct its shape—Luker thought that it might be the animated fetus of an elephant. Only that part of its head from the round flat ear to the round flat eye was visible. Its white pupil stared out into the camera lens.

"It makes me want to vomit," said India matter-of-factly.

The second photograph that India handed her father was of the bedroom on the second floor of the house. All the other pictures of that room had been marred by the reflections on the glass of the windows; but this one was not. The crosspieces of the window frame were visible, but it was as if the glass had not been there at all.

The photograph showed the chifforobe on the far side of the room; its door was open and the mirror on the inside of the door reflected a part of the room that was not directly visible from where India had stood. And against the outside wall of that bedroom a woman crouched in the edge of the dune of sand that had come through the broken window. She grinned into the camera; her eyes were black with white pupils. A parrot had embedded its claws into her shoulder, arched, and spread its wings.

"It's Nails," said India.

"And it's Marian Savage," said India's father.

CHAPTER 23

"Tricks," said Odessa, when she was shown the photographs that India had taken of the third house. "It's all tricks." She had looked at them cursorily and handed them directly back to India.

"But there are *pictures* here, Odessa. You can't look at these and tell me it's a trick of the light, because I know it isn't. There's something on the roof, you can see his chest and his chin and his legs; and there's something on the porch because it's looking right in the camera, and here's this dead woman upstairs—and I know who it is because I saw her in her coffin at the funeral!"

Odessa was adamant. "It's tricks. All of it's tricks."

India shook her head and looked to her father. "How can she say that?" she pleaded. "Nobody played tricks with that camera or that film. This film got developed at a drugstore, it all goes through a machine, they don't even *look* at it there! And I've looked at the negatives. All the images are on the negatives too."

"No," said Odessa, "wasn't nothing there. Spirits got in the camera, that's all. They wasn't there when you took the pictures. They got inside the camera and got on the film."

"I would have seen them if they had been there," said India weakly, and both Odessa and Luker nodded agreement with her. They sat in the glassed-in porch of the Small House early on Sunday afternoon, the second of July. Leigh and Dauphin had gone to a summer flower show at the Armory, this not only in order to please Lawton but also to keep an eye on Big Barbara, and make certain that her plastic glass contained ginger ale and not champagne.

Luker fidgeted for a minute, and when he spoke it was with a tone of voice that tokened unhappy resignation and giving-in. "India, listen," he said, "the images that you see on those photographs are images of things that weren't really there."

"I don't understand," said India plaintively, for she could tell that her father was sincere in this incredulity.

"It was the Elementals," he said quietly. "It was the Elementals playing tricks on you—playing tricks on all of us."

"I don't know what you're talking about. Elementals—what are Elementals?"

"That's the kind of spirits that's in the third house," said Luker. He had another drink, and had prepared India one as well. It was weaker than his own, but not much.

"You knew more about this than you let on," said India, and he nodded glumly. "You two have been treating me like a child! So now you tell me why I'm supposed to look at these photographs that have got monsters and dead people on them and say to myself, 'Hey, India, they weren't really there . . .'"

Odessa sat rocking with her arms folded across her breasts; she'd say nothing. Luker must talk.

"Well," he said, "you must know there are two kinds of spirits. Good spirits and evil spirits—"

"I don't believe in spirits," cried India.

"Shut the fuck up! You've got the goddamn pictures, and you want to know what's on 'em, well, I'm gone tell you, and don't give me this bullshit about not believing in things! I don't believe in things either. God's dead and the devil lives under a rock! But I know enough to know that I'm not supposed to go in the third house and that's what I'm telling you now, so sit there and shut up and don't be such a bitch! This is hard."

India was still.

"Well, to begin with, there're good spirits and there're evil spirits . . ."

India rolled her eyes and took a long swallow of her drink.

"And I guess you can guess what kind of spirits are in the third house. And the evil spirits in the third house are called Elementals."

"How do you know that?"

"Know what?"

"How do you know they're called Elementals? I mean, you don't seem to know anything about 'em really, but then you give 'em this big name, why—"

"That's what Mary-Scot calls 'em," said Odessa. "Mary-Scot went and talked to the priests and then came back and told us they were Elementals."

"And *you're* going by what a priest tells you?" India said accusingly to her father.

Luker shrugged. "It's a . . . *convenient* name, India, that's all. It sounds better than saying *spirit* or *ghost*. But really all we know is that there're presences in the house at Beldame, and they're evil."

"And they're called Elementals because they belong to the elements of nature or something like that?"

"Right."

"Big deal," she said. "So how the hell did they get in the third house?"

Luker shrugged and Odessa made echo.

"All right," said India. "So they're in there. And so there're three of 'em. And one of 'em is this thing that hangs out on the roof and one of 'em looks like an aborted frog that's the size of a collie and one of 'em is Dauphin's mother."

"No," said Odessa.

"No," said Luker. "That's the thing about Elementals. You don't know what they are or what they're like. They don't have any real shape. You don't even know if they have real bodies or not. They showed up on your film, but you didn't see 'em when you took the pictures, did you?"

"No."

"They might have been in the camera itself."

"Yeah," said India contemptuously, "maybe they came up and pasted pictures of themselves on the lens."

"Something like that," said Luker. "See, the point is you can't assume that spirits—and especially Elementals—work the way you and I do. Just because you get an image of them on your negative doesn't mean that they were really there. All it means is there were spirits in the house."

"But what do they *look* like?"

"They don't look like nothing," said Odessa, "they's just tricks and badness. They's this and they's that, and *this* and *that's* not ever gone be what you expecting. They look like anything they want."

"That's right," said Luker. "Maybe they knew you hated frogs so they put on their frog costume."

"I love frogs," said India. "It's lizards I hate."

"That's not the point. The point is they can look like anything. They can look like Marian Savage—"

"Or Martha-Ann," said India cruelly, glancing at Odessa.

"Or anything they want. See, they want to fool you, India. They want you to look at those pictures and say, 'My God, there's three of 'em, and they have this shape and this shape and this shape, and if I can avoid 'em, then I'll be all right.'"

India thought this over for several moments: the business was insane.

"But why don't they just show themselves like they really are?"

"Because they don't *have* any particular shape," said Luker. "Because they're just presences."

"So why do they go to all this trouble? I mean when you look at these pictures—and they're *not* faked—we're talking about a major work schedule for somebody. Why do they want to fool us like that?"

"Don't know," said Odessa shortly. "Don't nobody know that."

"Then are they dangerous?" asked India of the black woman.

Odessa regarded her sharply. "Look at your leg, child." India wore long pants; she slowly shook her head. Luker reached down and pushed up the corduroy pants leg. India's right ankle was badly bruised.

"What happened?" demanded Luker.

"I fell," said India meanly. "There was this Elemental, and it turned itself into a banana peel and it made me go and slip on it. Listen Luker, I want to know how much *you* know about all this. Have you had any run-ins?"

"Just one," replied Luker, "but mine wasn't so bad. It was poor old Mary-Scot who got the worst of it."

"What happened to Mary-Scot—and what happened to you, Luker?"

"India, why don't you leave well enough alone?"

"Goddamn it!" cried India. "It's not *'well enough'* so far as I'm concerned! I've got bruises, you saw 'em! Listen, Luker, last night Odessa and I went inside that fucking house and there were two bedrooms that had something in 'em. We locked the doors, and we were just going out when something knocked over a table right in front of me. There was something inside that dune. It tried to pull me under the sand. I've taken about five showers since we got back to Mobile, and I can *still* feel that sand on me. That's not what I call *'well enough.'*"

"You shouldn't have gone inside," said Luker primly. "I told you not to. And Odessa, you shouldn't have let her go with you."

Odessa shrugged. "Child can take care of herself, I—"

"I couldn't though!" shouted India. "I would have died in there, I would have suffocated or gotten eaten or something if you hadn't pulled me out of there! I tell you, I'm pissed! I'm pissed at the whole business! Why the hell did you take me to a place like Beldame? Why in the hell do Dauphin and Leigh and Big Barbara keep going back when you've got these demons—"

"Spirits," corrected Luker.

"These *Elementals* in the goddamn house, every one of 'em ready to pounce on you at any time of day or night? I mean, it's dangerous out there! Martha-Ann got killed, didn't she, Odessa? Martha-Ann didn't drown. Whatever tried to get me got Martha-Ann, but you weren't there to drag her out. And when I went up to that room on the first day I got there, it was Martha-Ann I saw inside. She's still there, she's dead but she won't lie down! Luker, next time you want a vacation why don't we just kayak to Iceland?—it'd be a hell of a lot safer!"

She breathed, heavily after her tirade, and Luker gently pressed the bottom of her glass to make her drink more. She swallowed too much, it went down wrong; she coughed and began to weep.

"India," he said softly. "You don't really think I'd take you to Beldame if I had thought it was going to be dangerous, do you?"

"But you knew about the Elementals—you said you did."

"Yes, of course I did. But when you're away you forget that you believe in them. Sure, when you first get to Beldame and you see the third house, you say, 'Oh, fuck, there's something inside and it's going to get me,' but then you forget because nothing happens. I was scared when I went to Beldame when I was real young, but it was just once that something happened to me, and now I can't really remember how much of it was just nightmares that came later, or my bad memory, or what—maybe *nothing* happened . . ."

"Then if nothing happened, tell me about it, Luker. Did you go in the house, did you just see something? What?"

Luker glanced at Odessa, and Odessa nodded for him to proceed. India couldn't tell by this signal whether or not Odessa knew the story. There were times she felt as if all this Alabama family had entered into a conspiracy against her, the only true Northerner among them.

"There's nothing to it," said Luker, with a deprecating wave of his hand. "Nothing really happened. It's just one time I saw something . . ."

"What?"

"It was one year early in the season and just Big Barbara and I were down there—we went down to open up the house or something like that and we were gone stay overnight, I guess. So I was out playing by myself. It was broad day and the sun was shining, and before I knew it I was standing on the front porch of the third house—that was when the sand had just started to come up that high, it probably wasn't more than a foot deep then. So I must have been nine or ten."

"But weren't you afraid of the house? Why'd you go up there all by yourself?"

"I don't know," said Luker. "I wonder why myself. I wouldn't do it now, and I can't figure out why I did it then either. I don't remember making a decision. I have an image of myself. I'm walking up and down on the Gulf side looking for shells or something, and then suddenly there's a jump-cut, and I'm standing on the front porch of the third house. I try to remember what came in between —but it's as if there were nothing in between. That's why I kept thinking of this as a dream and not as something that really happened. That's probably what it was, just a dream that I've confused with a memory."

"I doubt it," said India. "What did you do when you got up on the porch?"

Luker trembled as he said it. "I looked in the windows."

"What'd you see?"

"I looked in the living room first, and it was in perfect condition. None of the sand had gotten inside yet—"

"There's plenty there now," said India, glancing at Odessa for confirmation.

"I wasn't really scared," said Luker, "it didn't bother me, it was just this room that was in a locked house and that was all, and I thought, 'Well why have we been so scared of this?'"

"And then?"

"And then I went to the other side of the verandah; and I looked in the dining room window—" Luker glanced at Odessa and didn't go on. India saw that despite the air conditioning in the room, her father was perspiring heavily.

"What did you see?" she asked grimly.

Luker looked away, and when he spoke his voice was soft and halting. "There were two men sitting at the table right next to each other, one of them on the end. But I could see under the table, and they didn't have any legs. They were just bodies and arms."

"Were they real?" stammered India, "I mean . . . what were they doing?"

"Nothing. The table was set. Good stuff, china and silver and crystal, but everything right around where they were was all broken. Like they had deliberately smashed it."

"And they didn't have any legs? Were they like . . . freaks or something?"

"India!" cried Luker. "These weren't like people—you looked at them and you knew they weren't real people! You didn't say to yourself, 'Oh, those poor men they got their legs cut off in a train accident'! And you know what they were wearing?"

India shook her head.

"They were wearing flowered suits . . ."

"What? Like clown suits or something?"

"The material had these big flowers on it, camellias I think."

India sat very still a moment. "The drapes in the dining room of the third house have big camellias on them. I saw them."

"I know," said Luker. "They were sitting there wearing suits that were made out of the curtains."

"Did they see you?"

"They looked at me—they had black eyes with white pupils. They wanted me to come inside . . ."

"So they talked, they said something to you."

Luker nodded. "They whispered, but I could hear them even through the window glass. And when they talked, sand fell out of their mouths. Just sand. I couldn't see any teeth or tongues. But sand sprayed out when they talked. They said they had things they wanted to show me upstairs, things I could have if I wanted them. They told me I could look in boxes and trunks and have anything I wanted. They said there were boxes there that hadn't been gone through in thirty years, and there was great stuff inside them . . ."

"Did you believe them?"

"Yes, I did. Because that's exactly what I had always thought about the third house, that there were all these trunks upstairs with old letters and old clothes and stamp collections and coin collections and antique stuff."

"Nothing in that house . . ." whispered Odessa.

"Did you go inside?" demanded India.

Luker nodded.

"How did you get inside? I thought the house was locked, I thought—"

"I don't know. I don't know if I opened the window or went through the front door. That part is blank. The next thing I remember I'm standing at the foot of the table, and I'm holding on to the corners of the tablecloth and my fingernails are tearing holes in the cloth because it's so old and rotten."

"And those two men—"

"All of a sudden one of 'em jumps up on the table and I see he's got feet. No legs, just feet, coming right out of his hips, and he starts walking down the table toward me, kicking all the dishes and crystal out of the way. Everything breaks on the floor. And the other one hops down off the chair and starts coming round the table toward me and he's carrying a dinner plate like he wants me to do something with it. They're still whispering but I'm so scared I can't understand what they're saying. The last thing I remember is feeling sand hit me in the face—sand that was sprayed out of their mouths."

"But you got out," protested India. "You must have done something to get away. I mean, you're here now, you didn't get hurt. They obviously didn't kill you or anything."

Luker looked askance. "I dream about it," he said softly.

"They must have let you go on purpose," India persisted. "They had you there, they must have had a reason for letting you go."

"India, you're trying to make sense out of all this, and the point is there isn't any sense to it. I don't know if I'm remembering a dream or something that really happened. And that's *all* I remember. And when I remember it's not like I'm remembering what I saw, it's like I'm playing over a little film. I see me as a little boy walking along the beach, me as a little boy standing on the verandah and looking in the window. I've got camera angles and cuts and everything—it's not a real memory any more. I don't know what really happened."

"But things happened to other people too, didn't they?" protested India.

"Something happened to Mary-Scot one time, and she told me but I didn't believe it—I don't think I even believe it now. And Martha-Ann died, but really probably Martha-Ann just drowned. Nothing's ever happened to anybody really. Marian Savage never believed in any of it. You couldn't even talk to her about it, she'd just walk away."

"But something happened to me!" protested India, her ferocity dissipated and nothing but trembling weakness in its place.

Luker glanced away and clinked the ice in his glass. "It's never happened before, though. No one ever got touched by one of the spirits before. I always thought they were essentially visual manifestations—and of course I can accept anything that's essentially visual. You just pretend it's a photograph, that's all. An image is an image is an image. An image can shock you, but it can't hurt you."

India lifted her pants leg and showed her bruises.

CHAPTER 24

India could not get her father to continue the conversation of that afternoon. She wanted to hear Mary-Scot's story, but Odessa wouldn't let him tell it. "You heard enough, child. You heard plenty," the black woman said. Next morning Leigh took India out shopping with her, promising many new clothes and lunch at the best restaurant in town, while Luker spent this time at the home of a man he had gone to high school with. They had not been friends at the time particularly, but now they found they had several important things in common. Luker returned to the Small House refreshed in spirit.

Dauphin telephoned, wanting not Leigh, but Luker himself.

"Listen," said Dauphin, "I'm over here at your mama and daddy's, and you better come over."

"Why?" asked Luker grimly, knowing.

"Lawton's been talking to Big Barbara, and Big Barbara's upset."

"What'd he say to her?"

"Luker, listen, why don't you just come on over? If Leigh's there, tell her to come too."

Luker knew that his mother was drunk; nothing else could account for the guarded, tragic tone of Dauphin's voice. He left the house immediately, and gave word to the two maids that Leigh was to go to her mother's house as soon as she and India returned.

Big Barbara was in a bad way. When Dauphin got to her she had already consumed five large glasses of bourbon. She was morose and distracted, and the unaccustomed liquor was making her ill. She wept because Dauphin saw her throwing up in the bathroom.

When Luker arrived, Big Barbara said that Lawton had left an hour before. She had no idea where he was now.

Big Barbara sat sobbing at the foot of her bed. Luker brought a wetted cloth from the bathroom and tenderly wiped her face with it. Dauphin wanted to leave, but neither Luker nor Big Barbara would let him. He must sit opposite them, no matter his discomfort.

"Oh, y'all!" sobbed Big Barbara. "I'm so ashamed! Y'all worked so hard on me down at Beldame and I thought I was doing so good, and I'm back in Mobile for one day and look at me! I couldn't walk a straight line if it was painted with creosote! I don't know what y'all must think of me!"

"We don't think anything of you at all," said Dauphin soothingly.

"What did Lawton say to you, Barbara?" asked her son.

Big Barbara hiccoughed convulsively until Luker must beat her on the back.

"Luker," she wailed, "you were right and I was wrong!"

"He said he was gone divorce you," said Luker.

"When he came down to Beldame, he told me everything was gone be just fine from now on. And I come back today and he says he's changed his mind, and he's gone get a divorce come hell or high water. I told him I had quit drinking, and he said it didn't make any difference."

"Barbara," said Luker, "something must have happened to make him change his mind like that. What happened?"

"Oh, nothing! Not much!" she cried. "We were at that old luncheon this afternoon, Rotary Club or Jay-Cees or something, and I was sitting across from Lawton and everybody was talking about filing income tax forms. That's all they ever talk about at things like that—taxes and going out hunting. And everybody was complaining how much they had to pay, and I just said, 'Well y'all ought to come over and get some lessons from Lawton—you ought to see what Lawton can do with a 1040 form and a sharpened pencil . . .' That's all I said, honest to goodness. But Lawton looks at me like I was testifying against him on the stand.

"And then we get in the car right afterwards—he wouldn't even let me stay for dessert—and he starts talking about signing the papers again. He says that it doesn't matter—drunk or sober I cain't keep my mouth shut. I said, 'Lawton, are you telling me that you cheat on your taxes, really and truly?!' And he said, 'Of course, what did you think?' And I said, 'Well, I didn't think *that*! I was just saying how good I thought you were at itemizing deductions on the long form'—and honest to goodness, that's all I *did* mean by it! But he wouldn't listen, he dropped me off here and then said he was going to the lawyer's and I didn't even have to wave good-bye!"

"So you came in the house and ran to the liquor cabinet," said Luker grimly.

"Didn't even take off my shoes first," sighed Big Barbara. "In the car Lawton said to me there was no such thing as a former alcoholic, there was only alcoholics that *told* people they weren't drinking any more. He said I could have the house if I put up maps in the hall so I wouldn't get lost after my fourth bottle of the day."

"Barbara," said Luker, "you should have jabbed your fingers between his ribs and ripped his liver out—that's what I would have done. Then he wouldn't have to worry about a divorce."

"I know," sighed Big Barbara, "but I just wasn't thinking straight. But y'all know what?"

"What?" said Dauphin earnestly.

"I think," she said, looking at her son and son-in-law carefully and laying a hand on Luker's thigh as she spoke, "I think I just may let Lawton go on and get his divorce. I think it might do *me* as much good as it would him."

Luker didn't trust himself to say anything and just whistled.

"You think—" began Dauphin, then left off for he did not know what he had wished to say.

"And I tell you why I decided. It was because of this drinking thing. I'm not thinking straight now, but all yesterday and this morning too, I was. I wasn't even thinking about bourbon—alcohol didn't cross my mind. At breakfast this morning I drank a whole glass of grapefruit juice and it wasn't till after I had put it down in the sink that I thought about putting vodka in it. And if that's not being cured, I don't know what is!"

Dauphin nodded encouragingly.

"I was cured, I told myself. And you know, I did the whole thing for Lawton, because Lawton didn't want to be married to a drunk. I didn't care about me, in fact I *liked* getting sloshed every afternoon, and—I hate to say it—but it didn't really matter what all you children thought about it. If it had been just you telling me to stop, I wouldn't have listened. I'd have gone to a wedding reception with a necklace of pint bottles around my neck—I didn't care what other people thought! But Lawton didn't want to be married to a drunk, so I decided to give it up. All the time I was suffering at Beldame, I'd be thinking, now I'm not drinking any more, I'm not an alcoholic any more, and when I go back to Lawton, he'll say to me, 'Good God, Big Barbara, you can drive my chariot!' But it turned out that Lawton just didn't want to be married to me! He let me off in the driveway and he said, 'Go on inside and have a drink, Barbara, it'll make you feel better!'"

Dauphin shook his head as if in disbelief—though knowing Lawton McCray, the story was not at all improbable.

"You should have taken a spoon," said Luker, "and dug his eyes right out of their sockets."

"And I thought, if that's all that he cares about me, then there's nothing that I can do. Let him have his grass widow! If he gets elected to Congress, she's gone have a hard time in Washington, D.C. Grass widows with kinky hair don't have any idea what it takes to throw on a party for people in politics—they've got no idea!"

"You're gone live with Leigh and me," said Dauphin. "You let Lawton have everything he wants, I don't want you worrying about . . . things." He meant money. "Leigh and I are gone take care of you, we can all move into the Great House. Oh, we're all gone have such a good time from now on, I know it!"

"Now that you're finally sober again you can see what a turd that man is," said Luker.

"India picks up her language from you," said Big Barbara with a sigh. "Lawton says he's got papers he wants me to sign at Ward Benson's on Wednesday. He wants an uncontested divorce. I'm gone tell him I'd be happy to sign the divorce papers, I'd be happy to sign over to him all the stock I have in the fertilizer company, and all those mineral rights I have in Covington County. I'm gone tell him he can have everything—*except Beldame*. Isn't that smart of me, y'all! Beldame's gone be mine. That's the only thing I'm gone take. And that way we're not gone ever have to worry about the oil company coming in. I'll give Lawton the world and my good name, just as long as I can keep Beldame. I'll sign the papers on Wednesday morning, and we'll be back at Beldame by Wednesday night."

Through her weeping, Big Barbara smiled with anticipation of this happy prospect.

CHAPTER 25

Lawton McCray had kept company with Lula Pearl Thorndike for nine years—she had once been poor, but oil had been discovered in her modest pecan orchard only three weeks after Hurricane Clara had ripped up and carried away all but four of her trees. It was she who had put him on to the business of trying to sell Beldame by introducing him to Sonny Joe Black, the oil company's principal local representative for the Alabama panhandle. Sonny Joe Black told Lawton, in strictest confidence, of the proposed drilling off the Baldwin County coast.

Lawton expressed more than casual interest in the proposed transaction, and after conferring with his superiors, Sonny Joe Black brought back an offer of $2 million for Beldame, to be divided equally between him and Dauphin Savage. Dauphin Savage would officially be told, by the oil company, that Lawton had received a much smaller price for his much smaller parcel of land. In fact, the oil company would be paying Lawton for his assistance in the transacting of the sale. A million dollars would allow Lawton McCray to diversify his business; a man at his age, fifty-three, ought to be in something more than just fertilizer.

The first meeting that Lawton had held to introduce Sonny Joe Black to Dauphin had gone well he thought, but the second, in Mobile when Dauphin had come back for the reading of Marian Savage's will, had been disappointingly inconclusive. It didn't look as if Dauphin were going to give up the houses without a fight. Lawton had hinted to his son-in-law that he was just waiting for a high enough price to be named before he sold the house that he and Big Barbara owned, but this was bluff. The oil company could do nothing without the entire spit of land called Beldame; Lawton's deed included the house, but only fifty feet of beachfront and five thousand square feet of property. The rest was owned and controlled by Dauphin.

Lawton had a further disappointment in his plans. After she had talked to Dauphin and Luker in the afternoon, Big Barbara told her husband that she was going to allow him his divorce—on the sole condition that the house at Beldame came to her. "We got these scales here," said Big Barbara, "and on one side we're gone put in Beldame—that's my side. And on your side, we're gone put Lula Pearl Thorndike and about four hundred tons of fertilizer . . ."

Lawton saw that he had made a grievous error in pushing for the divorce from Big Barbara—for it worked as a lever only when she didn't want to be separated from him. And actually to lose his influential wife, his rich daughter and son-in-law, and Beldame too would be more than carelessness—it might be a fatal mistake. That night, when he contemplated the fireworks that burst over the battleship *Alabama* at a harborside festival, Lawton thought of a way of reconciling his family to the sale of Beldame.

He'd just burn the three houses down.

And once he had determined on a course, Lawton McCray wasn't a man to allow the grass to grow under his feet. Second thoughts and indecision were crippling to a man who wanted to get ahead in this world, and he had long ago learned the value of immediate action. He wondered, for a time, whether he ought not confide in Sonny Joe Black, who stood to make a great deal in bonuses and commissions if the sale of Beldame were effected. With this promise of wealth, Sonny Joe might well be persuaded into a little helpful conspiracy. But upon further reflection, Lawton determined to reveal his plans to no one. Arson was a desperate piece of business, and to admit his culpability even to one so congenial as Sonny Joe Black was doubtless an imprudence. He would do the job alone.

Two hours before the dawning of Independence Day Lawton arrived at the fertilizer plant in Belforest. There he placed five five-gallon cans of gasoline into the trunk of the Continental, and drove north to Bay Minette. He parked the Continental in the driveway of Lula Pearl Thorndike's big new house, and transferred the cans of gasoline to the back of a small pickup truck that was left over from Lula Pearl's days as a meager pecan-farmer; these he covered with a tarpaulin so that those who passed him on the highway would not know his cargo. For this operation, Lula Pearl herself came out; but she was better trained than Big Barbara, and did not pry.

"You coming back?" she ventured to ask when he was pulling out of the driveway.

"I got to," he replied. "I'm leaving the car here. Listen, Lula Pearl," he said, looking at her sternly, "I was here all last night. I got here 'bout midnight, and I'm gone be here till 'bout noon. You understand what I'm saying?"

"Every word, Lawton, every word," she replied, and turned uneasily to go back into her house.

The drive to Gulf Shores took an hour and a quarter. Inside the cab of the truck, Lawton wore dark mirrored sunglasses and a wide-brimmed hat. Despite his nervous haste, he did not allow himself to drive quickly, and took a residential route through Loxley, Robertsdale, and Foley, in order to avoid the police stations of those small towns. He was known. It was scarcely six o'clock when he reached Gulf Shores, and no one in that resort community was up yet. No one saw him turn onto the Dixie Graves Parkway. He left the highway before he got to Gasque and skirted those houses altogether; the pickup truck was not so happy a vehicle on sand as were Dauphin's jeep and Big Barbara's Scout, and twice it got stuck. Though the cab of the truck was air-conditioned, and the day was not yet hot, Lawton broke out into a terrible sweat. He couldn't relish being mired near Beldame carrying a load of gasoline in a truck that didn't even belong to him.

The tide was high when he finally reached the place, and thirty feet of rapidly moving water separated him from Beldame; but for this he was prepared. Also in the back of the truck was a small fishing boat equipped with an outboard motor. With some difficulty he took this out himself and carefully tied its towline to the bumper of the truck before he placed it in the channel. The water that poured in from the Gulf and made St. Elmo's Lagoon even saltier than it already was knocked the boat violently about.

Lawton loaded the five five-gallon cans, and at the last eased himself into the boat. He started the motor, untied the line, and the little boat, rocking precariously, was suddenly shot forward into St. Elmo's Lagoon. Away from the channel, the lagoon was calm—*dead* was perhaps a more accurate description of its reflective lifeless surface—and in five minutes more, he had pulled up before the Savage house. He had brought the tarpaulin with him and covered the cans of gasoline; though he was certain no one remained here, he felt he could not be too careful in such a matter as this. He pulled the boat onto the shore of the lagoon and tied it to a post that had been planted for that purpose.

He stood in the yard between the three houses and called out. No one answered. He banged on the back doors of both the Savage and the McCray houses. No one came to him. He looked from one to the other trying to decide which he should burn first.

Having no experience in arson other than the igniting of an overinsured two-family black tenement he had owned some years back, he decided that it might be as well to begin with the third house. It was in poorer repair than the others—it was in no repair at all, properly speaking—and there would be no wonder to investigators, if any investigators bothered to visit so remote a place as Beldame, that the house had caught sudden fire. In fact, looking at it now, Lawton idly wondered that the house looked as good as it did. His house here and the Savages' had required a little work every summer: some part of the roof replaced, windows reglazed, verandah supports shored up, rotten boards taken up and new ones put down. But that third house looked not much worse than the other two, and he was certain that no work had been done on it since he started to come to Beldame in 1951. Well, he considered, probably it was the sand that preserved it.

From the boat he took a can of gasoline and brought it on to the side verandah of the third house. He could empty one can in the third house, two in the Savage house, and two in his own; that ought to do it. Once the houses started to burn, nothing could save them. There wasn't a fire department within thirty miles. People on vacation at the beach—and they, nearest neighbors at Gasque, were six miles away—probably weren't even up yet, and even if they were couldn't do much more than come and watch. It was possible that some small fishing boat out in the Gulf would see the smoke and report it to the Coast Guard, but by that time Lawton would be long gone. In all probability the houses would burn to the ground and leave nothing but rubble and sheets of dirty glass where the sand had melted and been fused by the heat. Even if it were ever discovered that the houses had been deliberately set afire, Lawton had provided himself an alibi: Lula Pearl would say he had spent the night with her, and his unmistakable pink Continental in the front yard would be noticed by the nosy and early-rising neighbors. It was a perfect plan, and would bear him the perfect fruit of a million dollars in the bank.

He wished that he remembered more about this business; he hadn't set fire to a house in more than twenty years. He couldn't, for instance, recall how far he ought to stand back when he was tossing a lighted match into a pool of spilled gasoline, nor estimate the time it took a small and unhampered fire to gain irreversible control over a wooden structure. He needed to get away as soon as possible, and yet must make certain that the fires in the houses would not simply burn out. He was fortunate, he considered, in having a dry morning, though for this particular project he might have ordered a hotter one.

He was also nervous about this very beginning. He unscrewed the cap from the can, but hesitated simply to slosh the flammable liquid over the verandah boards. He didn't like the look of the dune at the end: what if a few of the boards were consumed and the porch gave way? The dune of sand might then rush forward and smother the fire that he had so carefully set; that obviously wouldn't do. It would be much better if the fire began in one of the back rooms of the third house, and ate inward, outward, and upward all at once. To his surprise the back door of the place was unlocked; he was pleased that he did not have to break a window. He walked through the kitchen, placed the can of gasoline on the table, and peered into the dining room. That room, at the front of the house, was almost filled with sand. It would do no good to start the fire there.

It occurred then to Lawton that he might as well take a look over the entire place. He had never been inside the house before and was somewhat curious to know what it contained; he was surprised, in fact, that none of them had ever bothered to explore it. And, since the floor plan of this house was identical to the other two, he might get some idea, looking over the rooms, of the best place to set his fire in all three. It might, for instance, make sense to pour the gasoline over the bedroom floors, thereby igniting both the first and second stories at once.

Leaving the can then on the kitchen table—he was surprised to find no dust there but only a fine layer of white sand—he went back through the dining room and struggled through the double doors into the living room, crunching on the glass of a lamp that had toppled over and smashed on the floor. He climbed the stairs carefully, fearful of rotten wood and not wanting to slip on the fine, undisturbed layers of white sand that coated each step.

On the second floor, three of the bedrooms' doors were closed but the fourth stood ajar, and the early morning sun through the eastern window lighted the landing dimly. Lawton pushed this door open farther and peered inside. The room was furnished in an old-fashioned manner, and the sand had penetrated here too, leaving everything beneath a ghostly layer of fine whiteness. He tried the other doors on the landing: all were unlocked, and each opened onto an old-fashioned, fully furnished bedroom. Only in the last had the sand entered to any great extent. The dune had built up against one of the windows outside, crashed through the lower panes and spilled a few cubic yards of sand onto the floor. He decided that the kitchen was the best place to begin after all; fire burned upward, so it made most sense to begin low. He turned around in the hallway, glancing once more into each of the four bedrooms and was about to descend the stairs into the living room, when a slight noise—like that of a single footfall—arrested his step and momentarily stopped his heart.

The sound had come from the third floor.

It was nothing, of course: the house reacting to the presence of a human being after thirty years of bearing no weight other than that of the gradually intruding sand. But he must see all the same, and more carefully than he had ascended from the first to the second floors did he now tread the steps that went from the second to the third.

There was no door here, only an opening in the floor. He paused with only his head through the trap and looked about. He could count six three-quarter-width beds, each with a rotting blue spread whose fringe dragged the floor. On all the boards the white sand lay a quarter-inch deep and entirely undisturbed. Nothing had trod that floor in thirty years, and he had heard the house resettling. Through the windows at either end of the room he could see only the bluish-white cloudless sky.

He turned himself around on the step and was about to descend again with complete reassurance—his thought was that he might not have to waste even the whole of a single five-gallon can on this house—when a small ring of metal, about two inches in diameter, rolled off one of the beds and onto the floor, in front of him. It left a little pattern of arcs as it spun to rest in the sand. Still thinking of the apportionment of the gasoline between the three houses, Lawton picked up the ring of metal: it was a chased silver bracelet, and evidently meant for a very tiny arm.

And it was warm.

He reached out for the spread of the bed from which the bracelet had fallen and jerked at it. The rotten fringe went to gritty dust in his hands.

With two high strides he mounted the rest of the steps into the room; he turned around, so little expecting to find anything there that he did not even bother to brace himself.

He should have. On the third bed from the western side of the house, cradled in a depression of sand, lay an infant. It was alive, but ought not to have been. It was large and fleshy with misshapen clawlike hands and feet. Its head, rather like Lawton's own, with a massive slack jaw and no chin to speak of, had indentations of flesh where there ought to have been eyes and a lump of unopened flesh where there ought to have been a nose. Its hair was red and thick with feverish perspiration. It breathed noisily through its mouth, which was filled with small fine teeth, and flailed its thick extremities in the sand that lay an inch deep on the bed. When it turned over in its pointless convulsive movement, Lawton saw that it had a rotting vestigial tail. He had never even dreamed of such a monstrosity.

What was perhaps most terrible about the creature was its dress: a dainty blue starched pinafore, though stained with urine and feces. There were rings on its misshapen fingers and bracelets on its thick wrists. Its monstrously large ears had been pierced and set with gold earrings. A single strand of pearls was chokingly embedded in the scaly flesh of its neck.

Its noisy breathing and movement left off of a sudden. It turned that unseeing head toward Lawton, and its arms reached out to him. Its mouth moved as if to form words.

Stuttering his terror, Lawton raced down the stairs to the second floor landing. He had put his foot on the first step leading down to the first floor, when he was suddenly stopped by what he saw through the window of the bedroom opposite. This looked out on to the Gulf of Mexico, and on the Gulf—about a hundred yards from shore—was a small sailboat with a bright red and orange sail. A man stood in the boat, holding jauntily on to the mast, and waved toward Beldame. *To me*, thought Lawton, and with that thought lost his balance. He slipped on the sand that covered the stairs, and fell all the way to the bottom. His leg was caught underneath him, and he registered first the loud cracking of his thigh and only then the excruciating pain.

He knew that his leg was broken—and broken badly. Still he must get out of that house: he'd crawl out, crawl to the boat, head around the lagoon and out to the Gulf. In the Gulf he'd ditch all but one can of the gasoline, and that would get him to Gulf Shores. He did not allow to intrude into his plans the thought of what that thing upstairs might be and how it might have got there; he was almost glad for the pain in his leg for it distracted him from his real fear.

Sweating and trying desperately to suppress his groaning—he did not want to give away his position to that thing on the third floor, for though it had appeared helpless, he could not think it altogether without power—Lawton crawled toward the narrow space that led from the living room into the dining room. He was lucky that there was no blood, he considered, though already his thigh was swollen to twice its normal size, and every step that he dragged it represented a long bolt of pain.

At last he reached the doorway and rested a moment on the mound of sand that lay a foot deep there; it was more comfortable than the bare floor. He wiped the perspiration from his brow and was carefully maneuvering himself to get through that narrow space when he heard another noise from upstairs. There were footsteps, slow and quiet but not surreptitious. Lawton tried to scramble through the doorway, but his leg was caught against the frame; he pulled and nearly fainted from the pain that tore up through his body. His head fell back but was cushioned by the sand; now he heard the doors of the bedrooms pushed farther open. Footsteps entered each of the rooms, again without hurry or secretiveness.

He was being sought for.

Once more Lawton pulled, and as he reeled and cried out in his agony, his broken leg came free of the doorjamb and he was wholly into the dining room. He heard the footsteps, light footsteps really, not those of an adult—and certainly not those of that monster on the third floor. Someone had been hiding on the third floor, someone had been beneath one of the beds, peering at him through the rotting blue fringe of one of those bedspreads. Under which bed had he been concealed, Lawton wondered, as he pulled himself toward the swinging kitchen door. Why hadn't he looked under the beds? *Someone* had to have put that thing there, it certainly wasn't capable of locomotion itself. *Someone*—

He knew when the footsteps reached the bottom of the stairs. There was a difference in the sound. He thrust one palm out toward the swinging door and pushed it, but he kept his eyes on the narrow vista he had of the living room. The kitchen door swung back and slapped against his open hand.

In the opening of the living room door stood a young black girl, whom he vaguely recognized. He felt suddenly reassured. "Martha-Ann," he said, her name coming to him suddenly—as names often came happily to politicians—"Martha-Ann, listen, I think I've done gone and broke my leg here. You got to—"

Odessa's Martha-Ann had died in 1969, drowned in St. Elmo's Lagoon. Lawton reached out for the swinging door again; when he pushed it open he could see into the kitchen. The sun through the windows gleamed on the gasoline can on the great table in the center of the room.

Martha-Ann smiled at him, but didn't come into the dining room. In fact, she turned to the side and disappeared. Lawton crawled toward the kitchen and got his shoulder against the door.

Martha-Ann stood in the doorway again. In her arms, pressed against her shoulder, was the thing that had been laid on the bed on the third floor. Martha-Ann's small body was tilted with the weight of it, but still she smiled. Her mouth opened wide in a grin and white sand spilled out of it over the back of the monster's pinafore. She brushed it off carefully with her tender black hand. She stooped and laid the monster belly-down in the sand, just inside the dining room. It began to crawl back toward her, but she turned it around, and pushed it gently in Lawton's direction.

It came carefully along the edge of the dune of sand. The hard yellow nails of its misshapen feet and the numerous rings and bracelets on its clawed hands clacked against the wooden floor as it approached. It hadn't eyes to see with and no nostrils to smell, but its ears were very large; and though Lawton McCray tried to remain still, it quickly found him out by his irregular, frightened breath.

PART IV

EYESIGHT

CHAPTER 26

On the morning of July Fourth Big Barbara McCray waited for her husband in vain. He had so often stood her up, however, that she did not attach much significance to his failure to appear. At the luncheon for local Republican dignitaries she sat across from Leigh and Dauphin, but it was Luker who took the place at her right-hand side. It was also without Lawton that the entire family attended a semiformal reception of the Mobile County Horticultural Society at Bellingrath Gardens that afternoon. Lawton wasn't present that evening at supper either, when Leigh announced to the family that she was pregnant.

At this unexpected news Big Barbara screamed and leaped up from the table to embrace her daughter. Odessa came too and hugged Dauphin. Luker and India, who had no particular liking for infants and—despite their own relationship—could not understand the joys of parenthood and childhood, added feebler congratulations.

"I just don't believe it," cried Big Barbara when she finally sat down again, "a child and a divorce in the same year! What family is as lucky as ours?" No news could have improved Big Barbara's spirits so much as that of Leigh's pregnancy. She was full of plans for the baby and for themselves; now she wondered how she could have lived with Lawton all these years. "Just him and me and not a baby in sight." On the spot she decided that when they returned from Beldame at the end of the summer, she wouldn't be returning to Lawton, but would move directly into the Small House—this assuming, of course, that now they were about to make a family, Leigh and Dauphin would remove to the mansion.

"Mama," laughed Leigh, "you got to take care of me. You're moving in with us." And Big Barbara blushed with pleasure at the invitation that Dauphin so warmly seconded.

"Well, y'all," said Leigh then, "when are we going back to Beldame? Up to me, I'd go tomorrow."

"Tomorrow's fine," said Big Barbara. "Sooner the better. I want everything to be just like it was before."

Leigh knew hesitation in her brother. "Luker," she said, "you don't have to go back to New York yet, do you?"

He shook his head. "Depends on India. If she wants to go to Beldame I'll go too, but if she doesn't, then we'll go back to the city." He glanced warily at his daughter, knowing what she had suffered her last night there.

"India," cried Big Barbara, "you got to go with us! It wouldn't be the same! And Thursday is Dauphin's birthday—we *got* to celebrate!"

"Barbara," said Dauphin, "y'ought to let India make up her own mind. She already knows how much we want her."

India sat very still in her chair and contemplated the happiness of those around her. In a measured voice she said; "This is what we'll do: We'll go back tomorrow, but I'm not going to promise I'll stay. Luker's got to promise that when I say I'm ready to leave, we'll leave that very minute. Luker, will you promise me that?"

Luker nodded, and no one thought it strange that a thirteen-year-old girl should have the power to impose such restrictions.

⋆   ⋆   ⋆

It was puzzling that Lawton didn't return that evening either, and Big Barbara even contemplated telephoning Lula Pearl Thorndike to see if anything were the matter. They all had been invited to a party at the Civic Center, but feeling that they had done their duty by Lawton all day long without his having the decency even to make an appearance, decided not to go. Big Barbara went home to pack and Leigh accompanied her. Luker went out looking for a decent bar and someone to lead astray, and India was left at the Small House alone with Dauphin. She watched television while he wrote checks at the long trestle table. When he had finished he sat down on the sofa next to her.

India looked meaningfully at Dauphin, and turned off the sound on the set. "Tell me what happened to your sister," she said.

"Mary-Scot?"

India nodded.

Dauphin laughed. "You just been sitting here waiting for me to get through so you could make me answer your question, haven't you?"

India nodded again. "Luker told me what happened to him in the third house, and he said something happened to your sister too—but he wouldn't say what it was. What was it?"

Dauphin was serious. "I don't think I ought to tell you."

"Why not?"

He shifted uncomfortably. "Why don't you ask Odessa?"

"She wouldn't tell me either. Tell me, Dauphin."

"Well, you know I had a brother—Darnley."

"He drowned. Like Martha-Ann."

"He went out in his boat, and he never came back," said Dauphin. "We *guess* he drowned—of course, what else could have happened to him?"

"So?"

"So that was about thirteen years ago. It was in the summer—August. Mary-Scot was about twelve or thirteen I guess. It happened at Beldame. He went out sailing one day and he just never came back. Coast Guard went out after him, whole shrimp fleet along the Alabama coast was looking for him—nobody ever saw him. Never found the boat. And Mama was always looking out the window, watching for Darnley's sail. We stayed at Beldame later that year than we ever had before. We stayed there till October first. On October first we were all packed up to go, but we couldn't find Mary-Scot. We called and called, and she didn't come. We looked in all the rooms of both houses and we couldn't find her, and Mama was mad—Mama could get real mad—and she started up the jeep and started blowing the horn and saying we were just gone leave her there. But Mary-Scot still didn't come . . ."

"Where was she?" asked India, knowing.

"She was in the third house. Mama and I never would have

looked there, 'cause we knew Mary-Scot was so scared of the place. But Odessa climbed in through one of the side windows—she had to break a pane to do it, but she went right on inside. Mary-Scot was in one of the bedrooms upstairs, in a chifforobe. She was passed out."

"What was she doing there? Was she playing hide-and-seek or something?"

Dauphin shook his head. "The chifforobe was locked—from the outside. And Odessa never did find the key. She had to break it open with a hammer and a table knife."

"Wait a minute. If it was closed and Mary-Scot was passed out, how'd Odessa know she was in there?"

Dauphin shrugged, as if to say, *How does Odessa know anything like that?*

"So who locked her in?" India persisted.

"Darnley," said Dauphin as if it were something India ought to have guessed. "Odessa got her out, and we just put her in the jeep and we took off. She didn't want to talk about it, she wouldn't say a word about what happened. But one time she told Odessa what had happened, and Odessa told me. Mary-Scot was looking out of the window of her room, and she saw somebody walking around inside the third house. She couldn't see who it was, just that it was a man. Then he came to the window and waved at her, and she saw it was Darnley, so she thinks he's come back and is hiding in the third house so he can jump out and surprise everybody. But he never comes out, so Mary-Scot goes around the third house, and up on the porch and right up to the window. And there's Darnley—he was twenty when he died—looking right out at her. But his eyes aren't right. They're black and they've got white pupils, so Mary-Scot knows something's wrong and she's about to run away, but next thing she knows she's inside the house and Darnley's got his hands all over her and he's saying things to her and sand is coming out of his mouth. She tried to get away, but she couldn't."

"And?"

"And that's all she remembered. She didn't come to till we were all the way to Gasque."

"When did Mary-Scot decide to join the convent?" India asked suspiciously.

"Oh, long 'bout that same time I guess. But Mary-Scot had always been big on confession . . ."

Next morning Big Barbara went to the lawyer's where she argued with him a while about the terms of the divorce settlement and wondered with him why Lawton failed to appear when the matter was of such importance. Leigh was at the pharmacy having prescriptions filled and looking over tanning lotions; Luker was at a bookstore buying indiscriminately; and Dauphin was at his office giving discouraging answers to Sonny Joe Black over the telephone. India and Odessa, who had long been packed and ready to go, sat in the swing suspended from one of the great arms of the live oak in the backyard of the Small House. It was dark here and cool, and the damp wind whipped at the Spanish moss that hung from the branches.

"Glad you decided to go back, child," said Odessa after a few moments of silence. "Don't do you no good to be scared. No good at all."

"But I am scared," said India. "I don't want to go back to Beldame. I think it's probably *stupid* to go back there, in fact. I feel like it's just sitting there *waiting* for me to come back, and all three houses are going to jump up and fall right on top of me."

Odessa shrugged. "You wasn't hurt the last time, and we're not gone be going inside that house no more, I can tell you that right now."

India laughed shortly. Her entering the third house again seemed as likely as being inducted tomorrow into the Baseball Hall of Fame. "Odessa, when I think about that house now and what happened when we went inside, all I can think is that it was a nightmare, and that none of it happened. Even the scratches on my leg—I tell myself they weren't real. It's like I could explain all that away, and I think I could go back now and look at that house, and say, 'Boy, did I have a nightmare about that place!'"

"That's right," said Odessa encouragingly. "That's what you ought to be saying."

"But then I look at those pictures—"

"Don't look at 'em!"

"—and those things don't go away. They're on the film, they

were in the camera. I was looking at 'em yesterday—"

"Ought to throw them things out!"

"—but before I took 'em out of the drawer, I said to myself, 'There's nothing on those pictures. I'll take 'em out and look at 'em again, and I won't see anything. It's all just shadows and reflections.' But then I took 'em out and I looked at 'em, and everything was still there, and it wasn't just shadows and reflections. And when I think about those pictures, then I'm afraid to go back. Listen, Odessa, I want you to tell me something—"

"What?"

"And tell me the truth. Is it dangerous for us to go there?"

"Been going to Beldame for thirty-five years," said Odessa evasively.

"Yes, I know, and eleven years ago your daughter was killed there. Your only daughter was killed inside the third house. I know that for a fact, Odessa, and don't try to tell me anything different. And last night I got Dauphin to tell me what happened to Mary-Scot. She would have suffocated inside that chifforobe if you hadn't gotten her out. And how did you know she was in there? If it was closed and locked and she wasn't making any noise?"

Odessa didn't answer the question. "Listen," she said, eyeing the Mercedes which was just then pulling into the long gravel driveway, "you don't need to ask me all this. They's no need. You don't think I'd let you go back there if I thought something bad was gone happen to you, do you, child?"

"No," said India.

"Child," said Odessa. She stood out of the swing and turned her back on Luker and Dauphin, who were getting out of the car a dozen yards away. Odessa loomed before India, blocking sight of her father and uncle. "If anything happens at Beldame," said Odessa, looking down at India sternly, "I want you to do something . . ."

"What?" said India, craning around to catch sight of her father. Odessa's tone and her suggestion that something else might happen made her fearful.

"If anything happens," Odessa said in a low voice, "*eat my eyes* . . ."

"What?" demanded India in a hissing whisper. Her father and

Dauphin were coming nearer. She longed for their protection. Odessa stepped closer to India, pressing her hands behind her to signal the two men to keep back. "What does that mean?" cried India desperately. "What do you—"

"If anything happens," Odessa repeated slowly, nodding her head with terrible significance, "*eat my eyes* . . ."

CHAPTER 27

It was sprinkling as they loaded the car. When Dauphin drove by Lula Pearl's house in Bay Minette to satisfy Big Barbara that Lawton was indeed there, the pink Continental in the red clay driveway was spattered with mud thrown up by the increasing shower. The drive through Baldwin County took half an hour longer than usual because of the severity of the rain. It churned the fields, beating down plants that were more than two feet high; it created vast pools across the road that threatened to drown the motor when Dauphin splashed through; in Loxley and Robertsdale and Foley the rain brought people to the screen doors of their houses and the front doors of their shops to watch the water pour off the roofs and awnings in thunderous destructive cascades. When they got near the coast the rain was even heavier, though five miles back that had seemed an impossibility; but its effects on the landscape were less severe. Any amount of water will fall on sandy ground and be immediately absorbed, and scrub pine may be blasted on the Day of Judgment, but nothing will harm it until then.

Along the peninsula they could scarcely discern where the rain left off and the Gulf began, so heavy was the water that spilled from the black sky above. Big Barbara turned around in the front seat and changed her mind every five minutes whether it was better or worse for a pregnant woman to wear a safety belt, and they had reached Gasque without mishap before she ever fell into any permanent decision. India and Odessa stood talking behind one of the closed doors of the garage of the abandoned gas station, staring out through the grimy windows; Luker sat inside the Fairlane, looking intently at a magazine that lay open on the seat beside him.

"Last week it was all heat," said Big Barbara, "so I guess this week it's gone be all rain."

"Don't say that," said India. "I've never seen rain like this. Will it turn into a hurricane?"

"Not the season yet," said Leigh. "It'll let up any minute now."

And so it did, in a quarter of an hour, to the extent that they were able to move the luggage from the Fairlane and the Mercedes into the Scout and the jeep. They waited ten minutes more, in which time the storm—which oddly had been without either thunder or lightning—abated further.

As they drove off in the two sand vehicles, India had the uneasy feeling that the curtain of water had drawn aside only momentarily, just long enough for them to get to Beldame. As soon as they crossed the channel she felt certain that the rain would begin again and they would be cut off entirely.

Though it was low tide, the channel was filled with rainwater to some depth; the jeep and the Scout splashed through and wet everyone's feet. This made little difference, however, since they were soaked anyway; when there was so much water in the atmosphere, metal roofs and raised windows could not insure dryness. As they neared the houses, India watched Odessa intently, hoping to discover by the black woman's expression whether things in Beldame were *all right.*

India proudly considered that she had developed a little intuition of her own. Before this summer she had never before admitted the possibility of anything existing that was paranormal, supernatural. Oh, of course there was ESP and psychokinesis, what they studied in Russia and North Carolina. These things she had known about since *Weekly Reader* days, but such things had nothing to do with Luker and India McCray and West Seventy-fourth Street in Manhattan. But Beldame was definitely out of kilter with the rest of the world. Something was at Beldame that ought not be there and India was sure that thing had never made an appearance at the laboratories in North Carolina and Russia. She had sensed it, she had heard it, seen it, even *felt* it—but still she did not entirely believe in it.

Certainly she did not think that Odessa's ideas were entirely accurate. Odessa didn't think straight, that was a fact. Odessa's ideas were confused and contradictory, and she said this and that about the third house, and this and that taken together didn't make an ounce of sense. There was something to it, of course, but not what Odessa suggested. India suspected that it was indeed the ghost of Martha-Ann inside the house, and that was all. Lots of houses had ghosts, she supposed—people had done research. Even the *Encyclopaedia Britannica* had an article on ghosts—so that was probably what it was. A decent exorcism would dissolve Martha-Ann, and all this business about Elementals and *"eat my eyes"*—whatever *that* meant—was a lot of confused hocus-pocus. Odessa couldn't help it. What with segregation and an illiberal state legislature, she had never had the educational benefits that India herself had enjoyed; it was even possible, she considered with a shudder, that Odessa had not finished high school. She meant to ask her.

But if India chose to discount Odessa's theories about the unreal occupants of the third house, she yet trusted the black woman's sensibilities. Odessa would feel these things before and more surely than India herself. India suspected that the third house was not always operative in the matter of ghosts and spirits—that at times it was relatively benign. Perhaps it was a matter of the tides or the phases of the moon or large-scale weather patterns. In any case, she hoped that this second part of their vacation would coincide with a period of low activity in the third house, and though the unnaturally heavy rain didn't augur well, it was with this hope that she searched Odessa's face.

In it she could read nothing, and Odessa refused to understand India's prods and winks. At last, when India was helping take groceries into the Savage kitchen, she stopped and asked Odessa directly, "Listen, is everything all right?"

Odessa shrugged.

"You know what I mean," persisted India. "You should be able to feel something. I want to know what you feel. Is everything all right or are we all going to be in trouble again?"

"I don't feel nothing," said Odessa at last. "When there's rain like this, when it's being like it's been today, I cain't feel nothing."

But next day, even India could sense the change that had come over Beldame. The rain had let off just at suppertime the night before. The moon had reached full on July second and was now on the wane; it shone through India's bedroom window and lighted the foot of her bed. Dauphin's thirtieth birthday had dawned splendidly clear; the lagoon was higher than usual and a dirty chain of detritus marked high tide on the beach, but there were no other indications of the previous day's storm. All the sand that had been blown against the house in months previous and lodged in crevices and dried against the windows had been washed away by the rain.

The third house appeared to be no more than it was: a house which hadn't been lived in or repaired in three decades or more, and which moreover was being slowly consumed by a dune of sand. It looked somber and picturesque, but not menacing. India even smiled when Luker dared her to peer through a window; but even the bright day and her intuition that nothing was wrong any more (perhaps Martha-Ann slept in the lagoon now) would not permit her to go so far as that. "Oh, no," she said to her father with a smile, "I've had just about enough of that place."

"But you're not afraid any more?"

"I'm not afraid *today*."

"What about last night?"

India shook her head. "I thought I was going to be scared, but I didn't even have any bad dreams. I got up once to go to the bathroom, and when I came back in I went to the window and looked out at it. And it was just a house. You know what I think the problem was?"

"What?" asked Luker.

"I think I got cabin fever. But it had never happened to me before, so I didn't know what to expect. I just went a little crazy, that's all. I *remember* what happened inside the third house, but it's as if it *didn't* happen because it was so crazy. Luker, I'm glad you raised me in New York. Alabama's weird."

"Yes," he laughed. "I guess it is. But what about the pictures? How do you explain those?" India's cavalier attitude toward the third house encouraged Luker to bring her fears into discussion, in hope they would all be dismissed.

"I don't know." India shrugged. "It was just one of those things,

I guess. I guess that part of it won't ever be explained. I left 'em at the Small House, I didn't see any point in bringing 'em back here just to scare myself. But when we go back to the city, what you'll do is blow them up real big, and we'll see what's really there. You can't really tell anything from a print that's only three by five. You'll make some eleven-by-fourteens and then we'll see what we can make of it. Till then, I just won't think about it."

"Very sensible," said Luker. He stooped and pushed aside the thick narrow leaves in a bed of greenery in the yard. "That's odd," he said.

"What is?" asked India.

"This day lily. It's already withering."

"I thought lilies died and then came back the next year."

"They do. But not till much later in the season, and certainly not till after they've bloomed. But this day lily is definitely withering."

"Maybe something got in the roots. It's a wonder they live at all in all this sand."

Luker pulled the plant up and examined the roots for insects or scale. "The roots look fine," he said. He knocked the heavy pendulous bulbs against his jeans to dislodge the loose soil. He tore off the dried and yellow foliage and tossed it aside.

"You think it's the bulb?" asked India.

Luker peeled away several of the cloves that surrounded the central bulb of the plant then, pressing his thumbnails into the top of the bulb, gently pried it apart.

It split suddenly open in his hand, and dry white sand spilled out over his bare feet.

CHAPTER 28

While India and her father were examining the strangely decayed lily in the yard, Dauphin and Odessa sat on the front porch of the McCray house, in the swing out of which Marian Savage had tumbled dead. "I'm glad we came back," said Dauphin.

"You got no work to keep you in Mobile?"

"Oh, 'course I got work. Always got work, Odessa, you know that. But cain't work all your life. If I was to go back to Mobile and work, I wouldn't 'complish a thing in this world 'cept make more money. And what's the point of having money 'cept to enjoy yourself and take care of the people you like taking care of?"

"I don't know," said Odessa, "I don't know nothing 'bout having money. Never had any, never gone have any."

"You got what Mama left you."

"That's right, but long as I work for you and Miz Leigh, I'm not gone touch that money. I'm counting on you taking care of it for me."

"You bet I will. Odessa, you know me and you know I'm not good for much. But there's one thing I can do, and that's make money. I turn round and there's money hitting me on the head. I don't hardly know where it comes from. I tell you, it's a good thing there's *something* I can do. I'll take care of your money and 'fore you know it, you gone have it rolling out your ears."

Odessa shrugged, lowered her head and rubbed the back of her neck. "Anyway," she said, "it's good you come back out here. You was always happiest at Beldame."

"I know it. Ever since I was little. Times I think I'm happy at Beldame and unhappy everywhere else. I'm sitting in that office in Mobile or I'm driving down the road or I'm listening to somebody talk to me about how much money I ought to lend him, and I think, 'Lord how I wish I was at Beldame right this very minute sitting on the porch talking to Odessa or Leigh or Big Barbara or somebody!' I'm just surprised I wasn't born here! 'Cause if I had my way I'd live here and I'd die here and I'd be buried here! When I get to heaven I hope there's a corner of it off somewhere that's so much like Beldame I cain't even tell the difference! I could sit on this front porch in heaven till the stars come falling down! You ever read in your Bible there's some place like Beldame?"

"Well," said Odessa, "there's 'many mansions'—so maybe they got a few of 'em on a beach somewhere for you and me."

"Oh, that's bound to be right, Odessa, that's just bound to be what it's like! Mama and Darnley are probably sitting there waiting for me right now. Darnley's out in the water—he's probably got a boat just like the one he had here—and Mama's lying down upstairs. And at supper they sit down and they say to each other, 'Where's Dauphin? Where's Odessa?' Listen, Odessa, you think they're thinking about us? You think they remember who they left behind?"

"No way to know what the dead are thinking 'bout," said Odessa. "Probably a good thing they not letting us know either."

And as they talked, a little breeze blew up from the west; and the wind sifted a glaze of white sand over the porch of the McCray house.

Leigh and Big Barbara had been in the living room of the Savage house all that morning, happily talking over their plans for the coming months.

"Mama," said Leigh, "I am so glad you are taking this thing the way you are!"

"You mean your baby! Well of course I'm happy about it, we're all—"

"No, Mama, I'm talking about your divorce. Luker and I were sure you were gone be upset, and have setbacks and get hooked on pills and I don't know what all, but here you are talking like you cain't wait to get out of your house and into mine!"

"Well I cain't!"

"Well good!" laughed Leigh. "I tell you it's gone be such a help to me to have you around. I've never had a baby and you've had two, you know what they look like and all that. I don't know a thing about 'em, and I don't think I want to know, either. Mama, when I go into labor I want you and Dauphin right there in the operating room. Dauphin's gone hold my hand and soon as that baby comes out, you're gone grab it up and run off with it. I don't even want to see it till it starts first grade!"

"Leigh!" cried Big Barbara, "you're talking about your child! You're gone love that baby! You're not gone want to let it out of your sight!"

"You take a Polaroid and send it to me and I'll stick it in my billfold. I think I'm gone go live with Luker and India till that child is six years old."

"Luker doesn't want you living with him," said Big Barbara with a laugh.

"I know," said Leigh. "There's a lot about Luker's life that he doesn't tell us about."

"Shoot! And don't I know it!" cried Luker's mother. "And I don't want to know it either! But I tell you something. India knows all about it. She's been talking to me—we've gotten real close in the time we've spent here together—and times are she starts to say something and then she holds back. That child has probably seen things and heard things that you and I never even read in those magazines you look at under the hair dryer."

They had wandered out on to the porch, but found that all the furniture there was filled with sand. Pools of it had gathered in the seats of the rockers and the glider and no amount of shaking and tilting could get rid of it all. "Yesterday that rain washed all the sand away, and it was so clean this morning! Now look at it! We're leaving prints everywhere we walk on this porch! Mama, let's walk down by the lagoon, and see how high the channel is now."

Big Barbara assented to this and mother and daughter strolled along the level shore of St. Elmo's Lagoon, their conversation reverting to the limitless ramifications of Big Barbara's divorce and Leigh's pregnancy. When they reached the point where the houses were small and indistinct behind them and the channel was just visible before them, growing wider and deeper as the tide rose, Big Barbara pointed suddenly at the surface of the lagoon.

"Law have mercy!" she cried.

"What, Mama?" said Leigh. "What is it?"

"Look there, Leigh. Don't you see it?"

Leigh shook her head, and her mother grabbed her arm and pulled her a few steps over. "You can't see anything from there because of the reflection on the water, but look here, look what's under there!"

What Leigh could see when she moved nearer her mother was a submerged truck. All they could actually make out was the top of the cab: the windshield, back window, and part of the door frame. The rest was buried in the sandy bottom of the lagoon.

"I never!" exclaimed Leigh. "Mama, have you ever noticed that before?"

"Well of course I haven't! 'Cause it wasn't there before! I would have noticed a truck in the middle of the lagoon if it had been there, don't you think?"

"I don't know. Except, Mama, it must have been there a long time to get buried like that."

"Then we would have noticed, wouldn't we? 'Course maybe it *was* buried a long time ago and that storm yesterday disturbed it and it came floating up."

"Oh, I bet that's what happened," said Leigh. "Listen, why don't I swim out there and look inside?" Leigh was already in her bathing suit.

"Oh, no!" protested Big Barbara. "Don't do any such of a thing! What if there's somebody under the dashboard, you don't want to be diving under the water and then run into a dead body or something. Maybe long time ago somebody got drunk on the Dixie Graves Parkway and lost his way and drove right in the lagoon—the highway's not more than a few hundred yards on the other side—drove right in and sank in and drowned. And nobody ever found out about it. If somebody drowned in that truck he's probably still in there."

"Then I sure am *not* gone swim out there and look in!"

"But I don't imagine that's what happened, really. It was probably kids, some kids from Gulf Shores getting drunk on Saturday night and driving a truck in the lagoon because it was a fun thing to do. It could have happened on July Fourth for all we know. I always suspected that bottom was soft. Poor old Martha-Ann! No wonder we never found her!"

Half an hour later the entire population of Beldame was standing on the edge of St. Elmo's Lagoon, peering into the water at the submerged truck. As soon as they had returned to the house, Leigh and Big Barbara had sought out the others and told them what they had seen. The discovery of a submerged truck in the lagoon was of more than sufficient novelty to draw them all out. The six of them in concert could make no better sense of it than Big Barbara and Leigh alone had managed. The truck had been there a long time, or it had not; there was a corpse in the cab, or there was not; someone had best swim out to look inside, or they had better remain on the shore. In any case, further investigation was put off until tomorrow—or the day after.

To India's eye, Odessa appeared disturbed by the discovery of the vehicle in the lagoon; and India then partook of some of that discomfort. However, when India asked Odessa if the truck *meant* anything, Odessa replied, "Mean, child? Trucks don't mean nothing to me."

"But wasn't it just an accident-like? What else could it be?"

Odessa whispered so that none of the others heard her words: "D'you see, child, how far out that truck was in the lagoon? Didn't nobody drive it out there. Somebody had, it would have gone down a lot nearer the other side—and it's right out there in the middle! Something *put* that truck there, put it where we'd see it and know it *wasn't* no accident—"

"But *why?*" demanded India.

Odessa shrugged and would say nothing more.

The curious discovery provided their conversation through most of supper—smothered steak and little white peas and fried okra. These were Dauphin's favorites, prepared in honor of his birthday. It was only toward dessert—a German chocolate cake with thirty candles that Odessa had baked before they left Mobile—that they returned to the infinitely interesting topic of the dissolution of the marriage of Lawton and Big Barbara McCray. They were all for it, and even Odessa, as she brought out a tray with five cups of coffee on it, ventured her approval in this manner: "Miz Barbara, I tell you, we sure are gone be glad to have you at the Great House. It was always a happy place when you was visiting Miz Marian there . . ."

Luker and India drank their coffee black; Big Barbara and Leigh and Dauphin took sugar and milk. Luker and India sipped at theirs and repeated the family litany of gratitude, "Sure was good, Odessa."

To which Odessa replied invariably, "Glad y'all enjoyed it."

Leigh took a swallow of her coffee and immediately spat it out all over her cake. "Good lord!" she cried, opened her mouth wide and energetically wiped the back of her hand across it.

"What's wrong?" cried Dauphin.

"Leigh?" said Big Barbara.

"Don't taste that coffee!"

"Nothing wrong with it," said India. "Mine's fine."

"So's mine," said Luker.

"It's got *sand* in it,' said Leigh. "I got a mouthful of sand! It's all over my teeth and my gums and I hate it!" She got up hurriedly and ran into the kitchen. In another moment they heard the running water from the sink.

"Ugh!" said Dauphin, tasting his own coffee, "it *is* full of sand."

"Must be in the sugar," said India, and they all stared suspiciously at the sugar bowl. Luker reached over and stirred the sugar with a wetted finger; he brought it to his mouth and tasted. "Almost all sand," he said with a grimace and wiped his tongue on his napkin. Beldame sand was *that* pure and white, that it could be easily confused with sugar. "Who's the joker?"

They looked at one another silently. Odessa sat in a chair against the kitchen wall; in a moment Leigh reappeared in the doorway. With no one speaking and everyone still for the first time that evening, another sound came to the fore.

"What's that?" whispered Big Barbara.

"Shhh!" said Luker.

They were silent again. There was a hiss, irregular and not loud, and it seemed to come from all sides of them.

They had begun supper when it was still fairly light out, but now it was deep dusk, and the room was dark and shadowed around them. At Luker's request Odessa switched on the overhead light.

From all the corners and moldings of the room fell a fine spray of white sand. It had piled up in a white line all around the baseboards. From the doorway Leigh looked up, and grains of sand spilled painfully into her eyes; sand spilled from the ceiling into Odessa's hair and she vigorously brushed it out again. When they hurried toward the table in the center of the room their sandals scraped across the glaze of sand that coated the floor.

CHAPTER 29

Sand had got not only into the sugar bowl, but into all the cabinets of the kitchen and spilled out when Odessa pulled open the doors. Even closed canisters of coffee and tea had got sand into them and the sink drains were stopped with sand. It was mounding at the ends of counters. Coffee and Dauphin's cake were abandoned on the table, and it didn't even seem worthwhile to clear the dishes.

Leigh and Dauphin went upstairs and found that in their bedroom, where the windows had been opened, sand had blown through the screens and left everything gritty and white. Leigh was glad that she had not yet unpacked, for all the clothes that had been left in the closed drawers of the dresser and chifforobe were filled with sand as well. In the other bedrooms sand had blown against the windows, leaving them opaque as with frost. They did not get up to the third floor at all, for the sand was falling so thickly there it proved an absolute shower down the staircase. The sound of falling sand, never letting up as they went room to room, was disheartening.

Luker moved around the first floor, shutting the windows and closing the doors. He stood on a tall chair and examined the ceiling all around, but could not discover how the sand gained entrance. It spilled from everywhere, and seemed to increase in intensity with every passing minute.

India and Big Barbara sat together very still on the wicker sofa in the living room, pulled away from the wall, and looked about them with distress. At last India stood, placed a newspaper over her head to protect her from the pure white and heavy sand that spilled from the molding and went to the window that opened onto the verandah. "It's piling up fast out there," she said quietly to Big Barbara.

"But how *can* it?" demanded her grandmother. "Like the house decided to fall apart just *bang*! And it's not like there's wind outside either."

"The house isn't falling apart," said India. "It's just beginning to fill up with sand, like the third house."

"But that was natural," argued Big Barbara. "That happened natural-like. The dune built up and took over. Look round India, the sand's coming out of everywhere here! How'd sand get in the sugar bowl when it had a cover on it? Where's all this sand coming from?"

India shrugged. "You think it's just this house, or is it the other one too?"

"Oh, lord!" cried Big Barbara, considering this dreadful possibility for the first time. "But we ought to go see!" She rose, but India took her hand.

"No, don't go yet. Don't go outside until . . ."

"Till what?" demanded Big Barbara.

India hesitated. ". . . Till we ask Odessa if it's all right."

Big Barbara considered this, then to India's surprise, agreed without demur or discussion. "Odessa!" she called out, and in another moment Odessa appeared from the kitchen.

"Odessa," said Big Barbara, "something awful is happening in this house—" As if in ironic emphasis there was a loud electric sputtering from the kitchen; when Odessa opened the door, they discovered that some of the electrical wiring had been short-circuited.

"Luker! Dauphin!" called Big Barbara. "Leigh! Y'all come on down here! Don't stay upstairs!" Big Barbara feared electricity.

"Something awful is happening," said India, repeating her grandmother's words. In places the sand was two inches deep along the baseboards. However, despite the sand's falling from the ceiling to the floor all around, there was no dust in the room: the sand was of uniformly heavy grains. "It would probably be best if we got out of here, but I don't know if it would be safe to leave. Odessa, is it all right to go outside?"

Luker and Dauphin heard this question from the staircase. Leigh just behind them asked, "What'd India say?" But for Leigh the question need not be put: she carried her suitcase in her hand.

Odessa said, "Ain't safe nowhere tonight."

The other lights on the first floor sputtered out, and their only illumination was from the bulb on the landing above.

"Y'all come on," said Big Barbara, and went for the door. Luker grabbed India's hand and dragged her forward. Dauphin and Leigh clattered down the stairs and followed after, brushing the sand from their hair. "Odessa," cried Leigh, when the black woman appeared to hesitate, "we need you, come on!"

There was a shower of sand spilling off the roof like rainwater, and they held their hands above their heads when they jumped through it. The six ran to the other side of the yard before turning to look back at the house they had just abandoned.

The night was dark, the waning moon hid behind a cloud. The Gulf waves broke behind them, but louder than that was the sizzle of falling sand before them. A single light was on in Leigh and Dauphin's bedroom, shaking and dim behind the curtain of showering sand. Soon it too shorted out and the house sizzled in darkness.

"I don't understand what's happening there," said Big Barbara. "Where's that sand coming from? It's not blowing in or anything. It's falling down from everywhere, it's like it's being poured down from the sky. Maybe if there was more light we could see something. If it was day maybe we could see what's happening. Is our place all right, you think?" She turned toward the McCray house.

"Yes," said Luker, "I don't hear anything. All the sand is at the Savage house, thank God."

"What's causing it?" said Leigh. "I mean, this is . . ." She trailed off in consternation.

Dauphin ran into the McCray house and fetched a flashlight. When he came out again he advanced across the yard and shone its feeble beam over the back porch and kitchen doorway. The sand was falling more heavily still but because it now accumulated on its own hills and mounds, rather than on bare wooden surfaces, it was quieter than before. "Y'all, I'm gone walk around the other side, and see—"

"Don't!" cried Leigh and "Don't do that, Mr. Dauphin," said Odessa.

"All right," he said, and retreated. "Maybe we ought to go inside."

"Maybe we ought to get the fuck out of this place altogether," suggested Luker.

"We cain't, it's getting to be high tide," said Dauphin. "It won't be low tide till almost morning."

"*Then* we're going for sure," said Leigh. "I'm not waiting round here to get covered up with sand in my bed, buried alive under a dune."

There was unanimity: they would leave at dawn, when the channel was sufficiently shallow for the two vehicles to get across.

"I hate this," whispered Leigh as they turned all to go into the McCray house. "I don't understand why it had to happen all of a sudden-like when we were just sitting there talking at the supper table."

"I think this is Lawton's doing," said Luker. "It's like him. Destroy the houses so that we *have* to sell the place."

"Luker!" exclaimed Big Barbara. "What are you saying? Are you saying that your father is sitting up on the roof with a pail and a shovel, pouring down sand on us? Is that what you're saying?"

Luker shook his head. "No, no—it's just that it's *like* something he'd do." He looked back sadly at the Savage house from the safety of McCray porch. "It took the sand twenty years to get at the third house, and this one's going to be gone in a single night. Dauphin," he said, turning to his brother-in-law, "maybe . . ."

Dauphin shook his head: there was no question but that the house had been usurped forever, and that for that loss there was no comfort.

Luker was the first inside the McCray house; he immediately started to lower all the windows in the house, and Dauphin followed him room to room, checking for accumulations of sand in the corners and along the baseboards. Odessa was the last; she looked once to the Savage house and attended to its sibilant destruction. She glanced at the lowering presence of the third house, an undifferentiated square façade of black against a black sky, stepped inside and locked the door.

CHAPTER 30

"I'm not going to bed," said Big Barbara. "I have no intention of lying down tonight. I'm gone sit right here on this sofa and wait for the sun and I would very much appreciate it if one or two of you would sit up with me."

They all would, they declared. No one could imagine sleeping. Big Barbara and Luker and India had packed their things, and brought down their suitcases and put them beside the kitchen door. Except for what was in Leigh's bag that she rescued from the Savage house, everything else there was abandoned. They sat at the Gulf end of the living room, and drew the curtains across the windows that looked out on the Savage house—though it was impossible to see what was happening there in the black night.

They simply waited, and when they talked it was not of Big Barbara's divorce or Leigh's pregnancy, but simply of the sand. In the silences they listened for the soft hissing fall that they feared would start up around them here. Odessa, after having set up several kerosene lamps against the possibility of electrical shortage here as well, sat a little apart, with her chin on the back of her fisted hand.

At midnight Luker said quietly, "We all saw what happened across the way and we all know what happened wasn't natural and cain't be explained. It wasn't the wind because there wasn't any wind. And it wasn't just sand that had always been caught in the timbers because why would it have all come out at once? And how did it get into things that were tight closed? Odessa said it even got in the boxes of food that we brought with us from Mobile yesterday."

"What are you saying to us?" asked Dauphin.

"I'm saying what happened wasn't natural."

"Good lord, Luker!" cried Leigh. "Don't you think we know that! Whoever heard of sand falling out of the ceiling?"

"But even if it wasn't natural," Luker went on, "I think something caused it, isn't that right, Odessa?"

Odessa raised her fist and that nodded her head.

"Now y'all," said Luker, reverting into a Southern accent to a degree that India had never before heard, "the night 'fore we left here to go back to Mobile, India and Odessa went in the third house—"

Here came exclamations of wonder and surprise from Big Barbara, Dauphin, and Leigh.

"—and fools they were to do it!" judged Luker.

"Out of their minds!" cried Big Barbara.

"Crazy!" said Leigh.

"—but they did," said Luker. "And there was something there. There was something upstairs and there was something downstairs and something grabbed India's leg. Show 'em your leg, India."

India raised her pants' leg and exhibited her ankle, which still was not quite healed.

"What was it?" demanded Dauphin. "Maybe it was some kind of animal that was living in the sand. Maybe it was a mole or a 'coon or something like that. Maybe it was a big crab—"

"It pushed over a table," said India calmly, "and then it reached out and it wrapped its fingers around my leg, and if Odessa hadn't been there it would have pulled me under."

"Now Odessa, is this true?" said Big Barbara, though she didn't for a minute doubt her granddaughter's word in this matter.

"Yes, ma'am," said Odessa.

"So what I think," said Luker after a moment, "is that whatever was in the third house and tried to get India is what's causing the sand in the Savage house. That's what I think."

"Whatever was in the third house has now got in my house," said Dauphin. "That's what you think?"

Luker nodded, and so did Odessa.

"Yes," said Leigh, "I think so too. I didn't say anything about it, but the other day I was over there lying down in the hammock all by myself and I heard these footsteps upstairs and I thought it was Odessa making the beds. I went upstairs and it wasn't Odessa and it wasn't even our bedroom, the footsteps were in that bedroom that nobody ever goes in, except the floor was covered with sand and nobody had been in there for five years. I guess that's when they got in. That's why I wouldn't sleep over there that last night. I don't know *why* we came back here. You'd think we'd have more sense . . ."

"Yeah, you'd think . . ." agreed Dauphin with a confused shake of his head.

"So what do we do now?" said Big Barbara.

"Just what we planned," replied Luker. "Get out of here soon as the tide goes out. Get out of here and never come back. Odessa, you think it'll ever be safe to come back to Beldame?"

"I don't know," she said. Her mouth was set and her hands gesticulated helplessly. Then she spoke at surprising length: "I don't know why y'all all the time coming to me with questions when I don't know much more than any of y'all. When I knew something was gone happen I did what I could to protect us. I gave us special things to eat—India helped me there. Those rolls I made one day, those were s'posed to protect us, but they didn't do no good. Then I went and locked doors, and I'm staying up half the night looking out the window and watching 'gainst anything happening, and it don't do no good. I keep on thinking, 'They in the third house, they not go bother us long as we keep out of the way,' but that's not how they thinking about things. Un-unh. They do what they want. They filling up the Savage house with sand, maybe they want the Savage house to live in. Maybe they got more of 'em and they need the room, maybe they's only one of 'em and always been just one, and he done got tired of the third house and wants to move. Maybe they's three and maybe they's seven, and maybe they's upstairs in *this* house right now. I'm tired of trying to think 'em out and I'm not no good at it anyway. Maybe they want revenge, 'cept nobody's done 'em no harm. Probably they just mean. Probably that's it, they just mean and want to cause grief."

"Are they gone let us out of here?" asked Big Barbara softly.

"Miz Barbara, I just got through saying I didn't know nothing! If I knew something to keep us safe, don't you think I'd be doing it right now? I used to think I knew what would keep us safe, but I don't any more. One time they gone see a cross and they gone back off, and next time they just gone laugh and make you feel like a fool. That's *real* meanness in a spirit. And I tell you, they laughing now, they laughing real hard."

Despite general agreement that it was high tide, Luker tried to persuade Dauphin to walk with him to the channel—perhaps they would find that it was shallow enough still to get across. But Leigh would not hear of Dauphin's leaving her, and Dauphin felt such pride in being wanted by his wife that he couldn't be persuaded. India couldn't be parted from Odessa, and finally it was Big Barbara who accompanied Luker.

They went out the front of the house and walked along the Gulf;

they could not see the Savage house except as a piece of blackness that blocked out the phosphorescence of St. Elmo's Lagoon, and the noise of the breakers covered the sound of the falling sand. In less than ten minutes they had reached the channel and found that it flowed deep and swift from the Gulf into the lagoon. With the moon still beneath clouds, the night was intensely dark and even the Gulf white-caps scarcely showed. There was only the shining green surface of the lagoon. "Maybe we can wade across," said Luker.

"No!" cried Big Barbara, and tugged at her son's hand. "Luker, you know what that channel's like—drag you under, drag you out! Remember what happened to poor old Martha-Ann!"

"Martha-Ann didn't die in the channel."

"Luker, you been coming to Beldame for thirty years, and you ought to know enough by now to know you cain't cross the channel 'cept when it's low tide."

"No, I don't know that, all I know is everybody *says* you cain't."

"There's reasons."

"What?"

"I don't know, but Luker, things are going wrong right and left out here, and now is not the time to start making 'speriments."

Luker pulled his mother closer to the channel. "Let me just stick my foot in, see how swift the water is—" He plunged his foot into the water, screamed, and fell back on to the ground. He pushed his foot beneath the sand.

"Luker, what's wrong!"

"It's hot! It's fucking hot! That's what's the matter, and I burned my fucking toes off. Goddamn . . ."

Big Barbara knelt at the edge of the channel; it was so dark she could not really see the surface of the water and lowered a single finger slowly. The tip of it touched scalding water, and she withdrew it precipitously.

"Well, I never!" she cried. "Gulf water never gets like this, Luker!"

"'Course not!"

They were silent for a moment.

"Let's try the Gulf," said Big Barbara. Luker limped along on his scalded foot, and Big Barbara dragged him. They stood on the shore and the waves broke coolly against their legs. "Well this is all right," she said. "I cain't see it but I think the channel begins 'bout twenty yards down there. Why don't we go down and see where the hot water begins, maybe we can get across there . . ."

Luker agreed, and they walked along through half a foot of water. As they went the Gulf grew appreciably warmer and by the time that they were perhaps five yards away from the place where the Gulf flowed across Beldame to St. Elmo's Lagoon, their legs were beginning to burn. A wave broke high against them and the water was as hot as that with which Odessa washed dishes. They ran frantically for the shore.

When they had recovered a little, Big Barbara said, "Is there any point in going over to the lagoon?"

"No," said Luker, "even I know enough not to go out in the lagoon. At night? And that truck—"

"Forgot about the truck," sighed Big Barbara. "We're gone be here all night, looks like."

"Looks like."

When they returned to the McCray house, they fashioned an excuse no one believed as to why their clothes were wet. It had seemed pointless to tell of the supernaturally heated water. Just that the channel was too high to be crossed—though this information came not unexpected—dragged on everyone's spirit, and they sat for a long while without saying anything.

The hours would be long until morning. India fell asleep with her head in Luker's lap, and he slept with his head tilted back against the sofa. Leigh and Big Barbara lay in the hammocks that were strung in the living room. Indicative of the severity of the night was the fact that Odessa went so far as to draw her rocking chair close beside Dauphin's on the braided rug, and then they rocked together, in rhythm and in silence.

CHAPTER 31

They had waited in the dark. They had listened in the dark for the sound of sand falling in the house until at last sleep had overcome them. When India awakened it was to find the room still dark, and herself blind in that darkness. Her head still rested on Luker's lap, and she felt rather than heard his breath. Behind the couch, she heard Big Barbara mumbling in the hammock—she dreamed, and not pleasantly. Leigh's breathing was rough too.

When her eyes had accustomed to the lack of light, India saw that Dauphin still slept in the motionless rocker. His hand, which had held Odessa's, dangled at the side. The black woman was not to be seen. India rose from the sofa without waking her father and went through the dining room into the kitchen. On the kitchen table were two of the three kerosene lamps which Odessa had prepared, set at lowest illumination. Through the panes of the back door India looked out at the Savage house.

The pallid light of the waning moon allowed her to make out the perfect cone of sand that had covered it—as if the house had been a tiny model at the bottom of an hourglass. India had seen such a figure in a museum of *curiosa* in the Catskills. The turrets over the verandah stuck out on the far side, the tops of the second floor gables were visible, and the third floor with the window of Odessa's room were still uncovered. But everything else, including all the doors and first-floor windows, had been neatly, malevolently, expeditiously inhumed.

It was no dune that had enveloped the Savage house, for dunes are irregular things shaped by wind and tide; and this was a cold geometric figure that had chosen to manifest itself in the same space occupied by the Savage house. Its circumference precisely intersected the four corners of the building. The peak of the cone was invisible but was obviously set somewhere on the third floor: as if all these hundreds of tons of sand had spilled out from another dimension of space and through a single point in the air above Odessa's bed.

"So that's what they wanted," India said in a whisper to herself, "all the time what they wanted was Dauphin's house. Well, now they've got it! I just wish I had my camera . . ."

India cautiously opened the back door, pushed on the screen, and then stood on the back steps of the house. She peered into the blackness, hoping to find Odessa. Seeing no one, hearing nothing, she walked out into the yard, nearer to the Savage house. Now she could see that the cone of sand was still growing, most quickly where the sand spilled through the open windows of the house.

Loose grains—millions altogether—tumbled silently from the top all the way down to the base.

India thought suddenly that Odessa might only have gone upstairs from the living room, and that her own venturing outside was therefore a piece of arrant stupidity. She turned to hurry back into the safety of the McCray house, when her eyes scanned over the façade of the third house—in comparison to the sudden tumultuous destruction of the Savage house, its familiar lowering presence had seemed almost innocuous.

A dull glow of amber light was visible in the living room window. It wavered, then disappeared. A moment later it showed itself again, but fainter, in both windows of the second floor.

With the kerosene lamp, Odessa had entered the third house and gone upstairs.

India didn't allow herself the leisure to think. She ran back to the McCray house and quietly re-entered the kitchen. From the drawer beside the sink, she took out a sharp carving knife and a meat cleaver—she found that these two weapons only might be carried in a single hand. From the table she lifted one of the kerosene lamps and increased its illumination to exactly what she judged Odessa's to have been. She slipped out into the yard, and unhesitatingly ran to the back door of the third house.

Inside, she shone her lamp on the red-painted can on the kitchen table. It had not been there the week before, and India was certain as well that it had not been among the items which had been brought to Beldame from Mobile. She sniffed the air, and judged the can had gasoline in it. She pushed it an inch or two across the sand-covered table, and found it full.

India looked around her, with less fear this time than the other. After all, now she *knew* that there was something unhuman inside the third house—at least she did not fear the surprise of *that* discovery.

India moved into the dining room, holding her knife and cleaver raised but without any tenseness apparent in her posture. She took a moment and curiously looked around in order to make out, by the superior light afforded by the lamp, those objects and shapes which had mystified her before. One bulky piece was evidently a large sideboard: a high carved corner remained uncovered and it bore on a tiny shelf a little silver pot, black with tarnish. The pictures on the walls were black with rot behind their glass, but looking closely at one that was on the near wall she could see that they formed a set depicting the important municipal structures of Mobile. A dinner plate of white bone china with a gold rim had been knocked off the table and was only half-buried in the sand. India reached down and picked it up. In the center was painted the initial *S*. The dune had come in farther, India judged, for the spilling sand had erased the prints that she and Odessa must have left the previous Tuesday night. Recalling suddenly the hallucinatory dinner party her father had once witnessed in that room, India dropped the plate back into the sand.

She jumped through the narrow aperture into the living room. She looked around, automatically cataloging the furniture, mourning the smashed lamp, and backing cautiously away from the dune that lapped toward her from the other end of the room. She searched the base of it for movement, and was prepared to sever the hand from any arm that reached out toward her ankle.

All at once India was overcome with the insanity of having looked over this place as if it were merely the home of one of Luker's new friends which she was visiting for the first time. Something burrowed through that dune toward her, moving slowly so as not to disturb the sand and give away its location. Something else waited for her in one of the four bedrooms upstairs, and it would not be in the bedroom she guessed. And if she stood on the stairs that led to the third floor, something would lean over the edge and peer down at her. And where was Odessa now?

India clattered up the stairs to the second-floor landing, and the white sand flew beneath her bare feet. Whatever was there was most likely to be in the room into which the sand had gained substantial entrance; something else had been in the bedroom that stood catercorner to it. The other two bedrooms were probably benign; their doors India tried first and found them locked.

"Of course," she said to herself aloud, "Odessa locked them the other night." But with that speech came again the thought: *Where is Odessa?*

"Odessa!" she called. Then more bravely and loudly; "Odessa! Where the hell are you?"

Turning the kerosene lamp up high and setting it exactly in the middle of the landing, she tried the door of the bedroom where she and Odessa had heard some heavy piece of furniture pushed up against the door.

The door opened. The piece of furniture had been a small vanity with triptych mirror, and now it was shoved out of the way again. India could see the tracks it had made being pushed about the sandy floor. There were no footprints, however, to show the nature of the creature moving it.

The room was furnished in only a rudimentary fashion; the only thing that stood out to India's occluded mind was a large red vase, which looked shining and clean and even new, placed at the foot of the bed. It stood on a patch of bare floor: the sand beneath it had been swept away.

India held on to the doorknob but turned back toward the landing. "Odessa!" the girl cried again, this time angrily.

There was no answer.

In frustration, India whirled around, lifted the vanity under the left-hand side drawers, and tumbled it over on to the floor. The mirrors smashed. Growling, she pushed the dresser across the sandy floor toward the red vase, but the knob of one of the drawers caught against an uneven board, and on this axis, the dresser simply turned in a circle. In another moment, India was staring into the landing. The door of the room across the way, the only room she had not tried, was now ajar. It had been shut before.

India clambered over the spilled vanity, and ran across the landing; she kicked the door fully open.

This room faced west. Odessa's lamp, dim and flickering, was placed on the dresser and provided but the scantiest illumination of the room. The black woman lay on the floor, on her back, with her head turned toward the window. When India moved forward she could see that Odessa's feet were buried in the dune of sand beneath the window. Haltingly, the black woman was being drawn into it. Her print dress caught on a nail; her back arched a little and then India heard the dress rip. Odessa's body fell back to the floor and her progress into the sand resumed.

Kneeling behind her and snagging her under the arms, India could feel with what surprising force Odessa was being pulled beneath the dune. "Odessa, Odessa," she whispered, "let me—"

The black woman was dead. India could feel that in the inert heaviness of her body, but that was only intuition compared to the proof afforded by the face that was suddenly tilted into the amber light from India's lamp on the landing. The black woman's visage was shiny with welling blood, no longer flowing but squeezed out by India's rough handling. The coagulating blood that had pooled in Odessa's empty eye sockets spilled out on to India's jeans when she suddenly let go the black woman's head.

Three thin arms, smooth and gray and slightly shining in the amber light, were thrust out of the dune. The dead woman's calves were clutched by many thick and nailless fingers. She was pulled beneath the sand more quickly than before.

Appalled, India let go Odessa and scuttled away toward the bed.

The hands soon disappeared back beneath the sand and Odessa was covered to the waist; there was some struggle to pull her all the way under but this failed. She lay still for a moment, then was jerked backwards—evidently by one of the hands thrust up through the sand and grasping the collar of her print dress. Now Odessa lay parallel to the wall, huddled against the dune. The sand began to spill over her. While India watched it was shaken over her face and it soaked up the blood there. It poured into her empty sockets, blackened for only a moment and then was covered with more sand that was white and pure.

India remembered the black woman's iterated injunction: *"Eat my eyes . . ."*

Only one arm lay entirely uncovered and it was thrust out from Odessa's corpse, resting on a bare patch of the rush matting, and convulsively fisted.

On her knees and leaning far forward, India pried apart the dead woman's fingers. Her eyeballs, one of them crushed and bloody and the other intact and still threaded with the optic nerve, lay on her bloody palm.

India took them up.

Odessa's corpse was swallowed like a black beetle into an anthill.

CHAPTER 32

Luker was gradually roused by the rising consciousness of India's absence—her head no longer heavy in his lap. He opened his eyes and looked slowly around. Seeing that Odessa was gone too, Luker guessed what might have become of the black woman and his daughter.

He rose quietly, went over to Dauphin and, clapping his hand over his brother-in-law's mouth, gently shook him. Dauphin rocked suddenly into wakefulness, tripping over a bad dream. Luker pointed to sleeping Big Barbara and Leigh in the hammocks and Dauphin understood the need for silence; he followed Luker into the kitchen.

"I know they've gone in the third house," whispered Luker shaking his head. "Goddamn 'em both, I just wonder whether Odessa took India or India took Odessa. They both got diced mushrooms for brains."

Dauphin was pained. "Why the hell would they go in there?"

"Because they thought they had to, because they thought it was necessary."

"Wait—" whispered Dauphin, who had suddenly remembered why they had all been together in the McCray living room. He went to the kitchen window and stared out at his own house across the yard. "Good God!" he exclaimed, too loudly, when he saw that it had been almost entirely usurped by a perfect cone of sand, gleaming yellowish-white now in the vivid rays of the setting moon and the first purplish-gray light of the dawning day. Already the cone, though it did not yet surmount the house, was higher than any dune that Dauphin had ever seen along the Gulf coast; and its perfect, unhesitating symmetry of form was unsettling, even mocking—as if they were all being dared to think it a natural phenomenon.

It was decidedly *un*natural.

"Oh, shit," whispered Luker when he came to the window. "Oh, shit!"

"You don't think they went back in *there*, do you?" asked
Dauphin, and Luker shook his head.

"They're in the third house. India's an asshole. Last week she got
scared shitless by that place, by something that was in there. She's
not gone let something scare her shitless without a fight. She's too
dumb to do the smart thing and run away. She doesn't believe in
any of this, she doesn't believe it's really happening. She thinks
she's in a fucking dream, a fucking film called *India at the Mouth of
Hell*, and she's gone jump right through the mirror because she's
been fucking telling herself none of it is real!"

"But Odessa's with her," said Dauphin.

"Odessa's no better. Odessa thinks she's gone protect us. If you
ran out of hot water, Dauphin, Odessa'd cut open her wrist and let
you bathe in her blood, you know she would! No matter what she
thought was in that house, she'd walk inside and wrestle it down
to give you time to get away. We got to go in there after 'em."

"Oh, Lord, Luker, I have *never* been inside the third house!"

"I've *got* to go in there after India—that asshole, I ought to
punch her out for a stunt like this. Listen Dauphin, I'm gone go in
there by myself, I'm—"

"No! I'll go with you, I—"

"You go wake up Barbara and Leigh. Then take these suitcases
out to the jeep. Get ready to go. I'm gone go get those two and
drag 'em out, and then we're leaving and we're not waiting for
coffee."

Taking up the third kerosene lamp, Luker went quickly out the
door, and did not look back at Dauphin. He did not look either at
the enormous cone of sand that had eclipsed the Savage house. He
moved slowly through the yard, despite his sense of the necessity of
haste. Something was different in the air of Beldame, something in
its breath that he had never tasted before: a stillness and heaviness
that had nothing to do with temperature or moisture. Astrono-
mers of old had thought that space was filled with a lambent ether
through which the stars and planets swam; and Luker thought he
moved now through just such an ether. It hadn't weight or heat so
much as a charged density that made even the drawing of breath
a difficulty. Holding aloft the lamp, he realized that there was no
dust in the air, no dancing motes. There was no dust at Beldame,

only sand, and that sand so heavy it all sank to the earth—or piled itself mockingly into unnaturally perfect geometric shapes.

The ether gave no real resistance to his movement, not the way wind would have, or water, but still as he mounted the back steps of the third house and reached for the handle of the kitchen door, he had the distinct sensation of parting liquid with his outstretching hand. The door was unlocked and he went inside into the kitchen.

He stared at the can of gasoline on the table and called India's name. There was no answer, and he called Odessa's. His voice rattled the panes in the windows. In the kitchen the air seemed of even greater density than outside.

He went into the dining room and was startled by the extent to which the room had filled with sand; there seemed scarcely room to breathe. He hurried into the living room and called out again for India and Odessa.

He went up the stairs slowly and stood on the landing. One of the bedroom doors was open. He held the lamp high before him, and called his daughter's name.

The room was empty.

His call was echoed from downstairs: "India! Odessa!" in Dauphin's voice.

"I'm up here!" called Luker, and tried the door of the next room. It was unlocked and Luker pushed it open.

Inside the bedroom—the same he had seen in his daughter's photographs—stood India, with one hand on the bedpost. Behind her was the small dune of sand which had broken through the window; and outside the window and over the dune, hung the engorged ocher moon.

"God!" cried Luker, "thank God! India, where's Odessa?"

India looked vaguely around the room, and had not answered when Dauphin appeared panting in the doorway. He was not used to running up stairs. He placed hands on opposite sides of the doorjamb and leaned inside as if fearful of placing a foot within.

"India!" Luker repeated. "Where's Odessa?"

India slowly turned her head toward the dune and the window. When she looked back to her father and her uncle, she said slowly, "Now I can see what she saw."

"Dauphin," said Luker, "I'll check the other two rooms on this floor. You go upstairs, see if Odessa's up there." He reached out, grabbed India's arm, and jerked her toward him, hoping that the small violence would wrench her from her stupor.

"I see—" she began.

"Don't think about what you saw," said Luker, pulling her toward the door. "It wasn't real. Nothing in this house is real. You know that, it's all illusion. Nothing is what it seems—"

He tried the doors on the other rooms on the landing; both were locked. He heard Dauphin's feet on the floor above; he was evidently pushing aside the beds, looking under them.

"India," said Luker, holding her close against his chest, "you've got to tell me where Odessa is! You didn't come in here by yourself, did you?"

She shook her head slowly, loosened herself from her father, and went to the locked door of the room at the southeastern corner of the house. Luker followed. India turned the knob and the door swung open. Inside, on the sandy floor of the room and behind the overturned vanity, stood a large red vase.

India's breath was drawn in sharply; she ran inside, stooped and picked up the vase in her arms, and then smashed it against the foot of the iron bedstead. Sand poured out, and mixed in the sand were disarticulated gray bones and tatters of cloth. India picked up what appeared to be a femur and threw it against the wall, crying out, "Oh, shit! Oh, shit!"

"India!" cried Luker, shocked.

She turned to her father weeping. "Luker! You don't know what's in this house! You don't know! Odessa knew! And now I know, I—"

From upstairs came the terrible noise of a bird beating its wings against the walls. They heard Dauphin cry out inarticulately. Then in a voice imitative of Luker's own came the pronouncement, *"Savage mothers eat their children up!"*

Something was thrown through the window, shattering much glass. Dauphin cried out again, and then something fell heavily to the floor.

"Dauphin!" called Luker, racing out of the room.

"Wait!" cried India. "Wait!" Luker hesitated at the bottom of the stairs; India ran into the bedroom where he had found her, and from the bed took up the knife and the cleaver. The knife she gave her father. "I have to go first," she hissed. "Let me go up there first."

"India," whispered Luker, "do you know what the fuck is up there?"

"Yeah," she said grimly, "I do. I told you, I know what's in this house now."

"Just call him down, just call Dauphin down. Dauphin!" cried Luker. "Are you all right up there? Come on down!"

There was no reply, but while they waited for answer, they made out a dry and furtive rasp.

"What is that?"

"Luker, stay down here," said India, and began to mount the stairs. When she looked back and found that he followed, she did not discourage him further. She went all the way up the stairs and into the room before she looked around.

All six beds had been knocked awry; the window at the northern end had been broken, something thrown through it. The rasp, no longer furtive, came from behind the sixth bed at that end of the room.

"Dauphin!" cried Luker as he rose into the room. "India," he said, "what's making that noise?"

With the cleaver raised, India went boldly toward the broken window. With her free hand she pulled back the last bed in a wide arc.

Luker had been close behind her with the lamp, but he had stopped with horror at what he saw revealed there.

Dauphin lay on the sandy floor, his throat slit open by a triangular shard of glass that was still embedded beneath his ear. His blood had soaked into the sand and formed a large red corona around his head. And on her knees, lapping up the bloody sand at the circumference of the unnatural halo, was Marian Savage. She raised her head and grinned. Her eyes were black with white pupils. Bloody sand spilled from her mouth.

India raised the cleaver swiftly, and brought it down squarely between Marian Savage's neck and shoulder. No blood but only more sand, pure and purely white, sprayed out. Marian Savage jerked and fell over. India wrested the cleaver out and plunged it deep into the woman's belly, cutting through her blue shift—it seemed to have been made of the same material as the bedspreads. A geyser of sand spewed up from the heart of the dead woman, sand that was wet and foul.

"India! Stop!" Luker was terrified and repulsed. He knew that Marian Savage was dead, knew that dead Marian Savage had murdered Dauphin, but still he could not but try to prevent India from destroying the woman. His daughter was grim and maniacal.

India stepped over Dauphin's body calmly and straddled Marian Savage. The woman dug her slender hands into India's ankles, and Luker saw his daughter's blood welling out beneath the dead woman's nails. India had pulled the cleaver free again, and this time she buried it deep in the woman's head; Marian Savage's face was split in half, and India worked the cleaver from side to side, until the halves were turned down to the floor. The sand inside Marian Savage's head was no longer pure and purely white, but gray and damp and lumped. The hands retained their grip on India's ankles, but they had no strength in them now and India carefully disengaged them, and as an afterthought, severed them from the wrists with two vigorous chops that lodged the cleaver in the floor beneath.

From her father India took the knife and methodically slashed through all the remainder of the shuddering body. When at last she stepped back from what was no longer recognizable as dead Marian Savage, bits of dry flesh and shreds of cloth were left, but most lay under a concealing spray of sand. Only the bare feet and severed hands remained whole, and these somehow didn't look real. However, poor Dauphin looked real enough, and India gazed on him pitifully. She stooped and carefully worked the triangle of glass from his neck. "We have to be careful when we lift him," said India matter-of-factly to her horrified father, "because the neck is almost cut through. See how much blood there was! And I've stepped all in it! Look," she said, standing on one bare foot, and exhibiting the sole of the other to Luker, "look how the sand sticks to it!"

Luker was certain that India had lost her mind. She had seen something downstairs that had deranged her—how else to explain her bravery in destroying the thing that had taken the form of Marian Savage? And now here *he* was, on the third floor of a house filled with evil and danger, expected to cart out the corpse of his best friend and protect his injured child. He pulled Dauphin's corpse away from the circle of blood-drenched sand, scattering the remains of what had murdered him.

"Luker! India!" called Big Barbara from outside the house. Luker didn't immediately reply, for he dreaded his mother discovering what had happened. India, however, stepped immediately to the window, and carefully avoiding the broken glass—after all, that was the way Dauphin had died—she craned her head out, and called down: "We're up here! Dauphin and Odessa are dead!"

"India, no!" cried Luker. "You don't want them to come inside this house! Get back!"

India ignored her father, and shouted to be heard over Big Barbara and Leigh's cries. "Stay there! Don't come up!"

"Why did you do that!" hissed Luker when India withdrew from the window. Dauphin's corpse lay on the floor between them. India stooped and closed the dead man's eyes with two fingers.

"Are you going to pretend that he isn't dead? Luker, listen to me and do what I tell you. Odessa is dead, and Dauphin is dead, and I saw what killed 'em."

"That *thing* in the corner. It looked like Marian Savage—"

"No," said India, with a smile. "Remember what you said, it wasn't five minutes ago, 'There's nothing real in this house.' Well, that's right. That wasn't Marian Savage, that wasn't one of the Elementals either. That was just a kind of scarecrow, it was sand and skin and cloth. That's why I could kill it, that's why I could tear it apart. That's what I took my pictures of. But there are things in this house that I *can't* kill with a cleaver, you understand?"

"No," said Luker, "I don't understand. How do you know these things?"

"Odessa knew 'em, but Odessa's dead and now I know 'em. Now listen, Luker, give me that knife and help me get Dauphin up on this bed."

"We got to get him out of here!" said Luker.

"We're not, though," his daughter replied. "We're going to leave him here."

"We cain't do that!"

"We have to," said India. "We can't drive him back to town like this, he's got his throat cut. It doesn't look like he died a natural death. And Odessa's downstairs, buried under about a ton of sand, and she doesn't have—" India broke off. She concluded. "We'd have a hard time explaining what happened to her too."

"But are we gone send the police down here?" her father asked, not even wondering why he should be asking his daughter's advice.

"No," said India.

"What are we gone say then? That Dauphin and Odessa just skipped town together? Do we tell people they went out of town for a while, and then wait seven years and hope everybody forgets that they ever existed? India, you're only thirteen years old, you really think you're smart enough to make decisions like this?"

"Luker, listen, it's not safe to stay in this house. But there's something we have to do before we go."

"What's that?"

India handed her father the carving knife and began to unbutton Dauphin's shirt with trembling bloody fingers. Her manner of calm suddenly altered to one of great agitation. "Hurry!" she cried. "Help me!"

Luker was loath, but India's glare forced his obedience. With their right hands placed on the handle of the carving knife, they plunged it into Dauphin's chest. It hit the sternum and glanced aside, shredding up a long flap of flesh and his right nipple. Luker pulled away, but India commanded him back; this time they turned the blade sideways and pressed it between two ribs to pierce Dauphin Savage's unbeating heart. Blood welled up along the blade. India withdrew the knife and picked up the cleaver with the same hand.

"Now," she said to Luker, "run downstairs, get out of this house. Don't look in any of the bedrooms, just get out—and wait for me three minutes."

"What if you haven't come out?"

"Then drive off!"

"You're not through in here?!"

"Get out, Luker!"

Luker ran down the stairs, splintering his hand on the railing.

On the landing two doors were open. Crawling toward him across the floor of the bedroom littered with fragments of broken red pottery was an abomination of a baby. It was large and malformed, without eyes or nose but with ears unnaturally large and teeth unnaturally small and numerous. Its hands and feet were fleshy and clawlike. The rings on its fingers clacked against the floor as it came.

"Get out!" screamed India from above, and Luker ran.

CHAPTER 33

India listened to Luker's progress through the house; she went to the window and peered out, and nodded with satisfaction when she saw him fly to Big Barbara and Leigh. She heard him begin his tale of woe long before he reached the two women, confirming the deaths of Dauphin and Odessa.

Because she had actually put into her mouth and swallowed the eyeballs that the black woman had gouged out of her own sockets as she was dying, India now saw what Odessa could see. The house was indeed inhabited by spirits, Elementals Luker had called them, and that name did as well as any other. But to give so definite a name to a spirit or spirits whose character was so distinctly indefinite was more misleading than convenient. And Odessa had been right: the Elementals were not what had shown up in her photographs. They did not take the shape of a toad the size of a collie, they were not Marian Savage and her parrot Nails, they were not an emaciated creature of bones and stretched flesh that crawled about the turrets—the Elementals were simply *presences*, amorphous and unsubstantial. They were indefinite as to number, size, power, age, personality, and habit—all India knew now for certain was that they partook of the air inside the rooms, they were in the sand. When storms came to Beldame and rain washed down the roof of the third house, the Elementals were swept over the shingles and spilled over the rotted gutters. When the sun poured into the rooms through the closed windows, the Elementals were in every degree of rising shimmering heat. They were the mechanism of the locks in the doors, they were the rot that destroyed fabrics, and they were the black detritus that gathered in drawers that hadn't been opened in three decades.

What had killed Dauphin, what had lapped at his pooled blood was something formed out of the air and the sand—the sand particularly. The Elementals had taken scraps of cloth and scraps of skin, sewn it and stuffed it with sand. It was an animated rag doll that India had destroyed with her cleaver, and afterward she had watched the shavings and the cloth shrivel with speckled rot.

The power of the Elementals waned and waxed; India could feel it in the quality of the air if she raised her hand from her side to her face. She could gauge it by the dimness or sharpness of a mirrored image in one of the bedrooms. For several minutes after she had split open Marian Savage, she and Luker had been safe. All the Elementals' energy had been focused into the creation and animation of that terrible effigy, and for a little time after that, the Elementals had no power to harm them.

However, just before she and her father had plunged the knife into Dauphin's breast, India had felt the Elementals rising in the room. To her eyes, the air seemed to grow thickly yellow with their exhalations. Odessa's eyesight was still new to her, and she could not yet interpret to a nicety; but she had realized it was imperative that Luker get out.

In the east the sky was beginning to lighten to a pinkish gray, though in the west it was still fully black. The moon was sinking below the horizon. Its last livid yellow rays were shed on the huddled group of mourners, and India could hear Big Barbara's sobbing, and Leigh's insistent and disbelieving questions. They seemed to have forgotten that she was still in the house. India looked out the window, not minding that she stood barefoot in the remains of the thing that had killed Dauphin—not minding Dauphin's corpse on the bed behind her. And as she watched her family below, she thought; and as she thought, she understood something else. That these effigies: the things in the photographs—Martha-Ann, Marian Savage and Nails, and the three hands that were thrust out of the dune in the bedroom below—were only the three-dimensional equivalents of hallucinations. They had form and substance, but they weren't *real*. Yet something had killed Odessa, and slowly enough that she had had time to pluck out her eyes; something had sliced open Dauphin's throat; and she remembered those nails dug into her ankles. Her ankles still bled. If they were only hallucinations in three dimensions, they still couldn't be got rid of with rapid blinking or brave anathema.

And something waited for her downstairs.

"Don't go back inside," pleaded Big Barbara.

Luker looked at her in dumbfounded surprise. "India is still in there. And whatever killed Dauphin and Odessa is in there with her."

Leigh started to speak, but was inarticulate.

"You two go on and get in the jeep. Get it started up. I'm going in and get her." Luker ran toward the third house, and Big Barbara and Leigh moved stuporously toward the parked vehicles on the edge of the yard.

Big Barbara and Leigh sat in the jeep, staring straight before them at the Savage house, watching as every moment more and more of it disappeared beneath the growing cone of sand. It was roseate pink in the dawn. Now you couldn't see the windows of the second floor at all, and the entire verandah was covered. Sand had spilled into the edge of the yard, and was smothering the vegetation there. Mechanically, Leigh backed the jeep up, and remarked to her mother, "We could just be sitting here and that sand would come cover us up, we didn't watch it."

"Oh, what we gone do, Leigh? What we gone do when we get out of this place?" She wept softly. "What we gone do without Dauphin?"

"Mama, I got no idea." She turned and looked dully at the façade of the third house—its windows glazed with the reflection of the pink sky in the east. "You think we gone lose Luker and India too?"

"India!" Luker shouted from the kitchen. "India! I'm gone burn this fucking house down and you in it if you don't get your ass down here!"

He unscrewed the cap from the gasoline can that was on the kitchen table—no longer wondering how it had got there—and cradling it like a baby, he splashed its contents all over the floor and along the counter tops. When it was empty he slung it vindictively through the back window breaking all six panes in the upper frame.

Despite the influx of fresh air, the fumes of the gasoline in the room were nearly asphyxiating. He opened the door into the dining room and called up again, hysterically: "India! Are you fucking alive! Answer me!"

"Luker!" he heard her shout from above, but her voice was distant. "I'm coming!"

She ran down the stairs from the third floor to the second-floor landing; she carried the knife in her left hand and the cleaver in her right. She looked down at the floor, fearful of being tripped, and held her weapons raised. She had not yet decided whether to stop and fight, and risk dying as horribly as had Odessa and Dauphin, or whether simply to run to Luker and flee Beldame. She smelled the fumes of the gasoline and began to hope that fire would destroy the house and the Elementals with it.

Though she had not intended, she stopped a moment on the landing and gazed into the two open bedrooms. She saw nothing, and more importantly, she *felt* nothing. Whispering her father's name as a kind of incantation for safety, she started down the stairs to the first floor.

The light of dawn penetrated but dimly into this part of the house, and India heard the thing before she saw it. Straining, she made out the creature's form on the stairs below her as it dropped clumsily from one step to the next toward the living room—and her father. India stood at the head of the stairs, too frightened to proceed and too courageous to call out to Luker for assistance.

She flung the cleaver at it, but it was the dull side that struck solidly against the creature's back. The weapon glanced off and fell between the balusters to the floor below.

The creature stopped and turned its expressionless unfeatured face to India. It presented one ear to her, and then the other; and then it began to struggle upward again.

India waited and held the knife poised. She trembled, and did not answer her father when he called again.

Luker appeared suddenly, climbing over the mound of sand between the living and dining rooms. "Goddamn it," he hissed, "India, why didn't you come on down, I was about to—"

With the lamp he had come to the foot of the stairs, and he now could see what was only three steps below his daughter. India knelt, with one hand gripping a baluster for her balance, and waited for the abomination to come within her reach.

Its small mouth worked, and she saw the grinding white teeth inside, tiny and countless. It turned its head from side to side, to catch her breathing first with one ear and then with the other. She could see the soft indentations where there ought to have been eyes, and even the vestigial bands of lashes buried in its doughy skin. Two small red scars it had instead of nostrils; beneath a pearl necklace there were scales on its thick neck, and thick red hair filled its ears. It stank.

Below, Luker had seen and retrieved the cleaver. He stood at the foot of the stairs, and called softly to his daughter: "India! India!"

India stepped back. When the monstrous thing was raising itself onto the landing, and reaching out at her with its bloated four-fingered hand, India drew back her bare foot from which Dauphin's blood had not yet been worn away and kicked the thing solidly in its exposed breast.

It tumbled down several steps, spewing bile and sand. It flailed blindly but one of its arms caught between two balusters and its progress was halted with a jerk. It had nearly recovered its balance when, with a strangled voice, Luker ran up the stairs and brought the cleaver down against the side of its head. The necklace it wore was snapped, and the tiny perfect pearls scattered.

Not sand but brains and blood exploded from the wound that Luker had inflicted. India ran down and plunged the knife deep into its breast. Thin stinking blood was geysered up along the blade and drenched her hands.

Luker grabbed India's wrist and started to pull her down the stairs, but she resisted. The baby still twitched, flinging sand and pearls.

She wrested out the cleaver, lifted it high, and brought it down against the creature's neck. But all her strength wasn't enough to sever it. The broken head only lolled down over the next step, as on a hinge. What contents of its misshapen head had not already spilled out began to seep through the wounds, and the unrecognizable and rotting internal organs pushed themselves out of the body through the opened neck.

India and her father fled the third house.

Luker set fire to it by tossing the kerosene lamp through the back door, which India held open. He took the empty gasoline can on to the verandah and with it knocked out all the windows on the first floor that were not covered with sand, to allow circulation of air through the place. By the time that he ran back to the jeep, where India was cowering in Big Barbara's lap, flames were leaping through the smashed kitchen windows.

Leigh wanted to drive away, but he cautioned her to wait. "Want to make sure it catches."

"No," said India, looking up suddenly. "We can't wait. We've got to get out of here!"

"India," said Luker, "whatever that was in the house, we killed it, we—"

"It's not just the third house," she said, "it's this whole place, we—"

"Oh!" cried Big Barbara, and pointed to the third house. There in the window of the bedroom that was over the living room— flames could now be seen on that side of the house as well—stood Lawton McCray. He was trying to raise the window, but it was evidently stuck in its frame.

"Oh, Lord!" cried Leigh. "Y'all have done gone and set that house on fire and *Daddy* is inside! Y'all didn't even say Daddy was inside there. Y'all—"

"Lawton!" screamed Big Barbara.

"It's not Lawton!" hissed India. "That's why I said get out of here!"

"It *is* Lawton!" said Big Barbara. "Lawton!" she shouted, and waved her arms wildly. "Luker, you got to get him out of there, you got—"

"Barbara," said Luker, "it's not Lawton. If India says it's not, then it's not. And even if it was," he added sullenly, turning away from the frantic figure of the man in the window of the burning house, "I couldn't do anything anyway. You—"

"Drive off!" cried India.

"Lord, India!' cried Leigh. "What kind of girl are you! That's

Daddy in there! Even if you don't love him the way Mama and I do, it's no reason just to watch him burn! And Dauphin's body is in there! Dauphin is dead and Odessa's probably dead too and now Daddy's gone die, and you want me to just drive off!"

India nodded. "Yes, that's exactly what I want. Just put it in gear, and drive off. Dauphin is dead, Odessa is dead, and we're going to be dead if we don't get away from this place right now. That's not Lawton standing in the window, because Lawton is already dead."

"How do you know that, child?" demanded Big Barbara.

"Did you see him?" said Luker.

India nodded. "In the dining room. I think it was Lawton who brought the gasoline can down. He's dead, there're three people dead in that house right now, and there's nobody who's alive. That's why you shouldn't look back. Don't look back at it, there's no telling what you'll see standing in the windows, there's—"

"Come on, Leigh!" shouted Luker, and Leigh drove off.

No one said anything as they drove the length of Beldame. They steadfastly kept their eyes ahead, and no one looked back to the three houses.

They came to the channel. They braced and were silent as the jeep plunged into the shallow water. Not one of them but half imagined that they would be stopped and never allowed to leave Beldame.

The jeep pulled up on to the sand on the far side. By the time they reached Gasque they could no longer see the gray smoke from the fire that consumed the third house.

EPILOGUE

At Gasque they exchanged the jeep for the black Mercedes. They drove to Gulf Shores and telephoned the highway patrol to inform them that during the night one of the three houses at Beldame had burned down, and that three persons had died inside: Lawton McCray, candidate for United States congressional representative; Dauphin Savage, third richest man in Mobile; and Odessa Red, a black woman in the latter's employ.

Luker, Big Barbara, Leigh, and India had determined on the implausible story that they four had returned to Mobile for a single day to do more grocery shopping and check on airline reservations and mail. When they returned early on Friday morning they discovered the third house in flames. Perhaps, Luker ventured to suggest, the three unfortunate persons had gone inside the place exploring, having heard some sound suggestive of burglars or intruders, and one of Lawton's cigarettes had ignited the dry rotting wood or the flimsy rotting draperies. All three had been overcome by smoke and were trapped.

It was a terrible tragedy, the highway patrol concurred, and it probably happened just that way. The third house had been burned right down to the dune and what little remained of it was a few walls and sticks of furniture that lay behind the glassy surface of that mound of fused sand. In the subsequent formal investigation three men from the Baldwin County fire marshal's office stomped about the blackened ruins of the third house for a quarter of an hour and later noted in writing that they had found nothing that pointed to the fire's being of anything but wholly accidental origin.

These three men in fact were far more struck by the strange dune of sand that seemed to have risen out of St. Elmo's Lagoon, on purpose to swallow the house there. Luker, Big Barbara, Leigh, and India, who had driven back along the Dixie Graves Parkway following the police, had seen from the road that the perfect cone that surmounted the Savage house had appreciably softened its contours. Now, by stretching one's imagination, one could judge it a natural if still improbable phenomenon of wind and drifting sand.

In two days' time three coffins were delivered to Mobile, though a man in the Mobile County sheriffs office privately cautioned Luker that they were empty. Not enough had been found in the wreckage of the third house to spear on the end of a pointed stick. This information was related to Big Barbara, Leigh, and India, who were more relieved by the information than not. Three funeral services were held in Mobile the following day, in three different churches. Early in the morning at the Zion Grace Baptist Church, Johnny Red threw himself wailing across the top of Odessa's empty coffin, and after the service begged Leigh to lend him a hundred dollars to tide him over until he could find a buyer for Odessa's house.

Dauphin's funeral was at the Church of St. Jude Thaddeus in the early afternoon, and no one was in attendance but the four who knew how he had died and Sister Mary-Scot. Leigh went up to her sister-in-law, whispered to her a few moments, and then Sister Mary-Scot put away the silver knife that was intended to pierce Dauphin's breast. She crossed herself repeatedly throughout the service. An empty coffin was sealed into the niche above Marian Savage. The day before, when preparing the mausoleum for an interment, the caretaker had discovered that the plaque memorializing Marian Savage had fallen from its place and smashed on the marble floor. A square of plywood preserved Leigh from the distressing sight of the foot of her mother-in-law's coffin.

Lawton McCray's service was held at the St. James Episcopal Church on Government Boulevard, where he and Big Barbara had been married and their children baptized. It was widely attended, and Big Barbara reserved the pew directly behind the family for the sole occupancy of Lula Pearl Thorndike, who wore a tight black dress with a gold-plated pecan fastened to the collar.

What with three ceremonies in three different churches, and three burials at three different cemeteries afterward, the four survivors were exhausted by that evening. They put a black wreath on the door of the Small House, turned out all the lights so that those who wished to proffer consolation would be discouraged from ringing the bell—there had been quite enough of that in the past three days—and sat very still on the glassed-in porch. They agreed that it was the hypocrisy of the day more than anything else that had been so enervating. They had mourned over three empty coffins: two blue and one silver.

"I don't even know what I feel," said Leigh, and in this she spoke for them all. "All that that happened down at Beldame, it was so horrible. It was so *wrong*. And there was nothing we could do to stop it. And since then, we've just lied and lied and lied about what happened. It's a wonder anybody believed any of it. But with all these lies I haven't even had the time to think what it all means, I mean, about Dauphin being dead. Every time I hear a noise, I look up, and I think it's gone be Dauphin coming through the door.

Or I wake up in the morning, and I think 'Oops! Time to go get Odessa!' Or I hear the telephone and I think it's Daddy, wanting Dauphin to do something for him. Y'all got to give me 'bout a month—'bout a month of waiting for 'em all just to walk in the room, and say, 'Hi y'all'—before I can bring myself to believe that they all really and truly died down there."

On Wednesday, the twelfth of July, Luker and India flew back to New York. Luker spent three days answering mail and returning phone calls, then he and India went up to Woodstock and stayed in the house of a friend who preferred Fire Island for his summers. It was cool and forested and lonely there, and Luker and India sought to recover themselves. They never talked of Beldame.

Leigh and Big Barbara made an extended tour of the western National Parks, staying four days at each. By the middle of November they had returned together to the Small House, and Luker and India came down for Thanksgiving. Between Christmas and New Year's Leigh was delivered of twin boys, whom she named Dauphin and Darnley.

Lawton's will was probated that February, but Dauphin's not until several months later—the Savage holdings were enormous, and the entire business was complicated by the fact that when Dauphin died, his mother's estate had been far from resolved. But as soon as she had clear control of the property, Leigh sold Beldame to the oil company that had wanted it, and the oil company was happy to have it—this was a full year after Lawton had first suggested the sale to his family. In the meantime none of them had returned to Beldame, and it was with misgiving that they crossed the Tensaw River into Baldwin County at all. Big Barbara had leased the fertilizer business to some of Lawton's relatives, who cheated her shamefully in return for the way that Lawton had treated them in decades past—and Big Barbara thought this only fair. She never went down to Belforest, because the ride and the name put her too much in mind of Beldame.

It was late that summer, six weeks after the oil company signed the papers on the property known as Beldame, that Hurricane Frederic slammed into the coast of Alabama. Ninety percent of the pecan trees in Baldwin Country, many of them more than seventy-five years old, were uprooted. What the crashing tides didn't smash in Gulf Shores, the wind and rains did. The Gulf waters simply broke across the entire peninsula there. It leveled the dunes and buried Dixie Graves Parkway. It shoved Gasque into Mobile Bay. Nothing at all remained to show where Beldame had been, not a stick of wood, not a foundation brick, not a tatter of cloth caught on a blasted sea rose. Sand spat up from the Gulf filled St. Elmo's Lagoon and it was now no more than a damp depression along the coast. The channel that had kept Dauphin and Odessa at Beldame the night before they were killed wasn't even a ditch now.

The oil company had to hire surveyors to tell them where the property was they had bought.

Luker and India made but one more trip to Alabama, in the autumn following the destruction of Beldame. India, however, expressed so great an aversion to the twins, Dauphin and Darnley, that she could not be persuaded to remain under the same roof with them. To Leigh, she said only, "I hate children. They make me break out." But to her father, India confided, "Remember, I can see what Odessa saw. And those babies aren't McCrays—they're Savages."

MORE CLASSIC HORROR FROM VALANCOURT

THE AMULET
Michael McDowell
Introduction by Poppy Z. Brite

THE MONK
M. G. Lewis
Introduction by Stephen King

THE ENTITY
Frank De Felitta
Introduction by Gemma Files

NIGHTSHADE AND DAMNATIONS
Gerald Kersh
Introduction by Harlan Ellison

RATMAN'S NOTEBOOKS (WILLARD)
Stephen Gilbert
Introduction by Kim Newman

THE MONSTER CLUB
R. Chetwynd-Hayes
Introduction by Stephen Jones

THE DELICATE DEPENDENCY
Michael Talbot
Introduction by Jillian Venters

THE GREAT WHITE SPACE
Basil Copper
Introduction by Stephen Jones

THE CORMORANT
Stephen Gregory
Introduction by the author

FOR A COMPLETE LIST OF TITLES AND ORDERING
INFORMATION, PLEASE VISIT US AT VALANCOURTBOOKS.COM

Milton Keynes UK
Ingram Content Group UK Ltd.
UKHW041259101023
430315UK00004B/82

9 781941 147177